THE
BOY
WHO
KILLED
GRANT
PARKER

ALSO BY KAT SPEARS

SWAY
BREAKAWAY

THE BOY WHO KILLED GRANT PARKER

KAT SPEARS

ST. MARTIN'S GRIFFIN NEW YORK

THE BOY WHO KILLED GRANT PARKER. Copyright © 2016 by Kat Spears. All rights reserved. Printed in the United States of America. For information, address St. Martin's Press, 175 Fifth Avenue, New York, N.Y. 10010.

www.stmartins.com

Designed by Anna Gorovoy

The Library of Congress Cataloging-in-Publication Data is available upon request.

ISBN 978-1-250-08886-4 (hardcover)
ISBN 978-1-250-08887-1 (e-book)

Our books may be purchased in bulk for promotional, educational, or business use. Please contact your local bookseller or the Macmillan Corporate and Premium Sales Department at 1-800-221-7945, extension 5442, or by e-mail at MacmillanSpecialMarkets@macmillan.com.

First Edition: September 2016

10 9 8 7 6 5 4 3 2 1

For Greg Andree's butt, second only to his beautiful, dangerous mind

ACKNOWLEDGMENTS

Once again, just when I thought a book idea could never possibly work, my amazing editor, Sara Goodman, made it a reality. I love this book, Sara. Thanks to my agent, Barbara Poelle, for consistently loving the wacky stories I pitch to her. It takes a certain level of crazy to appreciate some of my ideas.

Endless thanks (truly, impossible to thank enough) to Greg Andree for his encouragement, edits, suggestions, and enthusiasm for this book. I could not have finished a first draft without his help. When you find a friend who can appreciate a good Eva Braun joke, you keep them forever. I'm so glad to have found the entire Andree family because I think, though he can be hilarious, Greg's wife, Jess, is actually more entertaining than he is.

A shout-out to the strong, brilliant, and courageous

women in my life who never stop believing that I'm amazing even though on most days, I'm not. Deepest love for Jill Deiss, Amy Ferguson, Cristina Finan, Lydia Gershman, Annette Kielkopf, Erica Orloff, and Christina Sobran.

Thanks to the service industry heroes who give me what I want and then leave me alone to write books. I'm always happy to see the faces of Frank and Oyuka at The Tabard Inn, and Dana, Nathan, and Steve at Northside Grille.

And for Jack, Josie, and Ingrid, who continue to amaze me every day with their wit, charm, and senses of humor and keep our house full of love and laughter. Biology notwithstanding, they are the best people I've ever known.

God is dead. God remains dead. And we have killed him.

—FRIEDRICH NIETZSCHE

THE BOY WHO KILLED GRANT PARKER

1

When I imagined my first day of school in Ashland, Tennessee, it was me rolling up to the parking lot in a classic muscle car, the radio blaring with some hard-rocking song to match my awesome ride, sunlight glinting off of polished chrome, and heads turning to catch a glimpse of me, the mysterious new kid, at the wheel with sunglasses on.

The fact that I was an outsider would make me an enigma, a mystery to these sheltered, small-town, hopelessly backward hicks.

The reality was nothing like my fantasy.

It was the Tuesday after Labor Day, the weather still hot and dusty despite our proximity to the mountains and the calendar's promise of autumn. I had planned to ride my bike to school, but Dad insisted on driving me for my first day. He pulled straight up to the front of the building, flagrantly violating the buses-only restriction, in his mint-green RAV4 with a JESUS IS MY COPILOT bumper sticker.

I had been living with Dad for only two weeks, and things were still strained between us. It was hard for me to imagine that I would ever feel really comfortable with my dad. After all, because of my taste in music and the fact that I didn't accept Jesus as my savior, according to his belief system I was destined to burn in a fiery hell for all eternity. I had a feeling that was going to make Christmas dinner uncomfortable for at least one of us.

"Dad, you aren't supposed to drive up here," I said, my patience shortened by crippling embarrassment.

"Darn," Dad said, the closest he ever came to swearing, "I thought this was the entrance to the parking lot." He jerked to a stop and then, to make matters a hundred times worse, put the car into reverse and started to back out of the bus lane.

The bus pulling in behind us honked with alarm as Dad almost backed straight into the bumper of the giant yellow grille that loomed in the rearview mirror. Dad raised his hand in a friendly wave, as if genuinely grateful for the update that he was, in fact, the worst driver on the planet.

He inched forward but was now stuck waiting for the throng of students who poured in from the parking lot toward the main entrance. Every single person who passed turned to study us curiously, and I wanted to sink below the dash and disappear.

"I'll pull around and park," Dad said. "I want to walk you in. Make sure you find the office."

"You really don't have to," I said. "Mom hasn't gone with me for my first day of school since second grade."

"I think the school would expect me to be with you," he said.

"Dad. I'm seventeen. Not a child."

"You know," he said, ignoring my protest and circling back to our earlier conversation, "I specifically asked your mother to take you out shopping for some suitable school clothes before you moved. There isn't as broad a selection available here as there is in the city."

His tone when he said "city" conveyed disdain, as if Washington, DC, where I had lived for the past thirteen years, were the biblical Sodom or Gomorrah.

"She *did* take me shopping for school clothes," I said.

"Then why," he asked, "are you wearing that T-shirt for the first day of school?"

"She bought me this shirt," I said. A blatant lie. My mother had given me her credit card and told me to go out and buy clothes similar to the uniform I wore to the private school I had attended in DC. I had ignored her instructions, of course, and returned with only jeans and T-shirts and hoodies. I was sick of wearing a tie and collared shirts and blazers and considered the lack of a uniform the only advantage to attending my new public school.

Dad sighed wearily and waited for the students crossing the bus lane in a reluctant herd to clear.

"I'll be fine," I said, opening the door and evacuating before he could move the car.

———

A new student might have gone unnoticed for days or weeks (maybe months if he played his cards right) at my old school. Washington, DC, was such a transient city that people were always coming and going. But in Ashland, I might as well have been wearing a bell announcing myself as a leper. People stared and spoke in low voices to each other as I passed in the hallway.

If I heard laughter, I assumed it was directed toward me, as if everything about me was under scrutiny—my clothes, my hair, the way I walked, the Mount Vesuvius–like stress pimple that had erupted on my chin that morning.

The only thing I had going for me, maybe, was that my appearance was almost depressingly average. I might as well have been wallpaper. And that was exactly the way I wanted it—to blend into the background and go unnoticed.

I managed to find the office without asking anyone for directions, and the receptionist greeted me in a southern drawl so outrageous it seemed like it had to be a put-on.

"I'm Luke Grayson," I said. "I'm new here." Captain Obvious. As a stranger in Ashland, I stuck out like a boner in sweatpants.

"Well," she said, the word gusting out as she folded her hands on the desk and pressed them into her bosom, "I go to your daddy's church, and I never knew anything about Pastor Grayson having a son until we got word you were coming. Of course, he's such a busy man, what with all the goings-on we've had since Easter. Three funerals in as many months. Never a good sign if a church has more funerals than baptisms, wouldn't you say?"

I wouldn't, but I kept my mouth shut and tried to convey concern in my expression, though it was a lie. The tardy bell rang as she droned on about the business of my dad's church, and I feigned interest, while in my mind all I could really focus on was the fact that I would now have to enter class late and be even more of a spectacle than I already was.

"Principal Sherman wants to have a quick visit with you before you start the day," the receptionist said, once it was obvious I was going to fail miserably at making small talk, and then she picked up the receiver of the ancient desk phone.

As I was shown into the principal's office he came around from behind his desk to shake my hand and gestured for me to take one of the hard-backed chairs, though a leather couch along one wall offered a more comfortable option. He was middle-aged, with the paunch of a former football player, and his doughy hands clashed with the tailored suit he wore. His desk was an ocean of polished oak, and my chair was at least a few inches lower to the ground than his so that I felt small and insignificant sitting across from him. I disliked him immediately, feeling that he would have been more at home on a used-car lot than in a high school administration office. And once he started talking, I knew the disproportionate height of the chairs and the size of the desk were both power plays, his intention to make whoever sat across from him feel powerless.

"So, Mr. Grayson," he said as he crossed one leg over the other, shot his cuffs, and twitched his hand to settle a heavy gold watch against a meaty wrist. "How are you settling in?"

"Uh. Fine, I guess." My response came out as a wavering question since I wasn't sure how well I should have settled in during the five minutes I had been at Wakefield High School.

He just nodded at my answer, as if it was the response he had been expecting but wasn't really interested in whether it was true.

The ocean of wood between us housed only a phone and a pen holder with a faux-bronze nameplate on the front of it. The name LESLIE G. SHERMAN was inscribed on the plaque. I wondered what the "G" stood for and how he felt about having a girl's name. I could only assume the "G" stood for something worse than Leslie. I was distracted with trying to think of a name worse than Leslie that started with a "G"—*Garfield? Grover?*—when he startled me with his attack run.

"Since it's your first day here I'm not going to make a federal case out of it, but we do have a student dress code." He was looking so pointedly at my chest that I couldn't help but steal a self-conscious glance at my Death Cab for Cutie T-shirt. My stepmom, Doris, had already made a federal case out of my shirt that morning at breakfast.

"Oh. Really?" I asked innocently.

"Yes. Really," he said with such condescension that I wondered if he had kids of his own who hated him. "T-shirts with printed designs have been strictly forbidden since the Columbine tragedy." His expression conveyed the very real concern that my T-shirt would inspire a Columbine-like incident.

"Okay," I said as I tried to think of what shirts I owned

that didn't include printed designs. Did a Georgetown University sweatshirt count as a printed design? I wasn't sure. But it didn't seem the right time to ask.

"Mr. Grayson, I have a great deal of respect for your father," the principal said, changing the subject abruptly. He paused in anticipation after he said this, waiting for an appropriate response. I was still shifting gears from Columbine and printed T-shirts and I wasn't sure what an appropriate response should be, so the pause dragged on—from awkward to painful.

Finally I said, "Thanks." As if I was entitled to some credit for how respectable my father was.

"Ashland is a strong Christian community, as I'm sure you know since your father is a man of God." I was starting to get the sense that he had practiced this speech ahead of time. Like he had an agenda and had worked out in his mind how to approach it in a roundabout way.

"Yes. Strong," I said, feeling like an idiot as I said it.

My eyes wandered around the room as I tried to think of something clever to say to alleviate the impression that I was a moron. A large framed print hung on the wall behind the desk, the words THE PRINCIPAL IS MY PAL—THAT'S THE PRINCIPLE WE LIVE BY displayed in colorful block letters.

"I've been reviewing your records from your previous school," he said as he reached forward to lift the papers in front of him, the implied threat made all the more menacing because it was an alarmingly thick stack of papers.

I wasn't sure what to say. I decided to stay silent, not give anything away in case some things hadn't been committed to paper. Better to remain silent, not incriminate myself, than to start offering up explanations.

"Your grades were . . . unexceptional," he said, maybe still trying to be polite.

Unexceptional was putting it mildly, though I would often argue with my mom that a C average was just that—average. I didn't aspire to be anything other than average.

I kept silent, not wanting to do anything that would extend my stay in his office.

"It seems that you also like to challenge authority, Mr. Grayson," Leslie said as he frowned at the second stapled page of my permanent record.

"I went to an all-boys school when I lived in DC," I said with an innocent shrug. "Pranks are just the usual there."

"This seems much more serious than pranks." He looked at me expectantly over the rims of his reading glasses. "These notes indicate that on one occasion there was personal injury to another student and property damage to the school. Does that seem like just an innocent prank to you, Mr. Grayson?"

I shifted in my seat as I tried to let my anger dissolve before responding. If I came across as snide and pissed, it would just make the situation worse. But it was hard—the way he called me Mr. Grayson, the way teachers do as if they are showing a sign of respect for students as grown people when really they are just patronizing us.

As I waited for the acid to dissipate from my tongue before answering, I thought bitterly of Steve Moyo, my underachieving partner in crime for the debacle that had ultimately driven my mom beyond the point of no return.

That Steve had been stupid enough to light an M-80 firework while sitting on the toilet was his own fault. He had definitely been stoned and just hadn't thought through the sequence of events ahead of time. Trying to correct his mistake, he had dropped the firework into the toilet, not knowing it would land with the fuse above the waterline and continue to burn. Though the resulting damage to his ass and the underside of his balls was enough to keep him from sitting comfortably or jacking off for a few days (*a new personal record*), he wasn't seriously injured and his virility was intact. The explosion had cracked the toilet bowl and flooded the bathroom reserved for teachers. Teachers got to crap in private, didn't have to use the multistalled bathroom the students used.

At the moment of detonation I was in the teachers' lounge, loading a bag of contraband for later redistribution from the well-stocked snack cupboards. Steve's injuries prevented any kind of escape, and we were both caught red-handed. I was standing with the door to the toilet open while Steve writhed on the ground, holding his crotch and screaming, "Are they gone? Did I blow them off? Fucking tell me! Don't sugarcoat it, man!" at the precise moment when the track-and-field coach sauntered into the lounge, a newspaper folded under one arm, to take his morning dump.

"I asked you a question, Mr. Grayson," Leslie said, and brought me back to the present. "Does that seem like a simple prank to you?"

"No," I said finally, since it was the answer Leslie was waiting for.

"No, what?" he asked.

"Sir?" I hazarded a guess.

"I address you with respect," he said. "I expect the same in return."

Ri-ight. Respect.

Other transgressions on my record would be much more minor—tardies, maybe a mention of being caught smoking on school grounds once or twice, and repeated trips to the principal's office for mouthing off to my teachers— but really I had no idea how much information ended up in a permanent record. I wondered idly if this permanent record would follow me to college and beyond.

Leslie allowed his leather desk chair to fall forward on its rocker with an ominous thud. He blew out a weary sigh but said nothing for a long minute. The seconds ticked off on the wall clock as beads of sweat formed at my hairline.

"Let me be very clear," Leslie said, speaking slowly, as if I might be simpleminded. "If you give me any trouble. Any at all. I will recommend you finish your high school career at the juvenile reformatory in Purcellville. You get me, Mr. Anti-establishment?"

Since I had never considered myself anything even close to resembling a rebel, his threats almost made me giggle with nervous energy. Giggle or pee myself.

"Yes," I said, though I didn't really. Get him, that was.

"Yes, what?" he asked, his face crimson now.

The corners of his eyes creased into a menacing scowl,

and I unconsciously straightened in my chair and cleared my throat before saying, "Yes . . . sir. . . . I won't give you any trouble."

And even though I meant what I said, had no plans to cause trouble, by the end of the day, that promise would be broken.

2

I spent most of that first day cussing my mother in my head for making me come to this godforsaken town. Jesus, I had moved five hundred miles from DC to eastern Tennessee (actually, I had no idea how far DC was from Tennessee), but I felt like I had moved five hundred years. Principal Sherman had set the tone before my day even started, and now I was resentful and angry.

My mother really had no room to talk when it came to life choices. She had been a complete degenerate as a teenager and in her early twenties. She married my dad, a student at the Baptist seminary in her hometown of Richmond, Virginia, in a failed attempt to straighten out her life. Within a few years it became painfully apparent that my mom was not cut out for the role of preacher's wife, so she packed up me and her few belongings and relocated to Washington,

DC. After that, there had been a revolving door of weirdos in our house—Mom's friends and guys she dated.

My mom was actually pretty cool. I could tell her things most teenage guys can't tell their moms. But since she had been such a fuckup for most of her adult life, I also couldn't get away with anything. She could smell a lie from fifty paces, and she felt like she had some special license to try to make me turn out a saint after the havoc of her own young adulthood.

I had never lived with my dad. Hadn't even really seen much of him for the past thirteen years. He hadn't managed to do much to straighten Mom out. I'm not sure what she thought he could do with me.

It's not as if I were a total rebel or snorted heroin or anything. I just got bored easily. And a small town in eastern Tennessee is about as boring as it gets, so I'm not sure how she thought sending me here was going to keep me out of trouble.

And besides, the town kind of creeped me out. Nothing stayed open past 8:00 P.M., and there was nothing but white people as far as the eye could see. There wasn't even a Chinese restaurant. How the hell do you live without Chinese carryout? I didn't even know that was a thing.

I had no intention of forming attachments to this town. Ashland was my purgatory—nine months until graduation and my departure. Until then, I planned to phone it in.

I had known from the start that lunch would be the worst part of the day in my new school. A high school cafeteria is like Dante's vestibule of hell—shedding blood endlessly for nothing but more hell.

When the bell dismissed us to lunch, I hesitated stupidly in my seat and thought about my options. The idea of packing my lunch, which was the equivalent of social suicide at my old school, had been abhorrent to me that morning. Now I wished I had brought a sandwich so I didn't have to face the line for food in the cafeteria or the pathetic search for a place to sit by myself.

The cafeteria food was nothing like what they served at the private school I attended in DC. There, we had been offered fresh fruit and a salad bar and gluten-free everything. The Wakefield cafeteria offered extremely limited options—the color leached from the vegetables by overcooking, the meat the lowest grade rating approved by the FDA for human consumption.

It was obvious that most students at my new school brought their lunch from home, knew better than to eat the disgusting school lunch. I was one of the few who went through the full line.

The most mortifying moment of the day was when I turned away from the cashier with my lunch tray and stood, awkward and helpless, deciding where to sit.

I stutter-stepped as I tried to walk like I had some direction, my eyes searching desperately for a welcoming look or an empty table. Finally, I honed in on a table with only one occupant, a guy who didn't look old enough to be out of middle school and sat with his back rounded in the defensive posture of an inmate protecting his meal. He didn't even look up at me as I took a seat at the opposite end of the table. I kept my earbuds in to discourage conversation,

Modest Mouse playing at low volume so I could still hear the buzz of voices around me.

I scrolled relentlessly through my phone, sending out texts in rapid succession to friends back home, hoping one of them would engage me in some kind of conversation. I confirmed three times that I had received no new e-mails other than spam and, after opening my Web browser, quickly cleared the search history on my phone to keep porn sites from popping up at a bad moment.

However desperate I may have been for a social life at my new school, the first offer of friendship I got was not a welcome one. Even though I was painfully aware of how pathetic I looked sitting with just my phone for company, I was less than enthusiastic when a guy I dimly remembered from one of my morning classes approached me, his open and friendly expression demanding that I remove my ear-buds and engage in conversation. He was my height but slight, his wiry frame curved like a question mark, and his hair could have used a washing.

As he maneuvered his legs under the table across from me, he introduced himself by saying, "Hey, I'm Don. My family is Methodist, so we don't go to your dad's church."

"Hey, Don," I said. "I'm Luke. Agnostic."

"Hey," he said, his eyes lighting up with surprise, "that's pretty good."

Don had an unfortunate complexion that, if the lunch he was unpacking onto the table was any indication, was due to his poor diet and, possibly, lack of personal hygiene. I watched with mild distaste as he unpacked a Lunchable, fruit gummies, and a juice box that promised to contain at least 10 percent real juice.

"We never get new people in Ashland," he said as he shoved a plastic bag full of carrot sticks, the only organically created part of his lunch, back into the bag and set it aside. "You're, like, the first."

"Great."

"Josh," Don called to the silent, freckled boy at the end of our table. "C'mere," he said with a wave of his hand. The boy looked over at us from under a mushroom cap of wiry brown hair and then slowly, reluctantly gathered his food and moved down to join us.

Josh said nothing, didn't really even acknowledge me other than to give me an almost imperceptible nod, before resuming his lunch in Don's shadow.

"Josh doesn't talk much," Don said artlessly.

"Okay," I said, for lack of anything better, but was distracted by the sight of something across the lunchroom— long, buttery gold curls and a million-dollar smile. A petite girl, her delicate arms and legs brown from the sun, was laughing with her friends as she made her way across the cafeteria. Even from across the room I could tell her eyes were a vibrant sapphire. She was nothing like a DC girl. For one thing she was made up perfectly, like a doll, and wore a conservative plaid dress with a disappointingly high neckline.

Don followed my gaze and smiled knowingly when he saw what had captured my attention. "Penny Olson," he said. "You can just get that idea out of your head right now."

"What do you mean?" I asked.

He snorted. "I mean forget it. Every guy in school is crazy about her, but she's been going out with Grant Parker since last year."

"Yeah?" I asked. "Who's Grant Parker?"

"Grant Parker is God."

"If there is a God," I said, "I'm pretty sure he isn't from Ashland, Tennessee."

"Yeah, well, Grant Parker can do no wrong," Don said with a resigned sigh. "Star student, star athlete—and he looks like an Abercrombie model. His daddy owns the feed and farm supply, so they're the richest folks in town. And Grant's daddy's the mayor. Leland Parker is like the God of Ashland, and Grant Parker is Jesus Christ."

When Penny Olson walked by our table, I tried to keep my gaze fixed on Don or my food so I wouldn't be caught watching her. Just as she neared our table, a notebook that she held under one arm slipped and fell to the floor. Before she could shift her grip on her lunch bag and purse to reach down and retrieve her book, I was bending down to pick it up for her.

"Oh, thanks," she said with a sunny smile as she shook her hair back from her face in a practiced way.

"You're welcome," I said.

"You're the new boy," she said, and the way she said "boy" sent a shiver through my scrotum. "Ashland's a small town," she said, almost apologetically. "Word of anything new happening gets around pretty quickly." She laughed at this, and I felt an involuntary grin spread across my face.

"Yeah," I said. "I'm starting to realize that. I'm Luke."

"Penny," she said as she carefully shifted her belongings so she could offer her other hand to shake mine.

"It's nice to meet you, Penny," I said.

"I heard you were from New York City or something."

Her voice was eager and rose a couple of octaves at the end of her sentence.

"Washington, DC," I corrected her.

"Oh, well," she said as her face slipped easily back into a beauty-pageant smile, "it's nice to meet you, Luke."

"You too," I said, and meant it.

"I hope everyone is being nice and welcoming to you," she said. "It must be hard moving to a new place your senior year. I couldn't imagine if I didn't have my friends I've known all my life."

I'm going to be honest. When Penny said this, a small lump rose in my throat and I felt heat behind my eyelids. She was so . . . nice. And not in a way that was just saying the right words as a veneer of politeness. It was the first genuine human connection I'd had since moving to Ashland, and I wanted to stay in the warmth of her smile and, maybe, follow her around like a lost puppy.

"It's been . . . a big change," I said, hoping as I did that my smile seemed warm and genuine. "But I'm starting to think maybe there's hope for me in Ashland after all."

Her smile turned shy after I said this, and she dropped her gaze to the floor. "Well, it's nice to meet you. I'll see you around."

"Yeah," I said, since I had already used up everything interesting I had to say, then watched her as she walked away.

When I sat back down Don was shaking his head. "Take my advice," he said. "You steer well clear of Penny Olson. Unless you're some kind of MMA expert or carry concealed. Grant Parker can make your life miserable if he chooses."

"All I did was say hello," I said as I returned to my lunch, though my Tater Tots, the only appetizing part of the school lunch, were now cold.

"It doesn't matter," Don said. "Trust me."

Don had clearly suffered relegation to the lamest social level in school, but the only thing worse than accepting my place with him would have been sitting by myself at lunch. Don's other friend joined us soon after—Aaron, who was alarmingly thin yet had a mop of dark hair so thick it was a wonder he could hold his head up under the weight of it.

Josh didn't utter a single word during lunch. I wasn't even sure he could talk. Or had a tongue. It was up to Don and Aaron to carry the conversation at our table since I didn't have much more to say than Josh did. I didn't see any movies (other than porn highlights), didn't play any video games, and my experience with girls was limited to the aforementioned porn.

As Don and Aaron talked, I watched the wall clock tick through the longest forty minutes of my life. The day was still only half over, but I had assumed lunch would be the worst part of being the new kid.

I was wrong about that.

3

As if the day wasn't long and painful enough, the last period was reserved for a pep rally to kick off the football season. The entire student body was crammed into the home side of the bleachers, the manicured gridiron a vibrant green with fresh chalk lines. There was no lacrosse or golf or tennis at Wakefield High like there had been at my old school. In Ashland, football clearly ruled.

The press box at the top of the bleachers was nicer than Principal Sherman's office, and the manicured turf was devoid of any weeds. It looked like a freshly vacuumed wall-to-wall carpet.

As we filed into the bleachers I caught sight of Don, Aaron, and Josh seated near the percussion section of the concert band. Don was waving in my direction, but I was afraid to acknowledge him, afraid that if I waved back I would suddenly discover he was waving at someone just behind me.

I thought we would just file in and be seated by class, but people were branching off to take seats saved by their friends. I kept climbing toward the top bench, hoping to find myself alone in a private aerie. About five rows from the top I realized my mistake. Of course, the top bleacher seats would be reserved for the beta males. Not the athletically capable, as those boys would all be on the field introduced by number. The betas were the males who would view the football players with disdain, would ignore the cheers and chants of their classmates, and instead make plans for the joint they would smoke under the bleachers as soon as we were dismissed from the pep rally. I knew all of this instinctively because I had been a beta male at my old school.

I was not going to find a seat among them. It seemed too late to scurry sideways, find a place among my lunch comrades. I ditched, and took the first open seat I saw in a crowded section of bleachers. The seat I took had clearly been intended for someone else, but I tried to ignore the disappointed glances exchanged by the girls clustered around me. I was not the guy girls would be lusting after. *That* I already knew.

Principal Sherman took center field with a microphone to start the pep rally with a prayer, flagrantly disregarding any federal laws separating church from state.

Though a small town, Ashland had more churches than any other form of business. And not just churches in the traditional sense with steeples and bells and pews. Strip malls, abandoned bank buildings, and even a converted barn were all home to competing churches with large banners or signs inviting passersby to drop in and worship with them. I easily imagined oily haired evangelists and snake charmers overseeing flocks within these establishments.

As the pep rally got underway the cheerleaders ran onto the field, and I noticed Penny Olson among them, her thousand-watt smile casting the other girls in shadow. Each member of the football team was introduced by name and position, jogging onto the field in coordinated tracksuits. The final player introduced was the team captain, Grant Parker, Ashland's very own Second Coming of the Messiah. There was a murmur of anticipation, and then a roar came up from the crowd as he jogged onto the field, the sunlight winking off his even smile in a blinding eclipse.

Grant Parker ran along the line of his teammates, each of them reaching out to slap him five as he jogged past. Principal Sherman was waiting at the end of the receiving line, practically bro-ing out with a handshake and an affectionate shoulder grip for Grant. Even from my distant seat in the bleachers, Grant's charisma was glaring. His wave to the crowd was both friendly and full of humility, and he even took the opportunity to give a high five to the team mascot, a wildcat dressed in an oversize football jersey with the name WILLIE lettered on the back.

The enthusiasm was off the charts as everyone stomped and cheered, drowning out the chants of the cheerleaders. I was torn between showing some pride for my new high school, at least for the sake of blending in, or sitting in sullen silence waiting for the school day to end. Since I felt ridiculous raising my voice or stamping my feet when I didn't really give a shit about the Wakefield Wildcats, I went with the silent, sullen approach. And no one seemed to care.

When the dismissal bell rang I followed my classmates, all of them still singing and clapping as we spilled out of the bleachers. As I stepped off the metal staircase onto the field, things went suddenly and horribly wrong.

Willie the Wildcat was moving through a complex set of dance moves to wow the audience as they filed out of the bleachers. He had moved away from the field, following the crush of the crowd, and reached the base of the bleacher steps at the same moment I did. As he executed a hard spin he knocked into me, his significant bulk sending me flying. I sprawled onto the hard-packed earth, my arms splayed out in front of me to break my fall.

I scrambled to regain my feet, hoping not everyone had witnessed my fall. But I stood too quickly and lost my footing again, banging heavily into the padded belly of Willie.

People were paying attention now, and a few laughs rose up from the crowd at my unintentionally comic routine. Willie, clearly adept at pandering to an audience, took me by the shoulders and set me straight, then fell into a boxer's stance and started playfully jabbing his oversize paws in my direction, as if inviting me to fight.

Now everyone was watching and laughing. Maybe they were laughing at the way Willie had turned the whole situation into a joke, but I felt it only as ridicule of me, the new kid. I stood there with my fists clenched, wanting to knock the wildcat out for attracting an avalanche of unwanted attention. He danced around me playfully and swatted at me with his paws, first on my hip, then across the top of my head. When I took a moment to fix my hair, push it back to one side the way it was supposed to be styled, Willie came at me with a one-two punch.

Though his movements were playful, the blows knocked me off-balance again and I sat down hard on my ass. Sharp rocks bit into the heels of my palms and a shock of pain traveled up my arm.

The wound to my pride exacerbated the ache in my wrist, and I felt the prick of tears just behind my eyelids. That made me angry—the idea that my body would betray me in such a way and allow me to cry and subject myself to further ridicule. And instead of strengthening my resolve, my anger made me feel weaker. Impotent.

Willie jumped around, his arms lifted in the parody of a prizefighter who has just achieved a knockout. Now everyone—*everyone*—was laughing and cheering for Willie.

Willie had his back to me, accepting the applause of the crowd, alternating sweeping bows and fist pumps in the air.

I don't know what came over me then. It seemed impossible to just slink away from the whole situation, licking my wounds. However absurd it was that I was furious with a giant stuffed cat, I couldn't control my temper.

I'm not sure that I would have been able to take him down if it hadn't been for the element of surprise. Having no experience with contact sports, and given the wide girth of the anatomically incorrect cat, my attack was clumsy. I lunged at him, with what intent I have no idea. After all, what kind of psycho loser would attack a giant stuffed cat?

The truth is I didn't bother to think through the situation, just responded with anger, and I never could have imagined the scenario that actually played out. Willie was top-heavy because of his costume, and he fell forward easily, carrying me with him to the ground.

I landed on top of Willie, the cat fur and costume not as soft as you would think, totally ineffective for breaking my fall. My chin cracked against a rib or maybe a shoulder blade.

"What the fuck?" Willie's shouts were muffled from inside his costume. As close as I was, actually lying on top of him, I could smell his sweat through the mesh vents concealed by his mask.

Willie and I rolled around on the ground for a few minutes. He was on his back now, like a turtle in a shell, unable to roll onto his stomach to regain use of his arms and legs. I was struggling to extricate myself from the tangle of unruly limbs and cat fur so I could stand.

In my struggle to get free of Willie, I had momentarily forgotten about the crowd, but as I finally did break loose, spitting and using my fingers to remove offending tufts of cat fur from my tongue, the noise from the crowd was suddenly overwhelming.

Someone gripped my arm, just above the elbow, and lifted me to my feet. And then I was standing face-to-face with Leslie G. Sherman, still working my teeth against my tongue to get rid of the last piece of cat fur stuck in my mouth.

"Mr. Grayson," Principal Sherman said. "You sure don't waste any time, do you?"

"I wasn't . . ."

"Save it," Principal Sherman snapped. "We'll discuss it in my office."

With a defeated sigh, I let him take me by the arm and lead me back toward the school building, the shouts and laughter of fifteen hundred students a cresting tidal wave behind us.

4

Dad and Doris were waiting for me when I got home from
school that afternoon. Dad's face was set in grave concern,
which meant that Principal Sherman had already made the
promised call home.

Doris busied herself at the sink, but I knew she only lingered there to overhear our conversation. Though she had a
cleaning woman who came one day a week, Doris still spent
most of her time employed with domestic duties, wearing
one of her signature frilly aprons tied in a perfect bow at the
waist. By contrast, my mom spent most of her leisure time
in yoga pants and was always vowing to get her act together
and actually fold and put away laundry instead of storing it
in random piles designated as clean, dirty, and only a little
dirty. Mom had a demanding career, but she never hired
anyone to help her around the house. She said it would make

her uncomfortable to give up her privacy to a maid. As such, a domestic figure like Doris was completely foreign to me. Doris was up before the sun each day to prepare breakfast, with her hair styled and makeup expertly applied.

Before moving to Ashland I had only met Doris a few times, the first time at the wedding. Dad had asked me to be his best man. I was thirteen then, and our reunion had been awkward and horrible, especially since Mom had brought me and I got to see my parents interact, a rare event. It was almost impossible to imagine they had ever been in love, much less (shudder) had sex to produce a kid. But there I was, the product of a Southern Baptist preacher and a mom who acted like Keith Richards's love child.

Dad had a congregation in a suburb of Cleveland at the time he and Doris got married. Doris's family was from Kentucky, and she had a southern drawl as sweet as aspartame, with a kindness that was just as fake.

Mom had cursed under her breath when she found out it was a dry wedding. "I have to be in freaking Ohio for my ex-husband's wedding, and I can't even be drunk for it," she muttered to me at the reception. Except she hadn't said "freaking." Mom had the vocabulary of a sailor, a personal flaw she said she had tried to correct while married to my dad. "But cussing feels good," Mom always said to explain this particular vice. "Besides, there's nothing in the Bible that says you can't cuss. As long as you don't cuss and involve the Lord's name in it, you're all good."

In middle school I had found my mom's eccentric behavior humiliating. Now I missed the fact that I could swear without being called out for it in my own home.

"Luke," Dad said from where he sat at the kitchen table, a frosty glass of iced tea in front of him, "I had a very disturbing call from Leslie Sherman today."

I would think any conversation with Leslie Sherman would be disturbing.

This was not going to be a conversation. Dad was going to deliver a sermon, and I was going to endure it like I would any Sunday sermon he spoke from the pulpit.

"What is this about you attacking the team mascot at the pep rally?" he asked with a bewildered frown.

When he said it out loud it did sound ridiculous, more like the punch line to a joke than an actual event.

Like my life.

"I didn't attack him," I said wearily. "It was just a misunderstanding."

"He also mentioned your shirt. I told you this morning that shirt does not convey the kind of image you want to be creating for yourself in Ashland. A Death Cab? What is that? You know, the community has been concerned about violence in our schools ever since Columbine."

"Dad, I seriously doubt the Trench Coat Mafia was listening to Death Cab for Cutie. Those guys were from some backwater town like this one, and Death Cab wasn't even a big name until a few years after Columbine."

A squawk emanated from Doris's direction as she erupted with emotion, and she and Dad exchanged nervous glances.

Dad took a deep breath and looked down at his glass of iced tea, searching there for his next words.

"Look, Dad," I said, trying to ignore Doris, "moving here at the start of my senior year sucks. Okay? It sucks."

"I understand that, Luke," Dad said. "But you have to understand that Ashland is a conservative community. A small town. There just isn't going to be tolerance for anyone who . . ."—he paused as he considered what to say next—"well, for anyone wearing shirts like that. You're not helping yourself if you don't at least try to fit in."

"I don't want to fit in," I said. I felt myself getting angry and knew I was going to lose this argument. Again.

"Luke, I know when you're young it feels like things aren't ever going to change or get better. You have to be open to change. It's just like I tell my congregation. You have to be prepared to let the Lord into your life if you want to find real strength through his love."

He was retreating into dogma. An argument that was impossible to win. So I accepted defeat and went to my room.

My humiliation at the pep rally was not something anyone would soon forget, not least of all because someone had managed to capture most of the debacle on video. Don texted me to let me know. I wished he had kept it to himself. Of the forty thousand views the video got on YouTube in the first twenty-four hours, seventeen of those views were my own. I knew I shouldn't watch it, that it would just make me feel worse, but I couldn't help myself.

Though I already felt sorry enough for myself, I needed the replay of the whole episode to help me feel worse. I watched it on my phone in the privacy of my room and wondered if the person who had captured the video of my assault on Willie the Wildcat would need my permission before submitting it to *America's Funniest Home Videos*.

I looked painfully uncoordinated and lanky in the video, and had never noticed how thin my arms were before seeing them in the video seventeen times. My face was recognizable, but I hoped there was no way anyone at my old school would stumble upon it. After all, I wasn't friends with anyone at my new school on social media. It's not like they could tag me in a post.

As I lay in my bed, hidden in my room from the outside world, I could imagine the video going viral, shared among hundreds of my new classmates. A running counter in my mind spiraled into the millions of views and thumbs-up emojis before I drifted off to sleep that first night.

5

My assault on Willie the Wildcat had confirmed for Leslie G. Sherman on my first day at Wakefield that I was here looking for trouble. For everyone else, it offered clear evidence that I was a complete tool, a prime target for ridicule and dislike.

At least I now had the excuse of going to after-school detention every day for the next five days, where I could avoid other students—and Dad and Doris.

During the hour of afternoon detention I could not talk or read or listen to music, just stare blankly out the window, alone with my own thoughts. It was supposed to give me time to think about my crime and learn to repent. Instead, it gave me ample free time to think about how much I hated Ashland and everyone in it.

———

During that first week I rode my bike home by a different route every day. I was learning my way around town and, at the same time, trying to find the perfect route so that I would see the minimum number of people. It's not as if I had anything else to do, and I certainly didn't want to be at home.

Dad was only in his office part of the time because he made visits to people in the hospital or had to conduct a funeral or something. And since Doris didn't work, there was always the risk that I would run into her or, worse, she would have the Baptist Church Women (that's what they called themselves) over for sweet tea, with pimento cheese on Ritz crackers.

It was on the third day when I was on my way home, taking a much longer route that followed the train tracks through a nonresidential part of town, when I saw her for the first time.

A large junkyard surrounded by a chain-link fence took up a whole block near the main railroad crossing. Sitting on four bald tires was an old Camaro, a late-sixties model. The body was in great shape, if not filthy and coated in road dust. It was a ragtop, and from the street side of the fence I could see no tears or rips in the cover.

I walked my bike along the length of the fence that surrounded the junkyard until I came to a building with three bay doors and a black asphalt parking lot in front. ROGER'S AUTO AND BODY was painted on a sign hung above the glass entry door. A bell on the door announced my arrival, and I stepped into an empty office. The angle of the sun cut a path of light across the office, dust motes swirling in the current of air from the open door.

"Hello," I called through the doorway that opened into the garage bays.

A grunt and the clatter of metal were the only reply. I ventured into the well-lit work area, clean and orderly compared to the neglected office, and saw a Ford pickup gleaming under the overhead lights.

"Hello?" I said again, thinking maybe I had imagined the sounds of another human, or that the garage was haunted.

"You already said that," came a disembodied voice from somewhere below.

"Oh. Uh . . . sorry. Where are you?" I asked, feeling like a total idiot.

"Grease pit," was the reply. "That all you were looking to ask?"

I looked under the truck and saw a man standing beneath it in the grease pit, reaching up into the undercarriage of the Ford. The bay on the far side held a mechanical lift, an Oldsmobile perched on top of it.

"Actually, I was wondering about the old Camaro out in the yard," I said. "Is that your junkyard?"

"Who wants to know?" he asked. I couldn't make out any features, because the trouble light that hung under the Ford cast his face in shadow, but judging from his voice, he wasn't young, maybe not even middle-aged.

"I-I'm Luke. Grayson. I just moved here a couple of weeks ago."

"Pastor Grayson's kid, huh? I heard tell something about you moving to town." The grease pit was surrounded on three sides by a raised metal barrier to prevent objects from rolling from the garage floor over the edge. The fourth side of the pit opened onto a flight of metal steps that had once been painted yellow, but only a few flecks of paint remained.

Suddenly the man emerged from the grease pit and climbed the stairs while wiping his hands on a cloth that was more black with grease than the red of the fabric. My first reaction to him was fear. He was huge, big as an old oak, with long black hair that had grayed to the point that it was more salt than pepper. He wore a bushy beard, also shot through with gray, and the creases on his face and arms had been permanently blackened with car grease. "You don't look like your daddy," was his first observation.

"No, I don't," I said with some relief in my tone, since my dad resembled Ned Flanders from *The Simpsons*.

He almost smiled at that. At least his eyes did. His mouth was lost in the tangle of beard and mustache.

"What can I do for you?" he asked.

"The Camaro, the convertible out in the yard. Is that yours?"

He nodded thoughtfully as he tossed his rag onto the hood of the Ford and went to an old metal cooler that rested against one wall and pulled a can of beer from the ice bath within.

I tried to wait patiently as he cracked open his beer and took a long swig. He sighed with pleasure after he had emptied half the can and wiped his mouth with the back of his hand.

"Used to be my car," he said. "It's a chick magnet."

"A what?" I asked, hoping I had misheard him.

"A chick magnet," he said. "You know, it attracts women."

"Oh," I said as I contemplated a time in history when Roger, since I could only assume I was talking to Roger of Roger's Auto and Body, had been attractive to the opposite sex.

"Is it for sale?" I asked. I didn't want to sound too hopeful in case he was going to drive a hard bargain.

"Maybe," he said and took another swig of his beer. "You know anything about cars?"

"A little. Enough. I know enough."

My mom dated a guy for a while who lived with us. Clint. He was really into cars. Would take me to car shows and taught me how to do some of the basics. Older cars were less complicated, and I knew I could figure it out. "Does it need a lot of work?"

"Not much. Maybe a new radiator and hoses. The carburetor could use a good cleaning, spark plugs. Just needs someone to love her a little bit."

"I don't have a lot of money, but maybe you need some help around the shop. I'm looking for a job," I said. This wasn't really true, but the idea struck me as we stood talking. With an after-school job at least I would have something to pass the time. "I could earn what I can't pay you in cash."

He only nodded at this suggestion, giving me the impression he was the kind of person who didn't like to be convinced of anything. "Most people your age are pretty worthless," he said without any humor. "What are you, sixteen? Seventeen?"

"I'll be eighteen in December."

"Ooh," he hooted through his beard. "So you're all

grown. Might as well hire you while you still know every-thing."

"Does that mean you'll do it?" I asked, my voice rising in pitch with too much hope. "I'll do whatever you need. Cleaning, answering phones, whatever."

"I'll think about it. Come by tomorrow at the same time and I'll let you know."

"Okay," I said, taking that as a dismissal, and started backing toward the door. "I'll come by tomorrow on my way home from school. Same time."

He waved indifferently and tossed his beer can into an oil drum as he turned to reach for another. I was already forgotten as I let myself out to the tinkle of bells.

6

I was wrong to think of Ashland as my purgatory. It turned out to be my own personal hell. Not just the time I spent in school being alternately ignored or studied intently, like a specimen under glass in a museum, but the time I spent at home was hell, too. I rarely left my room, but when I did I was subject to Doris's saccharine smile or disapproving glances, depending on her mood and what shirt I was wearing. Dinner each night was torture. Dad and Doris would ask me questions in an effort to inspire conversation, but usually I stayed silent while they discussed the business of the parish—speculation about whose marriage seemed too perfect on the surface but was probably in serious trouble, or which caterer offered the best funeral wake.

It was Doris's ill-conceived idea to host a welcome-to-the-neighborhood party for me as an opportunity to introduce me to people from the community. I suppose she was hoping the party would serve as damage control for my initial impression on the neighbors as an assailant of their beloved wildcat.

Doris's idea of a party was not the same as my mom's idea of a party. For one thing, there was no booze. As Southern Baptists, Doris and Dad did not indulge in booze other than a bottle of medicinal brandy Dad kept in his study. For another thing, Doris prepared all of the food herself, didn't call for delivery from the local Italian deli or Lebanese restaurant the way Mom would have. Not that there was any such thing as an Italian deli or Lebanese restaurant in Ashland. Doris confined herself to the kitchen for two days, a never-ending collection of decorative aprons dirtied by her efforts, and created an impressive spread of ham biscuits and potato salad and deviled eggs and every other stereotypical southern food fit for a preacher's wake. Lemonade and iced tea were offered up in frosty pitchers, and there was a sickly sweet punch for the kids that stained the Styrofoam cups an electric pink.

I was expected to stand at attention with Dad and Doris and be introduced to everyone who came to visit us in our informal receiving line, though I immediately forgot any names that were told to me.

Though Doris had invited everyone in the immediate neighborhood, only the people who attended Dad's church showed for the party. Whether because of the threat of eternal damnation or social obligation, it wasn't clear. I got the sense that Doris made people uncomfortable, with her rural interpretation of Martha Stewart perfection and her icy smile.

There were only a few people I really remembered meeting at the party. One of those was Police Chief James Perry. He was exactly the person a Hollywood studio would have cast as a small-town southern sheriff—tall and broad through the shoulder, in good shape, and without the usual paunch of a middle-aged man. His black hair was cut with military precision, and his gray eyes seemed to suddenly know everything there was to know about a person with one fluid glance.

Police Chief Perry arrived in uniform, explaining to Doris as he greeted her that he would be heading in to work as soon as he left the party. When his gaze turned on me I experienced a twinge of guilt—for what, I don't know. But there it was.

"Hello, Frank," the police chief said as he extended a hand first to Dad, then to me. "This is your son, I take it. We're glad to have you here," he said to me, though the way his eyes appraised me implied he was still reserving judgment about how glad he was to have me there.

"Thanks. We're glad to have him here, too," Dad said affably.

Doris's smile never wavered, but she couldn't muster the enthusiasm to lie and say she too was glad to have me there. I clashed with her ideal public image the same way my Louder Than Bombs poster clashed with her plaid drapes in the spare bedroom.

"This is my daughter," Chief Perry said as he half turned to reveal a teenage girl who stood just behind him, her long hair matching his own in color. "Delilah, say hello," he said with just the hint of an edge to his tone, like the words he expected to come out of her mouth would be something less than polite talk for a man of God and his son.

"Hello," the girl said, looking bored, not giving either of us her eyes for more than a second.

"Well, hello, Delilah," Dad said, beaming at her, and I cringed mentally as I waited for him to make some cripplingly embarrassing remark. "We've missed you at church."

An awkward silence followed while Delilah said nothing, Dad grinned expectantly, waiting for her to say something in return about how much she missed church, and the police chief's jaw muscles bunched as he ground his teeth with restrained anger.

"Delilah, meet my son, Luke," Dad said finally to smother the horrible silence.

"Sure," Delilah said. "The wildcat slayer. I know you."

Chief Perry seemed puzzled by this comment, and I bit down on an angry retort. She let the awkward silence drag on for a minute while I stewed.

"Luke. That short for Lucas?" she asked me, her gaze now alert with sudden interest. Her eyes were the same color as her father's and held the same amount of judgment.

"No, just Luke," I said with a small shake of my head as I started to fumble the whole interaction by, one, forgetting to extend my hand to shake hers and, two, keeping my gaze on her longer than I should as I cataloged her features— long, wavy black hair, knockout smoky gray eyes, even if they did register only boredom when she looked at me. It was almost impossible to tell what kind of body she had since it was hidden beneath an oversize cardigan sweater and boyfriend-cut jeans. Her outfit wasn't grunge enough to qualify her as a rebel. More like she just didn't really give a crap.

"Yeah?" she asked. "Is that what people call you? 'Just Luke'?"

"Ju—Luke. My name is Luke," I said, now feeling like a complete idiot as she had me tripping over my own words while Dad and Chief Perry watched. Chief Perry's expression communicated that he thought I was an idiot and, at the same time, a threat to his daughter's virtue. I tried to keep my eyes from wandering to any part of Delilah's anatomy other than her face.

"Luke's a senior," Dad said, coming to the rescue as I found myself suddenly in the position of being less cool than a middle-aged preacher.

"Delilah's a senior, too," Chief Perry said, "and she's very focused on her studies." This with a meaningful glance at me to make sure I wasn't getting any funny ideas. I caught the roll of Delilah's eyes, but her expression remained placid and indifferent.

"I guess I'll see you around, Just Luke," Delilah said in a suggestive purr that raised Chief Perry's eyebrow—and his ire.

"Yeah, that . . . uh," I fumbled again, trying to be polite without showing too much interest in Chief Perry's precious daughter. "I'll see you around," I finished lamely.

The party graduated from awkward to painful as Doris tried to inject life into the whole debacle by entertaining people with small talk and forced enthusiasm. Her smile was practically a weapon. When she targeted people with it, they scrambled to engage someone—anyone—else in conversation, or made a quick retreat to the bathroom or the buffet.

I had taken up a stronghold in a corner with a cup of the sugary punch and kept rubbing my tongue around my mouth to scrub away the fuzzy feeling on my teeth.

Two elderly women I recognized from Dad's church sidled up to me and took up offensive positions on each side.

"Hello, Luke," the shorter one said.

"Hello . . . uh." I hesitated, not remembering either of their names.

"I'm Miss Wingfield, and this is my sister, Miss Mitze," the taller of the two said. She was regal in her tailored jacket and skirt. The silk flowers covering her hat in an uncertain heap were a major distraction. My eyes kept wandering up to study details like the obviously fake spray of leaves with white berries. The berries trembled each time she raised a hand to adjust the lapels of her jacket or to touch the brooch at her throat. "You may call me Miss Tucker."

"Okay," I said, for lack of anything better.

"Tucker is my Christian name, given to me because my mother's mother was a Tucker. Do you like my hat?" she asked with an arched brow. "I notice that you keep studying it."

"It's . . . interesting," I said.

"I do the design work for all of my own hats," she said. "Normally I would not feel it necessary to invite a compliment about one of my creations, but social graces don't seem to be your particular strength. You don't really have the . . . polished manners of your father, but I suppose that type of honesty is refreshing. People from the northern cit-ies are like that."

Washington was not a northern city by any map I had ever studied in school, but I let that one go.

"We saw you talking to the young Miss Delilah," Miss Mitze said with a crafty smile, and her sister shot her a look of disapproval.

Miss Mitze was as disheveled as her sister was polished. Miss Tucker's hair was a steely gray, shot through with one last stubborn streak of brown and pulled into a bun at her neck. In contrast, Miss Mitze's hair was a soft halo, with a faint blue cast to it that made me think of cotton candy.

"She *could* be quite lovely," Miss Tucker said, picking up the conversation. "I'm speaking about her appearance, of course. Her manners leave a lot to be desired."

"She takes after her mother in her looks," Miss Mitze said with a wistful sigh. "And maybe her personality too."

"Her mother was a Lefferts," Miss Tucker said, leaning in conspiratorially, though the name meant nothing to me.

"Mm," Mitze breathed in agreement.

"The Lefferts were always a bit eccentric," Tucker said diplomatically from my left.

"Insanity," Mitze clarified from my right.

"Yes. Though it usually skips a generation," Tucker said.

"You think Delilah is insane?" I asked, thinking maybe everyone in Ashland was crazy.

"Her grandmother was," Tucker said.

"Usually skips a generation," Mitze repeated. "But you never know."

"The cancer," Tucker said, and her expression softened

as she still looked at Delilah. Mitze nodded in agreement, her eyes shutting with dramatic effect.

Before I could ask for any explanation, Tucker continued: "It's hard to really know someone without knowing their family tree," she said, moving nimbly to an entirely new topic while I was still trying to get up to speed on insanity and cancer. She said this with an inviting look at me, presumably for me to disclose something worthwhile about my own family tree. Again our gazes tracked together, this time toward my dad and Doris, who were strong-arming an elderly couple into conversation. The husband kept glancing hopefully toward the buffet, while his wife sipped at her iced tea, nodding and smiling woodenly.

"Well," I said with a sigh, "if I have to be judged according to who I'm related to, I might as well give up the fight right now."

Mitze and Tucker both smiled but gracefully let the topic drop as we all continued to watch the party around us.

7

When I returned to the auto shop after our first meeting, Roger hired me to help him out after school—answering phones, keeping the office clean and organized, occasionally helping him with the cars for minor repairs like oil changes. There was only one other guy who worked at Roger's shop—a guy named Tiny who was anything but. He had wavy black hair to his shoulders, a grizzled goatee, rheumy eyes, and an impressive collection of tattoos, some of which might have been acquired in prison.

The Camaro was relocated to the driveway at home so I could work on it during my free hours in the evenings and on weekends. The exterior of the car was filthy, but the body was free of rust and the interior was in almost pristine condition. Doris blanched when the tow truck showed up at the house with the Camaro perched on its bed. "Where are you going to put it?" she asked, distaste evident in her tone.

"I told Dad," I said, "it will just be in the driveway until I get it running. I'll clean it, fix it up."

The Camaro stood out like a sore thumb against the backdrop of Doris's carefully pruned azaleas and hydrangeas. I felt like the Camaro and I had that in common. Neither one of us fit in to this life, this town. We were meant for each other.

Now instead of spending most evenings in my room with a book or watching television, I worked on the Camaro after dinner in the failing daylight. Roger had given me four almost-new tires, saying as he did, "If you end up killing yourself driving on those bald tires, I don't want the blame to get traced back to me."

The evening after Roger gave me the tires I was out in the driveway, working free the lug nuts, which had frozen after years of neglect. I was intent on my task so I did not even notice when Delilah Perry wandered into the yard and came to stand over me.

I don't know how long she had been standing there, watching me, when she finally spoke. I was listening to a new remix of an Andhim song on my iPhone and so hadn't noticed her approach. At the sound of her voice I jerked in surprise and looked up to find her appraising me with her cool gray eyes. She wore a pair of black leggings and an oversize hoodie, the hood up, forcing her hair to obscure most of her face.

"Hello, Delilah," I said absently as I kicked at the tire to loosen it from its mount. "What are you doing here?"

"I was just out for a walk," she said. "This your car?" she asked with a nod at the Camaro.

"Will be," I said, "once I get it fixed up."

I was mildly surprised when she sat down on the pavement near me and crossed her legs tailor fashion, plucking idly at the frayed drawstring of her hood.

"So how do you like Ashland, Just Luke?" she asked without any hint of humor as she buried her hands in the front pocket of her sweatshirt.

"Well, Delilah," I said, "I've got to be honest with you. So far, this place sucks pretty hard."

"People call me Del. No one calls me Delilah unless they're old."

"Well, I do," I said. "As long as you keep using that 'Just Luke' joke, I'm going to call you Delilah."

"Yeah, well, we're neighbors," she said as she pointed to the houses beyond the rear fence of my house. "I live on the street behind you. In fact, I can see into your bedroom window at night."

My face immediately flushed with heat at the thought of her watching me in my most private moments, even though I knew without a doubt she couldn't possibly. My bedroom was on the first floor, at the front of the house, and I always kept my shades carefully drawn. I spent far too much time watching porn on my phone to ever be inclined to let much daylight enter my room. The thought of the porn, and a girl knowing this intimate part of my life, kept the blush there long enough that Delilah got a full minute to enjoy it, the corners of her mouth turning up slightly with a triumphant smirk.

"You're very funny," I said. And she might have been, if her taunts were directed at someone else.

"My dad says preachers' kids are nothing but trouble," she said in almost a sigh, maybe from annoyance with her dad and his opinions, maybe because she thought I was a disappointment to this stereotype. "Told me I should stay away from you." After saying this she carefully studied my face, staring at me in a way I would soon learn to dread, her wonder and judgment evident, though her actual thoughts were hidden. "Is it true?"

"Is what true?" I asked, so disarmed by her stare that I had already forgotten her words.

"Are you trouble?" she asked.

Trying to recover some lost ground I said, matching her earnest tone, "In my experience, girls whose dads are cops are the biggest whores. Are you a whore?"

Actually, I had no personal experience with girls of just about any kind, least of all the daughters of police officers. But I was new in town. People only knew what I told them, or, in the case of Principal Sherman, what was in my school records.

"You sure don't talk like your dad's a preacher," Delilah said, unfazed by my rudeness. "Does your dad know you use words like that?" She was one of those people who expressed irony in a sincere tone, making it wrong either way you interpreted it.

"They say whore in the Bible all the time," I said as I sat back on one heel and squinted up at her.

Her eyes widened a bit as she cracked her gum and pushed her hair back from her face. "I'm from a town of twelve thousand people in America's heartland. You think I don't know my Bible?"

I snorted out a laugh and let the subject drop. Remembering my conversation with the Misses Wingfield I said, "The word around town is that insanity runs in your family. On your mother's side. That true?"

Delilah stiffened and her eyes went hard, and I thought I had made her mad enough to set her off, but after a few seconds she relaxed back into her confident slouch.

"It usually skips a generation," she said. "My grandmother was crazy."

"Crazy how?"

"She thought she was the illegitimate child of Robert E. Lee."

"How do you know she wasn't?" I asked.

Delilah gave me a wilting stare to articulate my stupidity before answering. "He died fifty years before she was born." And then, after a beat of silence, added, "I googled it."

"Well, you would have to, wouldn't you?" I asked.

"Anyway," she said, dismissing my comment with a wave, "the Wingfield sisters are a couple of old maids who love to gossip about everyone in town. They're nosy busybodies."

"I thought they were nice," I said with a shrug. "They were the only ones with anything interesting to say at Doris's party."

"Your stepmother is a disaster. At least my grandmother was legitimately crazy. Doris is just a snob and a backbiter. She's single-handedly setting back the feminist movement by several decades."

"So what do people do in this town anyway? Besides gossip."

"You mean people our age?" she asked.

"Yeah."

She shrugged. "The kids with money go down to the lake, ride their WaveRunners, and go waterskiing. They party down there by the lake. The rest of us mostly smoke a lot of weed and eat Hot Pockets." She paused to consider what other pastimes were immediately obvious but soon gave up the thought with a shrug and a grim, downward twist of her lips.

"Really?" I asked with some surprise. "You guys get weed here?"

Another wilting stare, as if I was possibly the dumbest person she had ever met. "We live in a farming community. Where do you think weed comes from?"

I took the question as rhetorical and didn't answer her, wondering at the time why it was physically impossible to stop a blush.

"Nice shirt," she said, suddenly changing tack. "Is that a hand-me-down from your dad?"

"My dad has terrible taste in music," I said, refusing to let her win this round, "and The Smiths rock."

"Sure," she said. "I wasn't judging you."

She watched me for a long minute, long enough that I grew uncomfortable and had to focus all of my attention on the task at hand to avoid feeling awkward. The silence didn't seem to bother her at all.

"Well," she said as she pushed herself up to a standing position in one fluid motion. "Guess I'll see you around."

"Yeah, sure," I said, but she was already walking away. When she looked back over her shoulder, she caught me watching her retreating form intently. Not because her baggy sweatshirt revealed anything of interest to watch. More like I was still trying to figure out if our conversation had been friendly or antagonistic. Either way, she caught my stare but ignored me and kept walking at the same languid pace.

8

The second week of school started out better than the first. Now I had a job, a car, and someone to sit with at lunch, even though the job didn't pay, the car didn't run, and Don wasn't really my first choice for a friend. Maybe not even a close third.

That Monday was also the day I met Grant Parker. I had seen him around campus, and we shared fifth-period American History. I was always on the lookout for Penny and her golden head of hair, and I usually saw her walking arm in arm with Grant or hanging around his locker. Before that day, Grant hadn't seemed to take any notice of me, even though I had physically assaulted his team's mascot.

I was sitting with Don and the dork squad when Grant stopped at our lunch table. It was almost like an after-thought, as if it just occurred to him that maybe it would be mildly entertaining to make our social status a little bit more painful. Grant had a buddy with him, a dark-haired guy who kept quiet and let Grant keep all the limelight for himself.

"Hey, Don," Grant said through a smirk. "Great haircut. Did your mom do that for you at home?"

Don's expression was one of weary resignation. This was a chore he had to face and was resigned to it even though it was a pain in the ass.

"Yeah, Grant," Don said. "She did."

"Nice," Grant said with a nod. "I thought so." Unable to get much of a reaction out of Don, Grant lost interest in him and turned his attention to me. Grant gave a slight roll of his eyes, quick and subtle so that I was the only one who saw it. He made it seem like we were sharing a private joke, an allegiance, at Don's expense. It gave me a warm feeling in my chest. With that subtle gesture Grant was acknowledging that Don was a total dork, but I wasn't like Don. I was different. Better.

"Hey, so you're the new kid in town, huh?" Grant said with a lazy smile as he extended a hand for me to shake. "I like that move you pulled with Willie," he said, as if my epic humiliation had been intentional, as if I had planned and executed a comical sparring routine with the wildcat and had somehow come out the winner.

"I'm Grant. Grant Parker," he said. "I'm the president of the student council, so I wanted to welcome you to Ashland."

Grant was standing so close to the table I had to bend my neck at an uncomfortable angle to really see him.

"Uh . . ." My voice came out as a squeaky gargle. I quickly cleared my throat, but the damage was done: the impression was there that I was self-conscious and weak. "I'm Luke Grayson."

"Good to meet you, Luke," Grant said with such warmth that I marveled again at how these southern, small-town people seemed to emerge from the womb with charm and manners to spare. "This is my buddy, Tony Hurst." A moment of awkward silence passed as Tony sized me up like a piece of livestock. He did not greet me with the same warmth Grant had, just stood in stony silence with one hand slung in his jeans pocket and favored me with only a nod. I felt his eyes take in my clothes—and my insignificant size compared to his.

"When did you move here?" Grant asked, oblivious to Tony's coldness toward me.

"About a month ago," I said.

"From where?"

"Washington, DC."

"Yeah? Why?"

I've been asking myself the same goddamned question for a month, dude. "My mom got tired of having me around, I guess," I said, that particular resentment still very close to the surface.

"Interesting," Grant said, though it wasn't really. Mom had said she wanted me to have a chance to get to know my dad before I left home for college and abandoned my childhood. She also thought that a positive male role model was something I was lacking, though Dad didn't offer anything remotely comforting in the form of a male perspective.

Tony, Grant's buddy, who still hadn't said a word, was well muscled and deeply tanned. He looked country strong, the kind of guy you see in a pickup truck commercial, with jeans that were faded almost white from age and abuse.

Grant parked himself next to me at the lunch table, one butt cheek rested comfortably on the edge of the tabletop, his boot planted on the seat. He placed his foot on the seat with cool and measured casualness, as if the bench—even the school itself—belonged to him and the rest of us were merely borrowing his things for a while.

"So like I was saying," Grant said, his voice a mellifluous baritone drawl, "that was a pretty good stunt you pulled the first day of school."

"Uh . . . yeah," I said. Did he really think I had humiliated myself intentionally? It was a brilliant idea, that. If I'd had any coolness factor at all, I would have played it off that way from the beginning.

"Since you're new around here," Grant continued, "Tony and I were thinking we should take you out, show you around the town."

Which will take all of about five minutes.

"That would be . . . cool," I said.

"So meet us at Parr's Drive-In Saturday night. About eight o'clock," he said as he stood and straightened his jacket.

"Drive-in?" I asked. "Like a drive-in movie theater?"

"A drive-in diner," Grant said, as if such a thing were so common I should know what that was.

"Like in the movies?" I asked stupidly, and wished I could take it back as soon as the words left my mouth.

"You've never heard of a drive-in diner?" Grant asked, maybe with a bit of impatience. "I thought you were from the big city."

"Yeah, we don't . . . we don't have those . . . drive-ins, I mean." God, it really was like I had moved five hundred years instead of five hundred miles. I still had no idea how far Tennessee was from DC, but it was starting to seem farther and farther every minute.

"We'll see you Saturday night, city boy," Grant said as he started to walk away, Tony falling naturally into place a half step behind him.

I returned my attention to my lunch but our table had gone quiet. When I looked at Don and his friends, they were all watching me in awe.

"What?" I asked.

"Nothing," Don said. "Just . . . I can't figure why Grant Parker would take an interest in you. I mean, you're . . . nobody."

"Thanks for saying so," I said.

"I just mean . . . well, you know, I'm nobody too. It isn't a *bad* thing."

I shrugged, trying to mask my own shock at this development. "Maybe he's just trying to be nice," I said.

Don gave an emphatic shake of his head. "Oh, no. Grant Parker doesn't have to be nice to anyone. It's weird that he invited you out like that."

"Like he said," I said as I pushed my lunch tray away, "he's the student council president. Maybe it's his job to welcome new people."

"It's possible," Don said doubtfully. "We've never had a

new person before, so maybe there's some kind of student council rule I don't know about."

"I still don't see what the big deal is," I said, feigning indifference, though inwardly I couldn't help but feel a little excited. I thought, *Maybe this is it.* Now the popular crowd would take notice of me. Once they got to know me, knew that I wasn't a toolbag like Don and his buddies, they'd accept me among the in crowd.

I glanced casually over my shoulder to study Grant Parker and his friends. They sat at the table closest to the large window overlooking the football field, hogging the only space in the room that was in a warm patch of sunlight.

I could absolutely imagine myself among them.

9

Saturday night I rode my bike to Parr's Drive-In. It really was a drive-in diner where you could pull into a parking space and order through a brightly painted speaker. The waitresses did not come out on roller skates—slightly disappointing—but they wore uniforms with short skirts that violated all principles of modern feminism. I was standing against the wall, trying to exude cool and nursing a soda I didn't really want, when Grant pulled into a parking space right in front of me in a shiny silver pickup truck with a king cab, a spotlight, and gun rack on the roof. The gun rack was empty, thankfully.

The door to the truck opened, and a waft of country music floated out onto the night air. Grant stuck his head out of the door and, without so much as a hello, said, "Get in."

I found myself crammed into the backseat of the king cab with two guys who were folded uncomfortably into the small space, both with cans of beer in hand. Grant threw introductions over the seat back, nearly lost in the noise from the speakers. Skip and Chet. Chet and Skip. It sounded like the name of a reality television show, like they could star in their own version of *Duck Dynasty*, hating gays and liberals for sport.

One of them, Chet or Skip, though I was unsure which, was blond, the other dark-haired. Their faces were largely hidden by baseball caps, both of them wearing hats with blaze orange accents. I wasn't country enough to know at the time what that meant, but blaze orange is the companion color of every man who hunts defenseless woodland creatures.

Penny was tucked in the front passenger seat and turned to look at me between the seat backs.

"Hi, Luke," she said with a sweet smile.

I smiled and said hello in return, then I noticed Grant's eyes on me in the rearview mirror, the ridge over his brow furrowed. I sat back so that my face was no longer visible in the mirror and looked out the window to keep my gaze away from Penny.

Grant drove us out of town with two cars caravanning behind us. The boys kept up a steady stream of chatter with each other, inside jokes falling like grenades into the conversation. They were so familiar with each other, had known each other for so long, that it made anything they said among them overtly private and exclusive. I sat silently, trying not to let my eyes stray to Penny, who scrolled idly through her phone.

Soon we were on a dirt road that wound over the hills. The road ended and I thought we would stop, but Grant kept on, the snick of dry autumn grass slapping against the body of the truck.

At the top of a small rise Grant shut off the truck but left the headlights burning and the radio playing. Everyone piled out of the trucks and cars, and Grant's buddies got to work building a small campfire under his supervision. The truck bed held several coolers filled with beer on ice, and everyone got down to the business of partying.

I took a can of beer and drank it quickly, grateful for something to do with my hands and my mouth, feeling like a conspicuous outsider. The old *Sesame Street* chant played in my mind: *One of these things is not like the others, one of these things just doesn't belong. . . .* I was the other.

While everyone gathered around the campfire, I sat with my legs hanging off the tailgate of Grant's truck and contemplated the size of the sky. It was as if I had gone my whole life without ever really seeing the sky before. In the city you can see only patches of sky between the rooflines, and even with a long view of the horizon, the city is so clogged with buildings and cars and bridges and exhaust fumes, the sky is only a backdrop.

But here, I was overwhelmed by the immensity of the sky, the horizon broken only by the rolling pastureland. Stars struggled against the gauze of the thin, low-hanging clouds. Though the moon was only a crescent sliver, the full roundness of its dark side was visible from where I sat, small and insignificant, on the Chevy truck.

I was on my second beer, and the alcohol was traveling quickly to my head. I wasn't drunk, but I felt a pleasant buzz, just enough to make me want to hurry up and finish the second beer so I could crack a third, knowing the first few sips would be cold and crisp.

The noise of the others talking and laughing faded into the background as I continued to study the sky, wishing that I knew something about constellations so I could read the stars. As I sat in comfortable silence, Penny settled into the seat beside me and offered me an unopened beer.

"Thanks," I said with a smile. "I was just thinking I would like another one, but I didn't feel like getting up."

The smile she gave me was partially hidden by a curtain of wavy blond hair that glowed even in the dim light cast by the moon and the campfire. "What are you doing?" she asked.

"Looking at the stars," I said as I turned back to the beauty of them, which had paled slightly in comparison to Penny's smile. "I just realized that back home I never really see the sky. Not like this. At night you see only streetlights and lighted buildings. In the city we've built up these walls around us, as if we aren't part of nature, as if we're somehow stronger than nature. Here—" I stopped suddenly as I realized I was babbling. I took a quick drink from my beer to cover my awkwardness.

"What were you going to say?" Penny asked as she gave my knee a nudge with the side of her hand.

"Nothing," I said with a self-conscious chuckle.

"No, really. Tell me. I want to know."

I shook my head but finally said, "I don't know. Here I feel so insignificant. Almost like you have to believe in a higher power because how else could you explain all of this." I waved vaguely at the sky and moon above us.

"I guess I never really think about it," she said, her voice soft. "But it's a real pretty thought." As she said this she shifted a little closer to me. It wasn't anything obvious, almost as if she was just resettling in her seat to get comfortable, but I was aware that now her hip and shoulder were touching mine. I became acutely aware of my posture and that my underarms were slimy with sweat. "Most people I know don't think about a world outside of Ashland," she said, her gaze still turned up to the sky.

"What about you?" I asked.

She laughed in a self-conscious way and rubbed her hands together as if to warm them. "I think about getting out of Ashland all the time. Leaving everyone and everything I know behind. But then I think . . ." She paused, and the silence dragged on for so long that I didn't think she was going to finish the thought.

"But then you think what?" I asked.

"I don't know," she said. "What would I do? Where would I go? How would I make new friends?"

"You've just summed up my entire life," I said.

"I know," she said. "You moving here, seeing you . . . have to adjust to a new life. It's made me think about it even more."

I was still formulating a response to Penny's comment when someone put a heavy hand on my shoulder and the weight of a knee in my back.

"Hey, city boy," Grant said, and I turned to find myself in the light of his easy smile.

"Hey, man," I said as I cracked the beer Penny had handed me. I held up the can I had just finished and said,

"Where are you putting the empties? You take them back to recycle?"

Grant took the can from my hand and flung it into the field as he dropped into a seat beside me in one fluid motion. "I can't tell if he tries to be funny or if he's just kind of simple," Grant said, leaning forward to direct his comment to Penny across my chest.

"You're hilarious," I said with a roll of my eyes. Though Grant came across as the typical jock douche bag at first, I regretted that I had been so quick to judge and dismiss him as a one-dimensional character.

As I sat there between Grant and Penny, sipping on my beer and swinging my legs off the tailgate, I found myself thinking that maybe my last year of high school wouldn't be so bad. Earlier that week my whole senior year had stretched out in front of me like a lonely abyss, but now I felt a certain warmth under my skin at the prospect of autumn nights out sipping beer under the stars, weekend fishing trips, and Friday-night football games.

Maybe it was just the beer talking, but it was the first moment since I had arrived in Ashland that I felt something other than anger, loneliness, or angry loneliness.

"All right, city boy," Grant said as he nudged me with his elbow. "Time for your initiation."

The unofficial nickname he had given me was starting to wear a groove in my patience, but he seemed to mean it in a good-natured way, so I didn't correct him. Instead I gave him shit in return.

"It doesn't involve having sex with barnyard animals, does it?" I asked as I turned to Grant again. "Because I know how you *country boys* like to get your kicks."

Grant was smiling at my joke, but I thought I detected the glint of anger in his eyes. Before I could really tell if I had insulted him with my comment about sexual relations with barnyard animals, the glint was gone and all that remained was his good-natured smile.

"If that's what you're into, you'll have to manage that in your own free time," he said as he slapped me on the upper back, hard enough that it actually hurt, but I fought back a wince. I didn't want him to think I was a complete wimp, which, if I'm being totally honest, I am. "Your initiation," Grant said as I felt the others go silent behind us, "is going to be your first cow tipping." A stifled laugh behind us from the group. I knew it wasn't Tony, since he never laughed at anything, but this seemed to generally amuse everyone.

"You're joking," I said.

Grant shook his head. "Nope."

"How the hell am I supposed to do that?" I asked.

"It's easy," Grant said. "Just walk on up to one of them out sleeping in the field and push it over. But you've got to really get your shoulder into it." With this he demonstrated as he dropped his shoulder and knocked his weight against mine in the parody of a football tackle.

Since we had arrived past dark I hadn't really taken much notice of the few cows scattered in the pasture. They were just part of the scenery. Now I turned to glance around the fields, only one or two of the cows now visible in the dark.

"Luke, you don't have to," Penny said as I sat considering what I should do.

"He wants to," Grant said. "He wants to prove he isn't just a city boy." Grant's voice held a warning, and I looked questioningly at Penny, but she just rolled her eyes and looked away.

"What are the chances the cow will kill me after I tip it?" I asked, trying to keep my voice casual to hide my unease.

"Mm," Grant said as if he were really considering the odds. "Slim to none. Just run real fast while it's still on the ground." He laughed after he said this, a laugh that invited me to join in. I tried to laugh along, but my heart wasn't in it.

"If I don't do this, you'll never let me live it down, right?" I asked as I suppressed a small sigh.

"Not likely," Grant said with a nod toward the closest cow, just a black hole in the absolute darkness beyond the light of the fire.

As I walked toward the cow I found myself high-stepping quietly through the grass as if I were a caveman sneaking up on a mammoth, or maybe Elmer Fudd sneaking up on Bugs Bunny. This was the closest I had ever been to livestock, and the experience was somewhat disquieting.

The cow remained still as I approached, and I silently prayed that it would not make any sudden movements, would not stampede and trample me to death or whatever it was cows do when they react with fear or anger. My heart was hammering so hard in my chest I couldn't believe the noise wouldn't wake every cow within a mile.

The headlights from Grant's truck cut on suddenly, startling me so much that I jerked in fright. I was so tightly wound that the abrupt introduction of artificial light was almost audible. My eyes had been adjusted to the dark, but now I could see the brown of the cow's coat and the white mask of its face. The light did not disturb the cow, and it remained still.

When I came alongside the cow, I paused to take a deep breath and steel my resolve. I turned sideways and dropped my shoulder in preparation for my attack. With one final glance over my shoulder at the group that hung clustered near Grant's truck, just a mass of silhouettes from my perspective, I planted my right foot and leaned into it, slamming my shoulder into the thickest part of the beast and pushing with all my might.

Almost immediately, I realized that I was doomed to fail. Pushing the cow was like pushing against a house or a car. The cow didn't even stumble but instead swung its head on the massively powerful neck to eye me curiously. Not docile and bovine, but self-aware and seriously annoyed.

The cow had not been asleep. It had merely been standing still, as any large animal with the same cranial capacity of a cow would, stupidly surveying its surroundings and contemplating the meaning of life.

The cow dropped its head as if it had a sudden interest in grazing, while I stood frozen, waiting to see how the situation would play out. Before I could decide whether to run or back away slowly and quietly, the head, bigger and heavier than an anvil, swung up and cracked me under the chin with the broad flat of its nose. My teeth cracked together and I saw stars, both literally and figuratively, as I fell onto my back.

My fall to the ground didn't really hurt anything other than my pride. The long grass was soft, and my fall was additionally pillowed by a pile of cowshit, made slimy from a recent rain.

I stood quickly to avoid being stepped on by the cow, now eyeing me menacingly as it waited to see what I would do. It took one threatening step toward me, and I was so scared I stumbled backward and fell again.

By now I was aware of the howls of laughter coming across the field from my audience, and I was so angry I forgot to be afraid. I stood for one minute looking at them all as they laughed; Grant was doubled over hugging his gut as he laughed the loudest.

I started to brush off my backside to remove the worst of the debris that clung to my clothes but I ended up just spreading the cowshit or grinding it into the fabric of my jeans.

Grant and his disciples continued to laugh with more enthusiasm than the situation really warranted. Instead of walking back to the circle of firelight, I walked toward what I hoped was the direction of town.

I heard my name called. Maybe the voice was Grant's, though I couldn't tell from that distance. The tone insisted on my return to the group, but I ignored it and kept walking. I wasn't sure I was headed home. I was just headed away.

I'll admit I was a little scared, afraid I would encounter a bear or even another cow, but going back to Grant and his friends was not an option. I was already embarrassed. If I had to face them now it would do nothing but compound my humiliation. I chose a cowardly exit while in my heart hoping that it conveyed only contempt and anger. My mortification manifested both mentally and physically, and I felt sick to my stomach.

———

Once I reached the road I walked quickly, my head down, angry with myself. Angry with the world. In my mind I was plotting the quickest way I could get back to DC. Maybe my mom would take me back. Maybe she would forget this idea of me forging some kind of relationship with my dad, would see that it was useless. After all, she had raised me, and she was nothing like my dad. I thought about calling her then. Calling to tell her I was done with Ashland and was coming home whether she liked it or not. I had friends in DC who would let me live with them. Maybe I could take the GED, graduate early, and get a job until I got accepted to some mediocre state university a thousand miles from either of my parents.

There were no streetlights on the outskirts of town, and the houses were dark and quiet, watching me with silent judgment as I passed. I had no concept of how far we had driven outside of town, but it took me over an hour to reach civilization on foot.

On the empty residential streets I wandered a circuitous route, so lost in my thoughts I didn't even notice as a car slid up alongside me, creeping at the same speed as I was walking. I half-turned to look over my shoulder, expecting to find Grant or one of his friends in the car, coming after me to apologize or try to make nice. I was angry enough to knock someone out but didn't like the idea of anyone, especially Penny or one of the other girls, seeing me covered in cowshit and shame.

The car was painted green and white, the colors of the local police department. The passenger window slid down and released a puff of cool air into the night.

"Evening," came the baritone drawl of the driver as he put the car into park and leaned one arm along the back of the passenger seat to look up at me. Chief Perry.

"Hey," I said through a sigh of defeat.

"Pastor Grayson's kid," he said, as if the title were an ironic compliment. "What's your name again?"

"Luke."

"Jesus Christ, boy, what is that smell?" he asked as I leaned over to look into the window and he caught a sudden whiff of me.

"It's shit, sir."

His left eye narrowed, and I could feel its cool judgment settle on me. "You getting smart with me, son?"

"No, sir. That smell is cowshit. I'm covered in it."

"What the hell have you been up to?" he asked, neither amused nor sympathetic.

"Just—" I bit off what I was going to say since any explanation I gave would either: one, make me sound like a complete idiot, or, two, take too much energy to explain when I didn't feel like telling the story in the first place. "I fell in a pile of cowshit."

"When you fell in a pile of cowshit did you also fall into a puddle of beer?" he asked without a hint of humor. "Because I can smell beer on you from ten paces."

"I had one beer," I said, hoping that maybe a little honesty would help to keep me out of trouble.

"They have different laws about underage drinking where you come from?" he asked.

"No, sir," I said, almost impossible now to keep the bite out of my tone. He was exactly like his daughter. Able to put me on the defensive with nothing more than a raised eyebrow or a question.

"You've been in this town all of two weeks and already you're looking for trouble. You some kind of overachiever?"

"Four weeks," I corrected him. *Each one of them an eternity.* "And I didn't go looking for any trouble. Trouble found me."

He ignored me, didn't ask me what had happened. "I'm not letting you in my vehicle smelling like that," he said, "but you'd better go straight home. I won't call your father this time, but next time I catch you drinking, you'll be answering to your folks and to the judge. Get on home now."

This was my dismissal as his window slid closed and he put the car into gear.

10

Monday I avoided any contact at all with Grant and his friends, but it was clear from the way people whispered and laughed behind their hands as they passed me at my locker that the story of my latest humiliation had already traversed the student grapevine. I seethed impotently.

When I entered my American History class at the last possible second before the bell rang, I studiously avoided even a glance in Grant's direction. He sat in the back of class and would occasionally make loud mooing noises when the teacher had her back to us. My face burned as the other students giggled at this childish joke. Though I wanted to haul off and hit him in the jaw, wanted to pound his face into a bloody pulp, I didn't turn to look at Grant, didn't acknowledge him in any way. I stared coldly ahead, trying to exude the vibe that the dry-erase board was the most captivating thing I had ever seen.

Delilah sat two rows over and one seat behind me, and I stole a few glances at her. She never looked up from her note taking and, I noticed, was the only person who ignored Grant's mooing.

When the dismissal bell rang at the end of the period, I took my time gathering my stuff, hoping everyone else would leave before I did so I didn't have to make my way down the hall with them.

Delilah was bent over her backpack, her long hair obscuring her face as everyone filed past her on their way out the door. Grant was making his way down the aisle past Delilah's desk, a smug smile on his face as he mooed again to get one final laugh out of everyone before they left the classroom.

As Grant passed Delilah's desk his feet became tangled in a combination of her feet and her backpack, and he pitched forward violently. His arms went wide as he tried to stop his fall, and his books flew in every direction. The desks groaned against the linoleum floor as his weight shoved them askew, and the sound of his body against the desktops was enough to tell me that the fall hurt more than his pride.

Grant was on his feet quickly, his face red and with murder in his eyes. "What the hell?" he shouted at Delilah, but she didn't flinch.

"You should watch where you're going," Delilah said coolly.

"You did that in purpose, you crazy bitch," Grant huffed, but Delilah just waited patiently for Grant to get out of her way.

"Everything okay, Mr. Parker?" the teacher asked. I swear she almost looked pleased.

"You're as crazy as everyone says you are," Grant muttered under his breath to Delilah. He summoned what little dignity he could and gathered his books. I felt his glare but didn't look up again until he was out of the room. Delilah left for her next class without saying anything to me.

I avoided the humiliation of the lunchroom that day, admitting to myself that Grant had won this round. His object was to put me in my place. And he had. Squarely.

At the end of the school day I took my time getting to my locker. I planned to wait until everyone was gone and Grant and his posse were safely at football practice before leaving the school building. The last person I wanted to see in this world was waiting near my locker.

Penny stood with one shoulder leaned against the wall of lockers as she scrolled through her phone. She looked up as I approached, and smiled in greeting.

"Hi," she said quietly.

"Hey," I said, my tone frigid. I was angry about my own feelings of inadequacy, angry because a girl like Penny would always choose a guy like Grant over a guy like me, even if Grant was an asshole and I was a . . . well, I wasn't sure what I was, but I sure as hell wasn't an asshole like Grant.

"I wanted to apologize to you. About the other night," she said.

"Apologize for what?" I asked.

"For the joke Grant and his buddies played on you. It wasn't very nice."

"Why should you apologize for him?" I asked.

"I knew what they were planning to do," she said with a sigh. "Grant told the guys that afternoon when I was there. I should have warned you or something."

I shrugged, as if the whole thing were no big deal, then worked the combination lock so I wouldn't have to see the pity in her eyes.

"They can be real jerks sometimes," she said.

"Just sometimes?" I asked. "I got the impression maybe they were jerks all of the time."

She laughed at that but didn't agree with me. "I hope . . . well, I guess I hope you and I can still be friends. I like talking to you. You're not like most other people."

"Because I'm not a jerk?"

"Exactly," she said with another laugh. "So? Apology accepted?"

"Like I said, you don't have to apologize for Grant."

"I think Grant just feels threatened, you know?" she said, her nose wrinkling. "You're new here and all. The girls all think you're really cute."

"Now you're just trying to make me feel better," I said, but I wondered if when she said "all the girls" she was including herself. There was no way to ask the question without sounding like I was fishing for a compliment, but I wanted to know. "Why do you go out with him?" I asked. "If he's such a jerk."

"Oh," she said, and now the tables were turned and she was working to avoid my gaze. "Everyone wants to be with Grant. But he chose me. That makes it special, I guess." She seemed to sense my judgment about this being a valid reason for dating Grant and quickly added, "Besides, he's not a jerk all the time."

"Well, that's good, I guess," I said as I slung my backpack over my shoulder and shut my locker door. "It doesn't seem right for a girl as nice and as pretty as you to be with a jerk."

She smiled at that and her eyes widened with sudden interest. "I . . . I guess I'd better get to practice," she said. "I'm late. I'll see you around, okay?"

"Yeah, okay," I said, and thought about her as I walked to my bike, and for most of the next twenty-four hours. I thought about her about as often as I thought about sex . . . so a lot. And sometimes I thought about both at the same time.

11

At home I spent very little time outside my room unless I was working on the Camaro. And I worked three days a week at Roger's garage. It wasn't much work, really. Once I had cleaned the office space and set up a desk calendar to schedule Roger's workload, there was only the occasional busywork. The phone rarely rang, as people would just drop in to see Roger for a quick consultation.

There was only one competing mechanic in town, a young guy who rode Harleys and had a mullet. As Roger told it, only the meth-smoking bikers used the other mechanic. Anyone who was respectable utilized Roger's garage.

For some inexplicable reason, Roger insisted on starting his work day at 7:00 A.M. By the time I got to the garage after school he would be winding down for the day, he and Tiny sipping on icy cans of Schlitz or Busch beer. Roger usually offered me a beer, and the three of us would sit to watch television in the office. Almost always we would watch episodes of *Law & Order,* and Roger would talk avidly to the characters on the screen, telling them who was really guilty. He was, almost without exception, always wrong about the solution to the crime.

Tiny, when he spoke at all, spoke mostly in grunts, so I had little else to do besides my homework.

"I heard about your run-in with Grant Parker and his buddies," Roger said to me one afternoon during a commercial break from *Law & Order.*

"What run-in?" I asked without looking up from my phone.

"Cow tipping," Roger said.

"You *heard* about that?" My voice rose with disbelief.

"That was the rumor going through the crowd at the football game Friday night," Roger said. "Football games and church are where we get all of the news."

"You never go to church," I said.

"I don't have to go to church. You see another qualified mechanic living within a hundred miles? No. Which means I do whatever the hell I want. And getting up for church on my one day off ain't one of the things I want to do."

Tiny emitted an affirming grunt and slurped loudly from his beer.

"Grant Parker is an asshole," Roger said. "It's in his genes. Leland Parker is an asshole too. We went to school together, though I was a few years ahead of him."

"Really?" I asked. "How old are you?"

"I'm fifty-one," Roger said. "Why?"

"I don't know," I said. "I guess I thought you were a lot older than that."

"Well, you ain't exactly pretty to look at neither," Roger said.

"What did you hear?" I asked. "About the cow tipping."

"Just that you're an idiot, but that part we already knew." Another affirming grunt from Tiny with the glimmer of a smile through his beard.

"Thanks a lot," I said acidly. "I hate this town."

"I don't mind it," Roger said. "Small-town folks aren't no different from big-city folks. Just less of them, so whatever they do gets amplified a million times. You must have had a kid like Grant Parker at your old school. There's always a Grant Parker."

"Sure. Yeah," I said, thinking of Jonathan Bryan III, a kid at my old school whose family had so much money he could afford to wear plaid pants and not get beaten up for it.

"And?" Roger pressed.

"I avoided him like the plague," I said.

"Well, then, maybe you aren't as dumb as you look. Avoid Grant Parker too."

"Hey, it's not as if I went out looking to get humiliated," I said in protest. "He came after me."

But Roger's attention had already returned to the television. "You gonna take her word for that?" he asked the fictional detective. "She's a hooker, for Christ's sake."

12

It was a Tuesday afternoon and I was hurrying to leave school, hoping to make it off campus without running into anyone.

Life at Wakefield High School had become ritualized torture. More horrible than being forced to listen to their god-awful hick-hop music, worse than enduring a class called Introduction to Agriculture, my reputation had been established based on my two encounters with animals—one wild, one domesticated. At least the Willie the Wildcat video had slipped into obscurity since the night of the cow-tipping incident, which, thankfully, had not been captured in digital.

When I wasn't being ignored by most people in school, I was being teased relentlessly for the cow tipping, mostly because Grant and his buddies wouldn't let it die. They per-

sisted in making mooing calls to me whenever I passed
them in the hallway or entered a classroom. And the mascot, Roland, who humbled himself at every sporting event
by dressing as a flea-ridden wildcat, would glare daggers
at me every time he passed me in the hallway. Sometimes,
if he was walking behind me, he would kick one of my
heels and make me stumble or drop my books. Roland was
surprisingly buff considering he was technically a cheerleader, so I didn't try to draw him into a disagreement, just
took my licks and avoided him when I could.

One afternoon I was almost home free, ready to escape
school without running into Roland or any of my other tormentors, when I saw Grant and his buddies approaching
the lobby at the same time. With a little luck they wouldn't
notice me and I could skate through. Maybe the next day I
could claim a stomachache and make it through forty-eight
hours without seeing anyone from school.

I missed the anonymity of my old school, where you
could get lost in the shuffle, fade into the crowd. The mis-
ery of loneliness is nothing compared to taking the brunt
of public ridicule at the hands of someone as powerful as
Grant Parker.

I shifted the weight of my backpack on my shoulder as
I filed out the main entrance amid a throng of other students, all chatting happily about their weekend plans. So
close. Only a short walk across the bus turnaround to the
bike rack. There was no god I could plead with to let me
reach the bike and leave campus unscathed, so I just grit-
ted my teeth and hoped.

And then they saw me.

"Hey, cowboy!" Grant shouted, his nickname for me now, his clever way of reminding everyone about my humiliation, while still relegating me to the position of "boy."

I think I preferred it when I was "city boy."

He projected his voice across the lake of people milling around. Many of them turned to look first at Grant, then me.

Crap.

"Hey, cowboy, you still smell like cowshit?"

As if it were conceivable that Grant wasn't directing his comments toward me, I kept my head down as I shuffled along, trying to get through the stalled traffic of people waiting to get on their buses. If I quickened my pace, Grant and his buddies would be on me in a second, like a pack of wolves after an elk that had separated from the herd. A blush started to creep into my cheeks as people studied me for a reaction.

"Hey, I'm talking to you, cowboy. What's the matter?" Now I could make out the laughter of Grant's buddies, their afternoon's entertainment.

Jesus said a man should turn the other cheek . . . but Jesus never had to go to high school in a small town. Or if he had, Jesus would have been the popular guy and not subject to the same humiliations I was. His ability to change water into wine alone would guarantee that.

Two girls stood off to one side, hugging their books to their chests, as the mob mentality shifted. Maybe no one really liked Grant Parker. Maybe people thought he was a bully and a creep. But the universal truth was everyone was glad I was the target instead of them. The distance between the entrance of the school and my bike suddenly became an ocean, and the probability of my survival lessened the farther I ventured from shore.

Something hit me on the shoulder and bounced to the ground in front of me. A pencil. A hail of other objects followed, meant to humiliate rather than hurt me.

And I was. Humiliated.

Red started to creep in around the edges of my vision, and my gut tightened like a blood-pressure cuff until I felt a vein throbbing in my forehead.

Who the fuck does he think he is?

My anger boiled up the way it had at the pep rally when I assaulted Willie the Wildcat. Grant's next comment was enough to set me off completely.

"Go ahead and run, faggot," Grant said. It wasn't the fact that he was accusing me of being gay, or even that he was such a cretin that he considered being gay an insult. It was the way this last comment was delivered—as a dismissal. He was done with me for the day. Somehow that made me angrier than anything else, that he had toyed with me, tired of me, and was now discarding me.

Grant and his friends were still walking toward me but were now laughing and joking among themselves. I stopped and knelt on one knee, setting my backpack down beside me on the ground. I made a show of tying my shoe, pretending I was indifferent to Grant as he approached.

I felt them behind me, felt their eyes on me with a question, wondering why I had chosen this moment to stop and tie my shoe as they walked past me, headed to their cars. Grant was just about even with me when I stood suddenly and swung a roundhouse punch with such force that if I had missed hitting Grant, the momentum would have sent me sprawling.

But I didn't miss. My fist landed in the center of his chest, and his breath gusted out with a rush. He was momentarily winded as he tried to keep his feet.

Time stopped. Grant's eyes went wide and he gasped for breath, his mouth working like a fish out of water.

Slowly his eyes traveled from my feet, to my hands clenched in fists at my side, to my face, and I couldn't decide which of us was more surprised by the fact that I had punched him. My hand hummed with pain from punching him on the hard bone of his sternum, or maybe his muscles were just so rock-hard it hurt to hit him anywhere, like a superhero in an armored suit.

The students around us started to circle, like scavengers around a kill site on the Serengeti. I noticed a few of them getting their phones ready to catch me being pulverized on video. I cringed at the thought of another video of my humiliation going viral. If you want a sense of your own self-worth, just contemplate how many hits the video of your untimely death would get on YouTube.

When Grant finally did find his voice, what he said was, "You're dead."

And the way he said it . . . not just a threat. A truth. A promise.

And I believed it. Like gospel.

Before Grant could lift a hand, there was a confusion of angry shouts and the figure of Principal Sherman burst into our little circle, red-faced and frothing at the mouth.

Sherman was pointing at me, his finger stabbing the air like a weapon as he moved to separate Grant from me. I sighed and hung my head, accepting guilt and defeat.

"Boy, you sure do know how to look for trouble," Principal Sherman said. I was no longer Mr. Grayson. Now I was merely "boy." "How many times do I have to tell you I'm not going to tolerate any funny business at my school?" Grant stood just behind him, and I kept my gaze fixed on Grant's smirk as Principal Sherman tore into me. "Fighting on school property is grounds for automatic suspension. I want both of you in my office right now." Then Sherman seemed to hesitate as he turned to look at Grant and said, "Grant, I'd like to hear your side of this." He said it almost deferentially, as if asking Grant's permission.

"Sure, Mr. Sherman," Grant said, his tone polite, his expression one of concern and innocence. He was too smart to smile in the presence of Sherman, but I saw the smug satisfaction in his eyes.

You motherfucker.

Sherman put a hand on my sleeve to usher me to the office, and I snatched my arm away, hot with impotent rage. Grant's mouth twitched with amusement when Sherman wasn't looking, and I wanted to smack the smile right off of his face.

In the office Grant gave his version of events—described how I stopped to wait for Grant and his buddies and attacked. Completely unprovoked.

Even if I was looking at the situation objectively, I would know this story was bullshit. Grant was a full head taller than I was. His neck was thicker than my arm. Only if I were an idiot would I go asking Grant Parker for a fight without provocation. And that's what these people believed. That I was an idiot.

"I was just walking to my car," Grant said, "and out of nowhere he starts insulting me, attacks me. I have no idea what provoked it." If I hadn't known for a fact that Grant was lying, I would have been tempted to believe his story myself. He was such a good liar, a brilliant actor.

I didn't bother giving my version of events. No one was going to rat out Grant Parker, and Principal Sherman already thought I was a troublemaker. Once again, I was plotting my escape from Ashland in my mind, ready to leave this place and never look back.

I suppose you could say that my silence only made me look guilty to Principal Sherman. But Grant Parker had done nothing but humiliate me from the beginning.

Principal Sherman sentenced me to two days of at-home suspension.

Since Grant was just a "victim," he would go unpunished.

Game, set, and match.

13

By the time I was free of the principal's office and got to work, Roger and Tiny were already sipping their beers. Happy hour, as Roger called it.

"Why are you so late?" Roger asked, but not in a way like he really cared. He wasn't paying me after all. It had cost him nothing to give me the Camaro, and I got the sense he was happy someone was giving it the love it deserved.

"I got in trouble. Had to go to the principal's office."

"Good old Leslie," Roger said. "Though I kind of feel sorry for the guy. I dated his wife in high school. She's a bitch and a half."

"Yeah, well, he's a dick."

"What'd you get in trouble for this time?" Roger asked.

"Fighting. Grant was giving me shit and I took a swing at him."

"Boy, you are about as dumb as they come."

"Well, he was messing with me. He thinks he can treat everybody any way he wants."

"He can."

"Well, anyway. Leslie is going to call my dad, and I'm suspended for the next two days. I don't want to go home. Ever."

"You can move in here, I guess," Roger said, as if he harbored juvenile delinquents in his garage as a regular thing.

"No, thanks," I said, thinking of the black mold that lurked in the corners, along with the accumulation of grimy air fresheners that no longer held any scent, in the garage's single bathroom.

When I got home that evening Dad was waiting for me. He pounced as soon as I came through the front door. Leslie had reached Dad at the church office, explaining that I would serve two days of at-home suspension for fighting on school grounds.

Because he was a spineless dweeb, Dad just took Principal Sherman's interpretation of events as gospel and ignored any arguments I made about my innocence. He lectured me at the dinner table about personal responsibility and the moral pitfalls of popular music and the Internet. As always, it felt distinctly as if he were delivering one of the sermons he had written and memorized for a Sunday delivery. After all, if Dad actually knew what I used the Internet for most of the time, there was no way he would allow me to keep my phone or my laptop.

Doris sat at the dinner table in grim silence as Dad sermonized his way through three courses, topped off with homemade peach cobbler. She and Dad sat at opposite heads of the table, Doris in a conservative blouse and skirt, her hair swept back in a neat bun, with a strand of pearls at her throat.

"Luke," Doris said once Dad had run out of breath, "your father is just asking you to live up to our important position in the community." Her voice was almost shrill and she looked to Dad for encouragement. "It makes me distinctly uncomfortable to entertain members of your father's church here when I never know what kind of music is going to be coming out of your room or whether the driveway will be a mess with your tools and car parts."

I almost felt sorry for Doris. It was hard to imagine how much time and effort she put into keeping Dad's house. There were meticulously embroidered pillows on the sofa in the den, artfully pruned lilacs arching over the front walk, and a hot three-course meal prepared every evening.

I imagined Doris's life was very much like that of Martha Stewart . . . while she was in jail. Ashland was Doris's prison as much as it was mine.

In Ashland, there was nothing but exclusion, humiliation, and loneliness. Even at my own dinner table.

I didn't get to move into Roger's garage or spend any time there for the next two weeks. While I was grounded I had to

sneak around if I wanted to do anything, a virtual impossi-
bility in a town as small as Ashland. On Sundays I had no
choice but to attend church. I had never spent much time in
church, since Mom was very anti-organized religion. Actually, she was very anti a lot of things. And instead of letting
me work at the garage, Dad made me spend time helping
him around the church. This involved everything from jan-
itorial work to helping with preparations for the annual
harvest festival, hosted by the Baptist Church Women.

It wasn't much of a festival. There were a few booths selling merchandise and a tent for food concessions. There
was a band that played Christian country music. I had heard
of Christian rock before, but Christian country was a new
one.

It took all of about five minutes to see the entire festival.
There was a livestock exhibit where you could pet goats and
baby pigs, but the stink made me keep my distance.

There were games for people to play, like horseshoes,
which I had heard of, and cornholing, which I hadn't. Cornholing, by the way, means something totally different
outside of an urban environment.

This was a church fund-raiser, and they made money
by selling tickets that could be used for cotton candy or lemonade or games with shitty prizes. I worked the ticket
booth most of the day, which forced me into contact with
people but at least kept me busy and didn't demand that I
have more than a passing conversation with anyone.

Even though I was grounded, the two days I had gotten
to miss school was like a vacation from degradation. I
dreaded the return to school, hated the idea of it.

My goal as the new kid, to avoid unwanted attention, had been an epic failure. I was a magnet for public ridicule.

And even though I was now even more of a target for Grant and his posse, when I returned to school I was amazed by the changes that had overcome my classmates. I had anticipated staring. I had anticipated feeling ostracized and excluded. I had anticipated the soundtrack of whispered comments about me as I passed people between classes.

And people did stare at me as I walked the halls, but not with shock or horror or dislike. It was more like they were finally seeing me, really seeing me, for the first time. As if I was a person now instead of just the punch line to one of Grant Parker's jokes.

The boys gave me a head nod, a few of them even a casual fist bump, in greeting. The girls made eye contact and smiled. As I moved through the corridors people got out of my way, the crowds parting like the Red Sea under Moses's command. When I moved up the aisles to take my seat in the classroom, other students politely removed backpacks from my path.

It was eerie, the way they acted. As if they respected me now, accepted me as one of their own. The classmates who had once treated me with indifference or disdain now treated me with deference.

As I walked into the cafeteria that day, I felt the climate shift. I sat at my usual table, with Don and Aaron, and things were like normal. Except they weren't.

A girl, a real girl, stopped off at our table to ask what I was doing that weekend, and a couple of guys stopped to

talk about the upcoming hunting season, a subject so foreign to me I had trouble hiding my absolute ignorance.
Even Roland—aka Willie the Wildcat—gave me a guarded
but almost friendly chin thrust when he passed our table.

It was . . . surreal. It was as if I, the lowly Luke Grayson,
was something . . . someone. Don explained it as best he
could.

"Nobody has ever stood up to Grant Parker before. It's
like . . . a brave new world," Don said, gesturing dramati-
cally with his Go-Gurt, the most nutritious part of the lunch
that day. And not just a Go-Gurt, but a *Star Wars*–themed
Go-Gurt.

He threw his Yoda wisdom at me as I finished my sandwich and tried not to look in the direction of Grant's table.

"I mean, sure it was a stupid thing to do, taking Grant
on, because now he's just going to bide his time until he
figures out the best way to kill you."

"Thanks a lot."

Don shrugged. "You probably should have stayed away
from the cafeteria for lunch. You need to lay low."

"This is ridiculous. You know, I don't care anything
about Grant Parker, this town. . . ."

Don just shook his head emphatically, his chin down and
eyes closed. "It doesn't matter. Look, you're new here, so you
don't know. But Grant is a serious sadist. You ever noticed
how Josh is really quiet?"

Before Don mentioned his name I hadn't even noticed
that Josh had disappeared from our lunch table like vapor.
Because he was always so quiet it was like he wasn't there
even when he *was* there.

"Yeah," I said. "Actually, I thought he was a mute."

"He used to talk," Don said, dropping his voice as he glanced around to make sure we weren't being overheard. "Used to have kind of a big mouth, actually. First week of sophomore year Grant was ragging on him, and Josh made some smart-ass remark back at him, embarrassed Grant a little bit. Grant didn't do anything right away. He waited, bided his time, then came after Josh one afternoon when no one was around. I don't know what happened exactly, because Josh hasn't said much since, but he spent the entire night locked in a gym locker. They found Josh during first period the next day in a puddle of his own piss. They never could get Josh to rat out who had done it to him, but we all know it was Grant. Probably with Tony's help."

"So you're saying," I asked as I pushed my lunch away, my appetite gone, "I'm like chum in the water now, attracting sharks, and Josh doesn't want to be around me? That's why he hasn't been coming around at lunch?"

"That's exactly what I'm saying. Josh is smart, even though he doesn't talk."

"And, by extension, the fact that I stood up to Grant Parker makes me an idiot?" I asked Don.

"Well, an idiot-hero, which isn't the worst thing, I suppose."

14

Against my better judgment I told Don I would go to a party with him on Friday night. Since I was grounded for two weeks after my "attack" on Grant, I had to sneak out of my first-floor window once Dad and Doris had gone to their room to watch television. Don met me a few doors down from my house. He was leaning against one of the massive old trees that lined the block, the only person I saw during my walk on an otherwise perfectly still evening. We walked through the quiet neighborhood until we turned onto a dead-end street with one lone streetlight. The pavement ended at a stand of trees, a natural path worn into the underbrush from the passage of many feet. As we walked beyond the edge of the woods, we were suddenly plunged into darkness, the tree canopy blocking the moonlight completely.

It was creepy quiet, with none of the background noise of a city. I fell in line behind Don as he moved confidently through the woods. My eyes adjusted to the dark, and the total blackness developed some recognizable shapes and outlines. After a few minutes, the sound of voices and laughter reached us—still distant, but at least guiding us in a direction.

If I had been regretting my decision to attend Don's party earlier, I was now rehearsing in my head excuses to leave. This was going to suck.

I don't know what I had been expecting. Maybe a few social rejects talking about *Star Wars*. Nothing could have prepared me for what the party turned out to actually be. Don and I entered a large clearing that looked as if it had been crafted by several generations of delinquents—an honest-to-God fort built in the middle of the woods. The clearing was lined with fallen logs, the surrounding vegetation beaten into submission. There was a lean-to built of two-by-fours sagging dejectedly against a large oak tree, in case they needed to take the party inside due to inclement weather. A large cooler served as a makeshift refrigerator next to the lean-to and had obviously spent at least several seasons outside.

The scene was *Brigadoon*-like, a spectacle so unlikely I thought at first I must be imagining the whole thing. A small bonfire cast a dance of light over the improbable gathering of people, who, though Halloween was still over a month away, were dressed in . . . armor? A few people, their gender indeterminate in the low light, wore long capes with oversized hoods; a few were dressed as medieval knights, complete with chain mail and swords. Still others wore costumes that could not be defined by any time or place, fantastical costumes with masks and other handmade accessories.

"What the hell?" I asked.

"Pretty cool, huh?" Don asked, a smile in his voice.

"Uh . . ." Cool wasn't exactly what I was thinking. *Pretty crazy*, my inner voice sneered. "What is this?" I asked.

"We're LARPers," he said simply, as if that statement could explain this alternate dimension.

"LARPers?" I asked, my voice rising to a squeak.

"Sure. Live-action role-playing. I thought you were from the city. You don't know about LARPers?"

"Sure, uh, yeah," I said, wondering if I should actually be concerned for my well-being, like this was going to turn into a parody of a bad horror movie—life imitating art. "I mean, I've seen YouTube videos, but I've never actually seen it . . . live."

"You want a beer?" Don asked.

"You have beer?"

"Of course," Don said scornfully. "What did you think? We're total dorks or something?"

No comment.

"Come on," Don said as he nudged my elbow, and I followed him across the clearing just as two of the knights prepared to engage in a mock sword battle. A girl dressed in a robe was lobbing Ping-Pong balls as if they were some kind of magical weapon against the faux-leather hide of a . . . well, I wasn't really sure what it was. Maybe a half werewolf, half dragon.

Jesus.

After Don handed me a lukewarm can of beer, I stood at the edge of the ring of firelight watching the mock battle. Don wanted to move in closer and gestured for me to follow him, but I just shook my head and stayed where I was. People were really into it, laughing and cheering for the combatants, and Don moved to a spot where he could get an unobstructed view.

When Delilah arrived at the clearing, I noticed her right away. Mostly because she was the only other person at the gathering who wasn't dressed as if she attended Hogwarts instead of a regular high school. She drifted through the crowd as if she wasn't really part of anything or there to see anyone, which, I was starting to notice, was pretty much how Delilah went through life.

As she drew close to me she still hadn't noticed me, so I said, "Hello, Delilah."

She turned with some surprise at the sound of my voice, but she was smiling as she said, "Hey."

"Does your daddy know you're here?" I asked, one eye narrowed skeptically.

"I snuck out," she said. "If he notices I'm gone he'll go out cruising all the places along the lake where couples go to make out in their cars. He seems to think every boy in Ashland is trying to get into my pants."

"Yeah," I said with a nod. "I kind of got that sense when I met him."

"How about you?" she asked. "Does *your* daddy know you're out partying?"

"I was nonspecific when I told him I was going out," I

said with an indifferent shrug. I kept to myself the fact that I had snuck out, too. Even though she had admitted as much to me, I still felt like I needed to reserve that information. "I'm surprised to see you hanging out down here."

"Why?" she shot back. "Because my dad's a cop? You think that means I don't know how to have a good time?"

"Clearly you have no idea how to have a good time if you're hanging out down here," I said, glancing around with mild distaste, still unsure why I had not turned and run in the other direction as soon as I saw what I was getting myself into. "I just meant I'm surprised to see you hanging out with Don and his buddies. I didn't get the impression they talk to many girls . . . or any girls at all."

"Well, I'm a total whore since my dad's a cop," she said, no sarcasm evident in her tone. "I prefer to deflower virgins, so, you know, I come down here because these guys have never been with a woman before. They're completely unspoiled when I get them."

"Awesome," I said.

"Are you wearing that shirt ironically?" she asked as I was still mining my brain for a better comeback. "Because if you are, I would totally respect you for that."

"Well," I said, with an involuntary glance down at my Beastie Boys T-shirt, "that's good to hear. Because your respect is what I live for."

I was rehearsing an excuse in my mind to walk away from her, was tired from how much work it was just to have a simple conversation with her, when she grabbed me by the hand and pulled me along with her. "Come on," she said. "I'll introduce you to some people." I followed her grudgingly, and she seemed to sense that I was irritated with her. "Don't be mad. I really do like your shirt. I was just teasing you."

I followed her outside the ring of firelight to where the beer was kept. Delilah grabbed two cans of beer and handed one to me, then gestured for me to follow her as she played hostess and introduced me to some of the weirdos who dressed up like characters from The Chronicles of Narnia or Harry Potter.

"These people are insane," I said to Delilah under my breath as we drifted among the crowd.

"Maybe," Delilah said with a shrug. "But I've grown up with all of them. They're nice people."

"They're wearing armor. It's insane," I said again.

"Well, you wear ridiculous T-shirts," she said. "You think you have room to judge other people?"

Instead of answering her I focused on drinking my beer and deadening self-awareness. How had my life gotten this fucked up? I was afraid that any minute someone was going to try to put a sword in my hand, challenge me to combat. I stayed close to Delilah, almost like she would protect me from the dork squad.

"So why are you here?" Delilah asked as she stopped and turned suddenly to face me.

"Um, Don invited me," I said.

"No, I mean here, here. In Ashland. Why did you come here?"

"Oh. My mom made me come. I was screwing up in school a lot. Getting in trouble . . ."

"By attacking the school mascot?"

I leveled a look of irritation on her, my eyes narrowed. "No. My mom just got sick of it. Thought I needed a positive male role model in my life. She called my dad, told him that it was his turn. Next thing I know I'm being shipped off to this shithole." My voice was bitter as I said this, and I gestured with my arm at the LARPer fort to illustrate my point about Ashland being a shithole.

"You do a lot of drugs or something?" she asked, and I suddenly felt like I was under interrogation. As if Delilah had learned to question suspects the way her police-chief father would. Though, as I imagined it, the worst crime wave Ashland ever saw was fertilizer theft, or rednecks driving drunk on deserted country roads, livestock their only potential victims.

"I've never done anything harder than weed or Molly," I answered honestly.

"Give it six months in this town," she said knowingly. "You'll be so bored you'll try just about anything."

"I'll be gone in nine months," I said. "I think I can make it that long without developing a meth problem."

"You think so now. We'll see. Besides, meth is so 2008." She blew out a weary sigh and seemed to be thinking about just how bored she really was. Maybe I was boring, too. Maybe she was so bored from talking to me she was thinking about where she could score some meth.

"What about you?" I asked. "You into hard drugs?"

"My dad's a cop," she said, her eyes rolling back with impatience as she returned her gaze to my face. "I have to pass a urine test every month."

"Are you serious?" I asked with genuine astonishment.

"No," she said. "Jesus, you're gullible. You raised in a cave or something?"

"No."

"My dad probably *would* make me take a urine test every month if it didn't violate some principle of decency," she said, her head tipped back on her spine in a world-weary pose. "He won't even let me watch R-rated movies at home. I'm seventeen, for Christ's sake."

"He's a scary dude," I said. "Your mom strict like that, too?"

"My mom's dead," Delilah said flatly. Not "passed away." Dead.

"Sorry. I didn't know."

"She died when I was nine. Cancer."

"I'm sorry," I said again. The most useless sentiment in human history. "You think that's why your dad is so over-protective of you?" I asked.

"No," she said with a shake of her head. "He's just an as-shole. My mom dying had nothing to do with that."

"Coming here," I said as I leaned back against a tree, one leg bent and my foot resting on the trunk. "It's been awful. People seem so friendly on the surface, but it's a lonely place."

"Yeah, it sucks," she said, almost sounding genuinely sympathetic. "Just don't snort any white powder. You'll be okay."

15

When I saw Grant around school he would glare menacingly at me, but he didn't come after me publicly anymore.
For a while I thought maybe the whole thing would blow
over, that by standing up to Grant I had convinced him to
leave me alone. Or maybe Don was right and Grant was
plotting my demise. This was the infinitely more likely scenario.

In class I spent most of my time fantasizing about the
ways Grant might try to ruin my life, and how I could avoid
him. I was doing my best to fly under the radar, but there
were new developments that prevented me from doing that.

People started inviting me to parties and to participate
in school functions. I was asked to join the 4-H club, but
since I had no idea what it was, I said that I would have to
think about it. Even after googling "4-H club" I was still

unsure what it was, so I didn't commit. I was even asked to join the Future Farmers of America, but my one interaction with livestock had convinced me this was not a career path I should follow.

The same week I was invited to join the 4-H club I got the shock of my life. Ballots were distributed during homeroom for the homecoming court, and there, listed alphabetically first under the nominees for homecoming king, was my name.

"Jesus!" I yelped without thinking.

"Is there a problem, Mr. Grayson?" Ms. Bartlett, my homeroom teacher, asked, as I had interrupted her midsentence.

"Uh, no—no. No problem." But there was a problem. A huge problem. I was competing directly for homecoming king with none other than Grant Parker. I couldn't imagine who had nominated me. But I knew that I needed at least three nominations to be put into the running. I wondered if Don was behind this, but when I saw him at lunch, he was as mystified as I was.

"What are you so concerned about?" Don asked. "It's not as if you'll win."

"I know that," I said, though to be honest I had entertained the idea as possible. I mean, after all, I was the guy who had stood up to Grant Parker. And I had yet to be shoved into a locker or run off the road while riding my bike to and from school. I had taken both of those things as positive signs.

I wondered if maybe Delilah was behind my nomination. It was exactly the kind of thing she would do. She'd love to stir up trouble without thinking through the situation. Or do it just to amuse herself.

"If it makes you feel any better, I didn't vote for you," Don said. "It would create more problems with Grant if you won. Because Penny will win homecoming queen, and then you'd be dancing with Grant's girl at homecoming. It would be a mess."

"Well, see? If you didn't vote for me then I'm sure no one else did either," I said. "I'm not worried about it."

And I wasn't. Even if people didn't make me feel excluded anymore, Grant was still the star quarterback, still the student council president. I couldn't, didn't want to, compete with him. On any level.

16

On Friday nights just about everyone in town turned out for the high school football game. Stores and restaurants closed, so even if you wanted to be somewhere else during the game, there was nothing else to do.

Don, Aaron, and I sat together at the game. We hugged the obscurity of the seats near the band, a safe zone where none of the in crowd would dare sit, so we could avoid mistreatment by any of Grant Parker's minions or risk another run-in with Willie the Wildcat.

Dad led the entire home side of the bleachers in a prayer, the crowd secure in its belief that Jesus was a football fan. And not just a fan, but a devout fan of the Wakefield Wildcats.

After the game, Don and the guys were heading down to the woods to drink cheap beer and, probably, engage in sword fights and other creepy role-playing games. Actually, their combat sessions did look kind of fun, but I would never admit that, even to myself, and I definitely would not participate. Sometimes I would catch myself thinking that they should throw a thrust when they went with a parry, but my face would burn with empathic embarrassment whenever I thought of them in their costumes.

We waited for the crowd to clear before starting the walk to our cars. Dad had left the RAV4 for me to drive, riding home with Doris in her camel-colored Volvo wagon. At least you couldn't tell the RAV4 was mint green in the dark.

By the time we were walking across the student parking lot, most of the spectators were gone, so the student parking lot was quiet. We heard raised voices coming from between two parked cars near the fence, and we all slowed with interest. That is, we slowed until we realized the people exchanging heated words were Grant and Penny.

Grant was still in his uniform, the silhouette of his boxy shoulder pads against the glow of the streetlights making him seem larger than life.

Though their words were not distinguishable from where we stood, it was clear they were both angry—Penny's voice loud and shrill, Grant's tight with impatience. In silent agreement we all kept walking toward our cars, minding our own business.

We loitered in the parking lot long enough to confirm our plans to meet down at the LARPer fort for a few beers, but our purpose for loitering was mostly to see the end of Grant and Penny's fight and overhear a few snatches of the conversation.

"If that's how you want it," Grant shouted, his words suddenly ringing clear across the entire parking lot, "then find another ride home!"

With that, he stormed off in the direction of the locker rooms and left Penny alone, her head and shoulders bent in a defeated slump.

The guys and I exchanged meaningful looks, but we were all silent, stealing only furtive glances in Penny's direction.

Grant's parting shot had been calculated. There was no other guy who was going to offer Penny a ride home, no hero willing to face Grant's wrath. A guy would have to be an idiot to offer Penny a ride home, risk someone finding out about it and word getting back to Grant.

The smart thing to do was to ignore her, turn the other way and leave.

"I'll catch up with you guys later," I said, back-stepping toward Penny and away from sanity.

"Are you crazy?" Don asked as it dawned on him immediately what my plan was. "Luke," Don said earnestly, "not a great idea."

"Don't worry about it," I said with a chin thrust, indicating he should walk on without me. "I'll catch up with you guys in a bit."

"You're a total idiot, Luke," Don called after me.

"An idiot-hero," I called back over my shoulder. And then I forgot about the guys as I approached Penny. She was leaned against the car door, one hand over her face, as she sniffled and her body shook with muffled sobs. "Are you okay?" I asked quietly, using the same voice you would use for an injured puppy.

As she turned to look at me she hiccuped out a little sigh and her lower lip—that full, sumptuous lower lip—quivered in a way that made me want to put my arms around her and keep her safe.

"Oh!" she said, her mouth forming a startled O. "Hi, Luke." She wiped at her cheeks, careful not to disturb her eye makeup. "Grant and I had a fight," she said. "Sometimes I can't stand him."

I know the feeling.

"Well, if you don't want to be around him right now I could . . . I could give you a lift home," I said, knowing as I did that it was a mistake, but not caring much.

"That would be great," she breathed. She followed me to the RAV4, and I unlocked and held the passenger door for her. She flashed me a coquettish smile as she smoothed her short skirt around her legs, looking at me through hooded eyes to see if I was noticing the bare skin of her thighs and calves. I was.

As we pulled out of the parking lot, Penny pointed me in the direction of her house and I turned on the stereo to cover any awkward silence between us.

"You want to drive down to the lake?" Penny asked after a minute, as she leaned forward to turn down the music. "We could just sit for a while and talk. I don't really feel like going home just yet."

"Sure," I said, immediately forgetting Don and my promise to catch up with him. He would understand. Bro code. The opportunity to get with a girl always trumps hanging out with a bro. I think. I hadn't had much opportunity to explore the truth of this before now. And besides, Don didn't technically qualify as a bro. Bros don't dress up like Harry Potter outside of Halloween. Maybe not even for Halloween.

I avoided the large gravel parking area near the public boat ramps and instead parked along the road that circled behind the trees bordering the water. A three-quarter moon hung in the sky, and there was very little wind so the lake was mostly still, though some small ripples captured the light of the moon and threw it back into the sky.

I kept the music on as we settled back in our seats.

"I told Grant I wanted to go someplace nice for dinner tomorrow night," Penny said as she crossed her arms over her chest, "and all he wants to do is go park somewhere and fool around."

On this point I sympathized with Grant Parker. Having sex with Penny in a parked car sounded pretty appealing.

"It's like he thinks that there's no other reason to be with me besides fooling around."

"That's crazy," I said. "I mean, I don't really know you, but I know you're beautiful, smart, and a nice person."

Her eyes misted over as she turned in her seat to face me. "That's the sweetest thing anyone has ever said to me," she said, and her voice trembled slightly with emotion.

I chuckled at that, a total cliché. "Yeah, right," I said as I shifted in my seat and fixed my gaze on the windshield. My face felt hot. "I know a girl like you has guys telling her she's beautiful all the time."

"No, really," she said quickly, with an earnest shake of her head. "Grant never tells me I'm beautiful. If anything, he's always telling me not to eat fattening food because it will ruin my figure. Or, like when Miley Cyrus cut her hair short and I said I might do the same thing, Grant told me I would look terrible with short hair and to keep it long." She seemed to deflate suddenly and sat back in her seat with a sigh. "And it's not like any other guy would ever tell me I was beautiful. They're all so terrified of what Grant might do to them, other guys won't even look at me."

There wasn't really anything I could say to that. If I told her she was beautiful again after that little speech, it would just sound fake, like I was putting sloppy moves on her. We sat in the murky silence, both of us lost in our own thoughts.

She broke the silence first by saying, "Except for you. You're the only guy who isn't too afraid of Grant." She was watching me out of the corner of her eye with such obvious anticipation that it almost made me snort out a laugh.

"I'm not a tough guy, Penny. I just think a girl like you"—I shrugged as I searched for the right words—"someone should treat you right. You know, you're the only person who has been really nice to me since I moved to Ashland."

She turned to face me again, and this time she leaned in toward me as our breath started to fog the windows of the car. "I don't think tough guys make the best boyfriends. I think sweet, sensitive guys who know how to talk to a girl with respect make the best boyfriends."

With her words and her body language, she was all but inviting me to kiss her, but I held off. Not just because of

Grant Parker, though it occurred to me to worry that someone might see Penny and me together. Penny was the only person who sympathized at all with my position. I wasn't hesitant to kiss her because I was unsure of how I felt about her.

There was just something nagging in the back of my mind, and I actually found myself thinking about Delilah, thinking that if she could hear my conversation with Penny she would be rolling her eyes and judging every word that came out of my mouth.

It was right when that thought of Delilah flashed through my mind that Penny suddenly threw herself at me, pressed her lips hard against mine, and put both hands on my chest. She caught me by surprise, so I don't think the first impression she got of the kiss was a very good one.

I had to keep reminding myself to close my eyes as I kissed her. It was so incredible to me that I was actually holding Penny Olson in my arms, I kept opening my eyes just to verify it was truly her. Within a few minutes we were both panting from the exhaustion of struggling to make out with the console between us, and the seat-belt latch was digging painfully into my leg.

Suddenly there was a loud rap against the glass of my window, and I jerked back with a yelp so quickly that I cracked my knee against the steering wheel. I turned toward the sound, and all I could see was a blinding beam of light.

"Oh, shit," Penny whispered as she sat up in her seat and smoothed her skirt against her legs.

I rolled down the window with one hand, the other held up to block the beam of light.

"Son, what are you doing?" I recognized the voice of Chief Perry even if I couldn't see his face around the flashlight beam.

"I . . . uh . . . well, this isn't what it looks like," I said.

"Miss Penelope," he said, ignoring my comment and turning his attention to Penny, "do your folks know where you are?"

"Hey, Chief Perry," she said, her voice breathy and sweet, putting on the act for his benefit now. Penny's methods seemed to affect men of any age, and Chief Perry's expression softened as he looked at her instead of me. "Luke was just giving me a ride home after the game."

"Is that right?" Chief Perry drawled. He stepped back from the car window, his shoe scraping against the gravel as he hitched his gun belt up on his hips. I fought the urge to tell him that I had not put the moves on Penny, that she had been the one to initiate our make-out session.

Right. Good strategy. Call her a whore. See where that gets me.

While I was still formulating excuses in my mind, Chief Perry said, "Son, step out of the car."

He took another step back as I got out of the car, one hand resting on the butt of his gun as if I posed some kind of potential physical threat. I wasn't sure if I should shut my door or leave it open but finally decided to just shut it gently and stand against it. I started to put my hands in my pockets, but Chief Perry tensed and so I let my hands hang at my sides.

"Have you been drinking?" he asked.

"No, sir," I said, fighting to keep the anger out of my voice. "I went to the football game. I was just giving Penny a ride home."

"A ride home? You lost? The Olsons don't live anywhere near here." He shifted his weight on his feet as he settled in to wait for my answer, and the stiff leather of his gun belt creaked.

"We were just . . . talking. Is there some kind of law against that?" I asked.

"Don't get smart with me, son," he snapped. "You take Penny on home. I'm going to follow to make sure you get there okay. You sure you haven't had anything to drink?"

"Yes," I said coldly.

"Yes, what?"

"Yes, I'm sure I haven't been drinking."

"Don't think that just because this is a small town that I'm naive or that I haven't dealt with your type before."

"My type?" I asked, almost impossible to control my temper now. "You don't even know me. You don't know anything about me."

"I know enough," he said, and turned on his heel to walk away, dismissing me without another glance.

Penny and I rode in silence on the way to her house, as if Chief Perry, following in the patrol car behind us, could overhear any conversation. At her house Penny flashed me a smile and said good night but didn't try to kiss me.

I waited to make sure she got to her door as I watched the windshield of Chief Perry's car in my rearview mirror.

I couldn't see him through the glare of taillights on glass, but I could feel his scowl on the back of my neck.

He followed me for a few blocks after I left Penny, and I was careful to mind the speed limit and use my turn signal. I headed home, defeated once again.

17

Saturday afternoon I was perched on a stack of tires that was waiting to be installed, looking at my phone, while Roger clanked around under the hood of a Buick. On Saturday afternoons Tiny took his mother to church for bingo and fried chicken, their weekly ritual, so it was just Roger and me.

"Heard about your run-in with the chief," Roger said, interrupting my search for new mixes on SoundCloud. "Didn't you and I just have a conversation recently about how you weren't going to be an idiot?"

"How am I an idiot?" I asked.

"Is this how you avoid Grant Parker? By taking his girlfriend out parking by the lake?"

"We weren't *parking*," I said, my tone emphatically denying the dirty implications of the word "parking." "And how the hell do you even know about that?"

"It was all the talk at the diner this morning when I stopped in for coffee with the fellas," Roger said, as if this were a perfectly reasonable explanation. "You can't ride home with a police escort in a town this size and expect people not to notice."

I shook my head with disbelief, my eyes squeezed shut. "It wasn't like that," I said. "I was giving her a ride home. She suggested we stop and talk by the lake for a few minutes. Chief Perry totally misread the situation."

"You really are kind of simple, aren't you?" Roger said, though I took the question as rhetorical. "Every village has to have an idiot. Aren't I the lucky one to have the village idiot working for me?"

He chuckled at his own wit, and I shot him a disgusted look. The look missed its mark, since Roger hadn't even bothered to turn his attention from the blackened engine of the Buick.

"Oh, hell, boy," he continued, as he must have felt my angry stare burning into his back. "I just look at it as a community service. Somebody's got to give you a job. Keep you out of trouble. Except you keep finding trouble everywhere you look."

"Oh, yeah?" I said. "So, let's say some gorgeous girl walked up to you and asked you to take her home. You telling me you would say 'no'? You'd turn that down?"

This got him to turn his interest away from the car engine, and he settled in with his rear end resting against the hood grill. The ubiquitous red rag materialized, and he idly wiped at his wrench while he considered his response. "Okay. Yeah," he said. "I get it. You're seventeen. When you're seventeen you have no control over your hormones. I was seventeen once, you know?"

"I know," I said, my eyes narrowing with the usual skepticism I felt whenever Roger referenced a youthful period in his life. "It's just so . . . hard to imagine."

He shot me a warning look but continued. "I'm old. My perspective is different. But you can't be an idiot and expect to live to be my age. If Grant Parker's girlfriend asks you to go parking by the lake, you say no."

"I couldn't help it," I said, my voice rising with frustration. "It's not as if my dick gives me any choice in a situation like that."

Roger chuckled again at that. "That won't change. But if you want to live to see eighteen, you'd better learn to start thinking with your other head. The big one."

"You're so full of crap," I said. "You expect me to believe you had sense enough to turn down a girl like Penny when you were my age? Hell, you wouldn't be able to turn it down now that you're a dirty old man."

He shook his head. "I can be smart now. At least, smarter than I was. I don't have to think about it as much at my age," he said. "At a certain point you just start to run out of boners."

"Please stop talking," I said as Roger's use of the word "boner" sent a shudder down my spine.

"It's true," he said with a dismissive shrug and turned back to the Buick. "You'll find out."

"I just want everyone in this town to mind their own business," I said, in a funk now and feeling sorry for myself. "Why can't everyone just leave me alone?"

18

It was late afternoon by the time I got home from work, but I still put in some time working on the Camaro. Delilah wandered into the driveway where I was lying on my back, my head and shoulders under the Camaro as I struggled to attach a radiator hose, cursing fluently to myself. Dusk was approaching, and it was getting too dark to see what I was doing.

It was unclear why she did it, but sometimes Delilah came to sit with me on evenings like this while I worked on the Camaro. Most of the time we didn't say much to each other, but she made herself useful by holding the light when I was working on the undercarriage. Though I wouldn't readily admit it to her, to anyone, I liked having her quiet company while I worked on the car.

As I was tightening the metal clamp over the hose, my

hand slipped and I raked a cut along my knuckle. "Ouch! Shit," I said, and sat up fast enough to crack my head on the undercarriage of the car. "Ah! Goddamn it."

I scooted out from under the car, rubbing my head as I looked at my knuckle and Delilah shined the light on it. "Blood?" she asked.

"A little," I said.

"You should wash it," Delilah said with a rare show of concern for my well-being.

"Yeah," I said, and was just standing to go to the utility sink in the garage when a red pickup truck pulled up at the curb next to the driveway.

"You expecting someone?" Delilah asked.

"No," I said, the pain in my finger and my head momentarily forgotten.

Tony Hurst climbed out of the truck and sauntered slowly up the driveway toward us. "Hello, Del," Tony said, some surprise in his voice at the sight of her there. If he'd been wearing a hat, I felt sure he would have tipped it at her.

"Hi, Tony," Delilah said, her tone uncharacteristically shy. Her head tipped forward so that her hair fell over half of her face, obscuring her expression. Tony watched her for a long minute, as if waiting for her to say more, and I sensed something between them—tension on Delilah's side and . . . something else from Tony. Maybe an expectation. He still hadn't even acknowledged my presence.

When his eyes finally did shift to me, they went dead, like the gaze of a wild animal. "I want to talk to you," he said.

"I'm listening," I said, trying to keep my tone neutral.

"You've got a serious problem," he said in a slow drawl. "You've pissed off Grant Parker, and he doesn't forgive and forget."

"I didn't do anything to Grant Parker," I said evenly, though my blood had started to simmer with latent anger.

"He knows you were talking to his girl. Penny told him you gave her a ride home last night after the game."

I felt Delilah's eyes shift to my face as Tony delivered this news, but I did my best to ignore her.

"Did he send you?" I asked as I reached into my pocket for the rag I kept to wipe my hands—a habit I had picked up from Roger. "Or is this just a friendly visit?"

"Consider this a warning. Maybe you haven't figured out how it works, but nobody fucks with Grant Parker. You keep playing it like you are, you'll end up paying for it."

"Is that some kind of threat?" I asked, feeling like I was acting out a scene from a movie.

"Take it however you want to," Tony said. "I'm just telling you that if you mess with us again, you're going to pay for it."

Delilah had watched this whole exchange in silence. She spoke up now with a toss of her hair over her shoulder. "Tony, you know Luke didn't do anything but stick up for himself when Grant was acting like a bully. And Penny's a big girl. It wouldn't be the first time she used some other guy to make Grant get in a sweat over her."

Tony turned his cool gaze to her, and his expression immediately softened. I was getting the vibe, definitely now, that they had some kind of history, some connection. The

way Delilah spoke to him told me that was the case, even if
the way Tony looked at her hadn't already. And I found myself feeling strangely pissed off about there being something between Delilah and Tony, though I was unsure
why.

"Stay out of it, Del," Tony said. "I'm not interested in seeing you get hurt. Does your daddy even know where you
are?"

"That's my business and none of yours, Anthony," she
said.

"You delivered your message," I said to break their focus on each other. "You can go."

Tony hesitated, like he might say more, but just turned
to leave. "You want a ride home?" he asked Delilah as he
stopped at the door of his truck, one arm leaning on the
open window.

"Not likely," Delilah said as she crossed her arms over
her chest.

Tony just smiled and shook his head, then climbed into
his truck and drove away.

I went into the garage to wash the cut on my knuckle. A
streak of blood had dried along the side of my finger. A co-
agulated drop at the tip washed away as I rubbed it. The
gritty Lava soap made the cut hurt worse, but I ground my
teeth and enjoyed the pain as it somehow made my anger
abate.

"Tony can be a real jerk," Delilah said as she leaned
against the counter and watched as I washed my hands, then
carefully dried the skin around the torn knuckle. "If he ever
thought for himself he might not be such a dumbass."

"I don't need you sticking up for me, getting in my business," I said, the words sounding colder than I had meant.

Her eyes flashed with anger, and she pushed off the counter with a gusted breath. "What's the matter?" she asked. "Did you get a bruised ego? Having a girl fight your battles?"

"Who is that guy to you?" I asked. "Did you used to date him or something?" Suddenly I wished I had kept my mouth shut. I wasn't angry because Delilah had taken up my fight against Tony. I was just angry in general, but Delilah was going to take the brunt of it.

"So what if I did? What do you care?" she asked, delivering it like a challenge.

"I guess I don't," I said, and not nicely.

She barely hesitated before she turned to walk out, leaving me standing there by the sink, holding a paper towel against my knuckle.

"Hey," I said and hurried to catch her as she left the driveway and turned up the sidewalk. "Hey, wait up. It's dark. I'll walk with you."

She snorted and tossed her hair at me with impatience but didn't argue when I fell in step beside her.

We walked in silence until I said, "I'm sorry. Okay? I was mad, and I took it out on you."

"You should listen to Tony. Just lay low and leave Grant Parker alone. He's . . ." She paused for so long I thought she wasn't going to finish but then said, "He doesn't fight fair."

"I can take care of myself," I said with more confidence than I felt. "Grant Parker doesn't scare me."

"Right. I forgot you're a macho gearhead." Then, after a beat, "And you listen to Morrissey."

"I listen to The Smiths. There's a big difference."

"No," she said. "There isn't."

"So, what's that guy Tony's story?" I asked, ignoring her invitation for a fight. "You guys used to date or something?"

She cast a sidelong look at me that I couldn't read. Guilt. Secrecy. "Or something."

I waited, but she wasn't going to give me anything else. It occurred to me to ask her if she liked Tony, but I thought it would sound too desperate if I did. I was unsure if I really liked Delilah or if she just exasperated me. Still, she had her moments, and she was the only person I knew in Ashland who seemed to get me as a person.

The porch light at Delilah's house burned a couple of hundred watts, and there were floodlights strategically placed to up-light the few trees and shrubs that dotted the manicured lawn. There was no place where a person could secret himself in the yard. She lived in a protected fortress with her heavily armed father, like a princess in a tower.

"I'd walk you to your door, but I'm afraid your dad would shoot me," I said as I stopped at the end of her front walk.

"He probably would," she said with a nod of agreement.

"You going to tell me what that was about? With you and that guy?" I asked, though I made a point of not looking at her.

She seemed to consider it but then just shook her head and said, "No."

"Good night, Delilah," I said, as I turned to walk away.

"Luke?" she called after me, her voice unnaturally high in pitch.

"Yeah?"

"Don't do anything stupid. About Grant, I mean. I wouldn't . . . Well, I just think you should be careful."

"You worry too much," I said, as I turned again to leave.

The truth is I was worried, too—knowing Grant Parker would be gunning for me for real now and that there was little I could do to stop him.

19

Other than compulsory attendance at church, I spent the whole weekend working on the Camaro and doing my best to avoid contact with other people, especially Dad and Doris. If avoiding Dad and Doris were an Olympic-qualifying event, I would have been a top-seed favorite for a gold medal.

Sunday night I tried to study, to catch up on the homework I had been ignoring all weekend. I fell asleep with my light on, my homework scattered on the bed, my music playing. I didn't sleep well in Dad and Doris's house, though I had finally grown accustomed to the quiet—no traffic noise, no sirens, no hum of a thousand transformers powering a city of light and sound.

When I opened my eyes it took me a minute to orient myself, another minute to realize what had wakened me. There was a scratching outside my window and then a rustling sound. At first I assumed it was a raccoon or some other animal, but then I heard a small cry of distress and a thud against the siding of the house.

I sat up so quickly the book that had been resting on my chest fell, but I had swung my legs over the edge of the bed before the book hit the floor.

"Who's there?" I asked, my voice choked with strain.

"Shit," was the reply, and I recognized Delilah's voice.

I went to the window and opened it all the way, then stuck my forehead up against the screen. "Delilah? What are you doing?"

"Tripping over bushes in the dark," she said, followed by a little giggle. Delilah never giggled.

"Are you drunk?" I asked.

"Maybe," she said. "Open the window."

I banged the side of my fist against the edge of the screen to pop it out of its frame. Delilah pulled the screen all the way out and tossed it carelessly on the lawn.

"Hey," I said in a sharp whisper. "Keep it down, will you? I don't need my dad any more up my ass than he already is."

She wasn't listening to me, was struggling to maneuver through the open window and reached for my arm to steady herself as she pulled in first one foot, then the other, from her seat on the windowsill. I could smell liquor on her, something sweet, like rum or spiced whiskey. With the amount of noise she was making, I expected Dad to start knocking on my locked bedroom door any second.

"What are you doing here?" I asked.

"Is that what you wear to bed?" she asked, ignoring my question.

My chest was bare and I was wearing sweatpants and socks with holes in them. I fought the urge to cross my arms over my chest defensively.

"Get dressed," she said. "You're coming with me."

"Absolutely not," I said with an emphatic shake of my head.

"Fine," she said with a little shrug. "We can hang out here." She plopped down on my bed and bounced two of my textbooks onto the floor.

"No, you can't *hang out* here," I said as I grabbed a sweatshirt from the top of my dresser and pulled it over my head.

"This is the first time I've been in your room," she said as she glanced around at the few posters I had hung in a halfhearted attempt to make the room more like home. "It's messy." She wrinkled her nose as if she smelled something unpleasant.

"I wasn't expecting company," I said as I sat down on the bed beside her to pull on my shoes. "Why didn't you text me first? Tell me you were coming over?"

"Because you would have told me not to come," she said simply. "Are you ready?"

I climbed out the window first and helped her so she wouldn't make as much noise going as she had coming. She bent down to pick up a bottle of liquor she had left on the ground near the wall of the house. It was only half full and she held it out to me, the bottle swinging by the neck between two fingers.

I snatched the bottle before it fell and smashed on the driveway, then followed her down the street. Delilah was quiet now as we strolled along, me stealing occasional glances over my shoulder, convinced Chief Perry would ride up on us any second in his squad car.

"Will you tell me where we're going?" I asked.

"We're going for a walk," she said.

"Why are we going for a walk in the middle of the night?"

She sighed but didn't answer and reached for the bottle to take another long swig. Her eyes squeezed shut at the burn from the liquor.

"I can't believe you're drinking this," I said as she handed the bottle back to me. I studied the label before taking a swig.

"I stole it from my dad's liquor cabinet. He never drinks this stuff."

"With good reason," I said and helped myself to another sip. "It's disgusting."

We had reached the dead-end street where the path into the woods beckoned us like the gaping mouth to hell. This time I was prepared for the total blackness of the woods and was slightly more sure-footed stepping among the tree roots and stones that interrupted the path. We continued on in silence, passing the point where I thought the turn-off for the LARPer fort would be, but Delilah showed no sign of slowing down or stopping.

"Seriously, Delilah, this is how people end up eviscerated in horror movies," I said as a branch brushed my arm and I almost jumped out of my skin with fright. "Where are we going?"

"It's a surprise. Come on."

I decided I was probably stupid to follow her but kept

walking anyway because, honestly, at this point I had no idea how to get back home. She slipped through a dense group of shrubs, and I lost sight of her for a few seconds. "Delilah," I called softly, wondering why I was whispering since we were so far out in the woods no one could have heard me scream, even if I wanted them to.

The shrubs fought me as I tried to follow her, and I almost fell when I pushed through and suddenly met air. Delilah turned back to look at me from where she stood at the edge of a clearing, an open, rolling field covered in autumn-gold grass that glowed dully in the moonlight. The moon was almost full, so close you would swear you could reach out and touch it, and the sky was a blanket of stars.

The planes of her face caught the moonlight, and I could make out the angles of a smile. "Beautiful, right?" she asked as she turned her face back to the sky and took a long swig from the bottle. For a moment I thought she was asking me if she was beautiful, because it was what I had been thinking. Somehow I had never noticed Delilah was beautiful before. Maybe it was the liquor. Or the moonlight. She wiped the back of her hand across her mouth, put the cap on the bottle, and dropped it in the grass at her feet.

"Yes. Beautiful," I said, still speaking in almost a whisper.

She took a deep breath and blew it out slowly. "I saw the moon earlier from my window. Figured it would be nice out here. There's a pond," she said pointing into the blackness against the opposite tree line. "My brother and I used to come down here to fish and swim. When we were kids," she added, and I detected sadness in her voice.

"I didn't know you had a brother," I said.

"You wouldn't. Nobody talks about him. He went to Afghanistan," she said to the stars. "Came home three months later in a box. He would have been twenty-one today. Figured I'd have a drink in his honor."

"I'm sorry," I said, knowing as I did that it was worthless.

"What an idiot, right?" she asked with a mirthless laugh. "I mean, who joins the army in the middle of a war?"

There was nothing to say.

"Anyway," she said, oblivious to my silence, "I wanted to come down here but I was afraid to come alone. Ghosts," she said, then betrayed her emotions with a self-conscious laugh.

For a while we listened to the crickets and the wind whispering through the trees. I kept turning my head to look around us, convinced someone would happen onto us, more afraid to run into another human than I was to see a wild animal.

"I miss him," she said finally, her words slurred a little, letting me know she had already been pretty drunk before coming to my window. "Do you believe in heaven?"

"No," I said. I cleared my throat as I said it but had not hesitated, didn't consider lying to make her feel better. Most of the time I felt like that was my dad's whole job. Lying to make people feel better.

"Me either," she said with a sigh. "Sucks. It must be easier for people who believe."

She turned and came to stand right in front of me, close enough that I could feel the heat from her body on my arms and neck. Close enough that my body reacted to her and I wished I had brushed my teeth before leaving the house.

"Do you want to kiss me?" she asked.

"I wasn't really thinking about it," I said.

"Why not?" she shot back quickly.

"What do you mean, why not? You just told me about your brother. It's not like that would turn me on or something."

"What about before that?" she asked, somewhat impatiently. "Before I told you about my brother. Were you thinking about kissing me then?"

"No. I was thinking that you're going to end up getting us killed or busted by your dad, dragging me out here in the middle of the night." I said this with another cautious glance around us, though I was unsure if I was more afraid of meeting Chief Perry or an ax murderer out here in the dark.

"Really?" she asked, incredulous. "Like it never even occurred to you?"

I shrugged. "You don't like my shirts. Remember?"

She dropped her head to one side and twirled a lock of hair around her finger. "You're so sensitive. And I never said I didn't like your shirts. How much time do you need to consider it? Kissing me, I mean."

I cleared my throat and felt ridiculous, just standing there, not really knowing what to do. There were plenty of guys who would have grabbed Delilah and kissed her, probably would try to get to second base, or even a runner into home, without worrying about lying down on the ground where piles of wild animal poop probably lurked unseen.

Those were the guys who ended up getting laid all the time because they weren't afraid to take the initiative. And here I was, a girl asking me to kiss her and I couldn't even say yes.

"You've been drinking," I said.

"So?" she pressed.

She leaned in and put her lips against mine, grabbed me by the shoulders, and lifted onto her toes as she wrapped an arm around me. The liquor was sweet on her breath. My nose and mouth filled with her smell. And she was kissing me with tongue, putting everything into it.

The kiss had come so suddenly I hadn't even been able to prepare by taking a breath, and found myself suddenly starved for oxygen. That was, until I remembered I could still breathe through my nose. When I did take a breath it was loud in the stillness of the meadow.

Delilah took my hand, still hanging uselessly at my side, and guided it under her shirt. At her invitation my hand went straight for her left breast, and when I felt the soft roundness of it, I was instantly hard. Now my other arm was around her waist and pulling her closer so I could press myself against her, an unconscious action that surprised both of us.

She laughed softly, and it was enough to break the spell. I pulled away so suddenly that she pitched forward and stumbled against me. "We shouldn't do this," I said as I wiped my mouth with my hand.

"Why not?" she asked, her voice sleepy now.

At that moment I could think of a million reasons why we should and not a lot of reasons why we shouldn't, so I didn't answer.

"Because you don't want to?" she asked in a whisper as she leaned in against my chest.

"No," I said but took her by the shoulders to hold her at arm's length. "Because you've been drinking. Because you're . . . upset. We wouldn't even be here if you were sober."

"Oh, God, you're not gay, are you?" she asked with a moan. "I didn't just make a fool out of myself, did I? Throwing myself at a gay guy?"

"I'm not gay," I said. "Guys can have other reasons for not wanting to fool around with a girl."

"Not any guy I've ever met," she said.

"Look, you chose me to come out here with you because you knew I wouldn't make any moves on you."

"Hmph," she said, hating that I was right.

"If you want to talk about your brother, I'm listening."

"There's nothing to talk about," she said, sounding almost angry, but I knew her anger wasn't directed at me. "He's dead. That's it. That's the end of the story."

"What was he like?" I asked.

"Oh," she said with a dismissive wave of her hand, "you don't really want to know about it."

"Sure I do," I said. "If you want to tell me."

She cast a sidelong look at me for a minute as she built up the nerve to say more. "Jeremy was . . . hard to explain. Everything he did was larger than life. Big laugh, big heart, big personality. He was really good-looking. All of the girls had crushes on Jeremy."

"Sounds like a cool guy," I said, fighting the urge to yawn. The dark, the liquor, the warmth of her body next to my arm were all making me sleepy.

"You don't want to listen to this," she said. "And I don't want to talk about it."

"Come on," I said. "I'll walk you home."

She turned her back to me, hugging her arms to herself. "In a minute," she said. Her voice quavered, telling me she was close to crying, when she said, "I just want to stay with him for a minute longer."

I held her hand as we stood and watched the moon cast shimmers on the pond, the night sounds loud now that we had fallen quiet.

Though I insisted on walking her home, I didn't have the courage to get anywhere near her house, just watched her from a few doors down to make sure she got in okay. As I followed the now-familiar path home, I thought about a girl who had lost half of her family before she was eighteen years old, and for the first time in months, I felt pity for someone other than myself.

20

By Monday the whole town seemed to know by instant osmosis about the drama between Penny and me after the football game. I assumed Penny must have been the one to say something about our failed romantic moment by the lake. I couldn't imagine Chief Perry blabbing anything about it, and I knew I hadn't told anyone. Maybe Penny had told her girlfriends about it. By the looks I was getting from my schoolmates, I knew the story had already made the rounds to everyone. People looked at me as if I were a ghost—already dead or soon to be.

I almost didn't want to face the lunch hour with Don and the dork squad. For one thing, hanging with them was kind of boring. When they talked about girls, it was almost always about girls who didn't really exist, like Cortana and Chell from video games they played. And for another, sitting with Don and his buddies was my daily reminder that I was permanently relegated to the lamest social clique in school. Not only that, but I was the most pathetic and newest member of the lamest social clique.

Don asked about Friday night, the outcome of me giving Penny a ride home. I told him the things Penny had said about Grant, that we kissed but nothing else. I left out the part about Chief Perry cock-blocking me and about his patrol car escorting us home.

"And Grant already knows about it," he said, his brow wrinkling in concern. "You're an idiot. No one else in Ashland is dumb enough to make the moves on Penny."

"I didn't make any moves. I don't have any moves," I said impatiently, and truer words were never spoken. "All I did was give her a ride home. *She* kissed *me*."

"Are you trying to tell me that Penny Olson date-raped you?" Don asked skeptically. "Is that what you're saying? That she forced herself on you and you were just an unwilling participant?"

"That's not what I said."

"What about Del?" Aaron asked.

"What about her? I mean, we hang out . . . sometimes . . . but there's nothing going on between us." Aaron and Don exchanged skeptical glances but said nothing about my protests. I was more concerned about the threat from Tony on Saturday than my feelings regarding Delilah, which were, as always, a mess of confusion. Half the time she was cutting me down in that ironic way she had, always making me wrong no matter how I interpreted what she was saying. The way a girl's mind works is like chaos theory: the only predictable factor is unpredictability. "What's the story with Delilah and that guy Tony?" I asked suddenly, remembering the way Tony and Delilah had interacted.

"They used to go out," Don said. "Del used to hang out with Grant and all of those other douche bags. She broke up with Tony after her brother died. It was a long time before she talked to anyone after that. I think later, Tony wanted her back, but she's kind of a loner now, has been since Jeremy died."

"You mean she was different before Jeremy died?" I asked.

"Very different. For one thing she used to brush her hair, dressed like a girl. She would even smile. Guys were always asking her out, even Grant, but she never really gave anyone the time of day. Girls wanted to be her friend so they could get close to Jeremy. She was really popular, in fact. But that all changed after Jeremy died. She and Jeremy were pretty close. Practically the whole town turned out for his funeral. Everyone came. Jeremy was the only person from Ashland we lost in Iraq or Afghanistan. At least so far. Everyone came to the funeral except for Del. She didn't leave her house for two weeks."

"Her brother—you knew him?" I asked.

"Jeremy? Sure," Don said. "Small town. Everybody knows everybody."

"Delilah told me. About Jeremy. He would have been twenty-one yesterday."

"Really?" Don asked. "I mean, really, she told you that? I'm surprised. She never talks about him. Did she tell you why Jeremy joined the army?"

"No," I said, and it had not occurred to me to wonder about it before. I figured that's just what boys from small towns in America's heartland did. Go off to war.

"I don't know how it all went down, but the story goes that Jeremy was running away. That was how he ended up in the army."

"Running away?" I asked. "Like running away from home?"

"Maybe," Don said with a shrug. "Running away from home, from life, from Ashland. Take your pick. We all fantasize about it. Getting out of this town. Chief Perry is a strict guy. Jeremy was a little wild. Not bad. Not into drugs or anything like that. Just a little out there."

"So the police chief's son runs off to war to get away from his dad and ends up killed," I said thoughtfully. "I'd almost feel bad for Chief Perry if he weren't such an angry son of a bitch. He's been out to get me since I got here."

"Well, you do have a lot of weird shirts," Aaron said. "You aren't exactly going to blend in, dressing the way you do."

"Your problem, Luke," Don said around a mouthful of Rice Krispies Treats, "is that you are caught up in the classic Archie dilemma."

"The what?" I asked with a frown.

"Archie," he said with some impatience, like I was a complete moron. "As in the *Archie* comics. Betty and Veronica."

Aaron was nodding his head knowingly as Don spoke.

"Archie has two girls who are into him," Don said as he leaned forward earnestly and put both elbows on the table. "Betty, the girl next door who is nice and down-to-earth and not stuck on her looks, and Veronica, who's catty and mean and a total bitch but rich and beautiful. Archie is always falling all over himself to get with Veronica and keep her happy, but the girl he should be in love with is Betty. She cares about him and just wants to make him happy."

"Is Betty ugly?" I asked, and Don grimaced.

"She's a cartoon, Luke." This with a weary roll of his eyes. "But no, I don't think she's supposed to be ugly. Anyway, Del is not ugly. She's totally hot."

"Delilah has never had anything nice to say to me," I said. "She's stubborn and difficult to get along with. She makes me nuts. Delilah is not a Betty."

"She's supposed to make you nuts," Don said, his voice rising to a squeak. "That's what girls do. But Penny is just like Veronica. She doesn't really care about you as a person. You think she's so in love with Grant? She just wants to be with him because he's the best-looking guy in school and his dad has a lot of money."

"How do you know?" I shot back. "Penny's not like that. She's nice."

Don looked unconvinced and only shrugged. "You don't have to listen to me. I'm just saying that you should appreciate your relationship with Del. She's awesome, even if you can't see it because you're so infatuated with Penny."

"Delilah and I don't have a relationship," I said, maybe too forcefully. "I told you. There's nothing going on between us."

The conversation with Don and Aaron left me feeling irritated, though I wasn't exactly sure why. Delilah was a sore point for me. Sure, she was pretty and more like a guy friend to me than any girl I had ever known, but every time

I was with her she did her best to trip me up and make me feel like an idiot. And her dad was a total nightmare. Even if I did want to have a relationship with Delilah, her dad would make it impossible. Just like Grant made it impossible for me to be with Penny. If I wanted a girlfriend, I was going to have to find some other prospect.

21

At the garage that afternoon there wasn't much to do. I sat and chewed the fat with Roger and Tiny while they drank their afternoon beers. When the sun dipped in the sky they saddled up and rode home and I was finally motivated to do something. I put away any stray tools, loaded shop rags into the ancient washing machine that would clang angrily through the spin cycle, and was just going to shut down the lights in the garage bay when a car pulled up out front. The headlights burned through the slitted windows in the bay door, but that was all I could see. A few beats after the headlights extinguished, there was the tinkle of bells as the office door opened.

"Roger's gone for the day," I called out across the bay.

There was no answer to my greeting, but then Grant Parker stepped through the office door into the garage.

"Hey, asshole," he said.

"What are you doing here?" I asked.

"Well, I'm not here for an oil change," Grant said, and stepped down into the recessed floor of the garage. He moved toward me deliberately and I was suddenly afraid.

"I'm just closing up. You shouldn't be here."

"I'll go wherever I want, whenever I want to," Grant said. "I don't know what the rules are like in the big city where you come from, but here, if you make a move on another guy's girl, you're going to pay for it."

"I didn't make a move on anyone," I said. "I don't have any moves."

"Boy, you got that right," Grant said.

"You've been a dick to me since the first day I got here," I said. I sounded like a whiny baby now, but it was hard to keep my voice level and stay calm.

"What? Are you still mad about that whole cow-tipping thing?" he asked scornfully. "It was a joke. You can't take a joke?"

"It wasn't my idea of a good joke."

"So, what?" he asked. "You got it in for me now? Is that it? You think you're a tough guy."

"No," I answered honestly.

It seemed that the talking portion of our program was now over. Grant shrugged out of his jacket and tossed it on a pile of tires waiting to go for recycling. "I'm going to make you wish you were never born."

If you've ever been punched in the face, you know that the chances of getting hit a couple of times and coming back with your own slugs isn't really the way it goes down. You get hit in the face a couple of times and that's it. You're out. Down for the count.

At that moment I was completely focused on avoiding Grant's fist as it came flying at my face. He lunged for me and I dodged left. It never even occurred to me to take him on, to swing my fist. I just ran like a coward. I spun on my heel, looking wildly around for a tool or something else to use as a weapon. Not that I intended to use it on him, but I thought that if I was holding a wrench or a crowbar, I'd be able to scare him off.

In the eternity between him lunging for me and me recovering my balance, there was a bloodcurdling scream, a loud clang, like we were trapped together inside an enormous bell, and then silence. The silence was so complete I could hear my own breath and the roar of adrenaline in my ears. My breath caught and I held it for a long minute. The world swam in front of my eyes, and I may have blacked out for a second. My conscious awareness had not caught up with what my subconscious already knew.

Grant was gone, had disappeared like a magician, without the telltale puff of smoke.

I'm not sure how much time passed before I worked up the nerve to move to the edge of the grease pit, the hole in the garage floor that opened to the work area below. I couldn't bring myself to look down into the mouth that had gaped with silence since Grant's fall.

Look. Just take one quick peek. You don't have to keep looking, but just take one glance, to confirm what we already know.

I can't. Can't look.

Yes, you can. On the count of three.

Oh, Jesus.

Ready? One . . . two . . .

Human bodies, for all their athletic ability, grace, and amazing feats, can only look like that when they are dead. Legs and arms don't turn in those unnatural angles when there is a living presence inside them.

Grant Parker had lunged for me, had not calculated my cowardice, had thought his body would meet the resistance of another person almost his equal in size and weight . . . and had missed. He had plunged headfirst into the grease pit, his head connecting with the air compressor that lay like a monster coiled in its lair.

"Dead." The word played through my mind over and over again until it lost all meaning. Life had no meaning, and I wished suddenly that the fairy tales my dad told each Sunday were true, that there was something to believe in.

Had I been a character in a movie, or had I any presence of mind to do what was right, I would have run down to the lower level and felt for a pulse, attempted to cajole life back into his body with CPR or mouth-to-mouth or anything else I had been taught in various health classes I'd sat through in school. But I knew he was without salvation, knew it the way you know the sky is blue or that the Earth turns on its axis.

I spun quickly on my heel, unable to look at Grant Parker's lifeless body for another second, though the image was burned onto my retinas forever. I turned, so suddenly that the room spun crazily, my hand clapped over my mouth. Vomit ejected from my mouth with such force that it sprayed between my fingers.

And that was the last thing I knew for a long while.

22

Grant Parker wasn't dead.

He was seriously fucked up. But not dead.

Broken spine? Maybe. Brain damage? Also a real possibility. But nobody was telling me anything.

Though I didn't remember much of what happened after Grant fell into the grease pit, somehow I must have had the presence of mind to call for an ambulance. And because I mentioned Grant as the accident victim by name, the entire Ashland emergency response team showed up at Roger's. A fire truck, ambulance, and all four patrol cars crowded the street, all with roof lights rotating and casting a kaleidoscope of yellow, red, and blue. The junkyard seemed alive with the movement of light, and watching it for too long made me feel stoned.

I was asked, and answered, questions but could only

give one response. "He fell. He fell." I kept saying it over and over again. Once it became obvious to them I wouldn't, couldn't, say anything else, I was largely forgotten in the clamor of emergency responders.

I had been biting the skin around my thumbnail obsessively since the police arrived at Roger's garage. Gut-tightening fear had dumped an almost lethal dose of adrenaline into my bloodstream, and I was still trembling and sweating, my legs bouncing when I tried to sit still. As the paramedics rolled Grant Parker out on a gurney and loaded him into the back of an ambulance, I could see that Grant's neck was held in line by a red brace, his torso strapped to a body board.

Leland Parker, who was called by the police as soon as the ambulance had been dispatched, showed up in his Sedan DeVille. It was my first time seeing him up close, because Grant's family didn't go to Dad's church. Leland Parker was a big man. Huge. Made to seem all the more so from my position as a prisoner in the back of Chief Perry's patrol car.

Leland Parker wore a tweed sport coat and a crisp blue Oxford cloth shirt. These were awkwardly out of sync with the dark blue jeans and dusty work boots he also wore, but somehow he made the outfit work. He looked like he had just walked out of the pages of a cigarette ad, snowcapped mountains and horses as his backdrop.

It wasn't clear if I was under arrest. They hadn't put me in handcuffs. Just stowed me away in the back of the car while everyone tried to figure out what to do. Every once in a while Chief Perry's eyes would stray in my direction to pierce me with an arrow gaze. My face would get hot with shame, though shame about what . . . I wasn't sure.

After all, I hadn't really done anything wrong. Other than stick up for myself against Grant at school, a fact that would make me look guilty as hell.

I wanted to scream out my innocence, tell them I had done nothing to hurt Grant. Hadn't even touched him.

Would that make me look guilty?

I tried to think about all of the suspect interviews I had ever seen on crime shows. Wondered if Chief Perry would use some special interrogation ploy—a good cop/bad cop scenario, for example—to get me tripping over my words and admitting that I had actually caused the (*let's face it*) possible impending death and almost certain permanent vegetative state of Grant Parker.

Once the ambulance left to deliver Grant to the hospital, Leland Parker riding shotgun in the cab, the attention of the four sheriff's deputies turned to me. They held a brief conference, all of them staring at me as they spoke, and then Chief Perry came to get behind the wheel of the car.

His judgment hung heavy between us, but something told me to keep my mouth shut. No matter what. Keep my mouth shut and wait until my brain was functional again before speaking.

But Chief Perry didn't ask me anything. Didn't really even acknowledge my presence at all on the short drive to the police station. I wanted to ask him things. Wanted to know about Grant's condition and whether my dad had been called. But I didn't say a single word. I needed to pee but wasn't even comfortable admitting that. Any words or action, even taking a piss, seemed like an admission of guilt in my confused and tortured mind.

At the station, Chief Perry escorted me to a small room. Not an interrogation room like you see on television, just a shitty little room with a couple of filing cabinets, a scarred wood table, and a water cooler that was dusty from disuse. Chief Perry stood across the table from me in the cramped room, his hands tightening and loosening on the ladder back of a chair as if he were imagining my throat in his grip. He seemed wary of me, the way a person would act with a poisonous snake or an unfriendly dog.

When Chief Perry thought the worst offense I had ever committed was trying to make time with his precious daughter, he had looked at me as if he wanted to kill me. Every time he saw me, his eyes would turn sharp and his left eyelid would narrow, as if he were sighting my head through the scope of a rifle.

Now that he believed I was an attempted murderer *and* I was trying to sleep with his only daughter, he still looked like he wanted to shoot me. And I got the sense, definitely, from the glint in his eyes, that he enjoyed the idea that his suspicions had been proven correct, that I was nothing but trouble.

He still hadn't said anything to me, and I realized he probably wasn't allowed to ask me anything since I was only seventeen and still a minor. Or maybe I should be asking for a lawyer, though asking for a lawyer would also make me look guilty as hell. Every way I turned in my mind, trying to decide what to do, what to say, all I could see was an appearance of guilt.

As Chief Perry stared at me I kept my gaze fixed on his hands, unable to meet his eye. I fought the urge to tell him that I hadn't put the moves on his daughter, that I hardly even thought about Del in that way since I had seen Penny Olson in her cheerleading uniform. Del never wore anything even remotely revealing. Before I had been given the opportunity to touch one of them, I hadn't even been sure she had breasts. Thinking about Delilah's breasts reminded me of our heated embrace on her dead brother's twenty-first birthday.

When was that? Yesterday? It seemed like a lifetime ago. The sudden thought of our fevered groping and kissing under the moonlight gave me a half hard-on, and I shifted uncomfortably in my seat.

Jesus, what was wrong with me? What kind of sick, depraved individual gets a hard-on at a time like this? The fact that Delilah's father was actually in the room with me at the moment just made the whole thing so surreal I wondered if this was just a nightmare—a nightmare–wet-dream combo, which wouldn't be a first.

When he finally broke the silence, I knew immediately that in *his* mind, I was already tried and convicted.

"What I find most disturbing, Mr. Grayson," Chief Perry said as I gnawed at the side of my thumbnail, "is that you haven't even asked me about Grant's condition. Aren't you at all curious if he's alright?" Chief Perry's southern drawl made the question sound downright polite, a veneer of courtesy that made almost everything these southerners said come across as sinister.

I knew the thumb gnawing would also make me look

guilty, but I couldn't help myself. I was dying to smoke a cigarette and guzzle a forty-ounce can of some shitty domestic beer. Maybe follow it up with a bong rip and a hit of Molly—shit, anything to get me out of this situation and into an alternate reality.

I didn't answer him, but my eyes narrowed into slits as I tried to see through his guile. Thanks to Roger, I had watched enough episodes of *Law & Order* to know Chief Perry was probably just trying to trick me into giving up some damning evidence. Appearance of guilt or not, I kept my silence.

The chief reached my dad at the church during Bible study, and Dad and Doris arrived at the police station in such a state of shock and confusion that I almost wished they hadn't come. Almost. At the very least they created a distraction from my status as an assailant.

We were all crammed into the room, Doris's clip-on earrings garish under the fluorescent lights and her cloud of perfume expanding to fill the small space. Chief Perry was very formal, called them "Reverend and Mrs. Grayson." His formality made me nervous, as if he was intentionally putting distance between himself and Dad because I now held status as a perp. I was wracking my brain, trying to remember if Chief Perry usually called them Frank and Doris.

"I've been waiting for you to get here before I asked him anything," Chief Perry said. "But let me just say that Grant Parker's condition is bad. Your boy has managed to get himself into some serious trouble. And right now we only have his word to listen to. There were no other witnesses, and Grant Parker can't tell us anything."

"Luke," Dad said turning to me, "I can't believe it. First a call from Principal Sherman about you fighting at school. Now this?" I wanted to kick Dad for saying something so damning in front of the chief.

Chief Perry's eyes widened slightly, like a bird with a hit on prey. The fistfight story was news to him. Maybe there hadn't been time for that story to spread through Ashland like kudzu. Or maybe Chief Perry's sources weren't as good as Roger's.

"Answer me, Luke," Dad said with a gulp of air, genuinely upset. "What is going on with you? This isn't the big city, son. Here we obey the word of the Lord as it was written."

I wasn't aware of anything in the Bible that prohibited fistfights at school, but I got the sense Dad was bringing the Lord into the conversation to remind Chief Perry that we were God-fearing people. At least that's what I hoped. I hoped that Dad didn't also believe I was a murderer, which was what everyone else seemed to think of me.

Now, murder, they do get specific in the Bible about whether that's a good or bad thing. They even gave that rule a number so you could use shorthand to remember it.

"Tell us what happened," Chief Perry said.

I tried to start by recounting everything that had happened up to that point—the cow tipping, giving Penny a ride home, the threats and abuse from Grant and his friends—but it all came out sounding garbled and ridiculous. The sense of burning humiliation and status as an outcast was a big part of the story, but not something I could explain adequately. And I was losing my audience, Chief Perry barely listening to me as he sized me up, watching for indications that I was lying.

Eventually I gave up trying to explain the past few weeks and just told the events as they had happened that night. I hadn't touched Grant. He had come after me, tripped, and fell. It was so simple, really. So little to tell. It was the confusion of events leading up to Grant's attack that came off sounding unbelievable.

When I got to the part about the vomit and calling the ambulance, Doris had a complete and total meltdown. She started crying and wailing like a crazy person. "How?" she asked. "How am I supposed to host a women's club function at church this Friday when I have a stepson who is in jail? I've already confirmed a seated dinner for forty people with the caterer. It's not like they are going to refund our deposit." She turned helplessly to Chief Perry, her hands held out in supplication as if to beg him to understand. "His mother is not a fit role model. I've done the best I could to help him to be a better person. Can you talk to the caterer?"

"Uh . . . no, ma'am, I'm afraid that's not something I can do," Chief Perry said, looking uncertain for the first time. He hooked his thumbs in his broad leather gun belt and rocked back on his heels as he tried to figure out how to handle this new development.

"This is your fault," Doris said, turning to me, her voice lowering to a hiss. "You've ruined everything! Your father told you not to wear that shirt on your first day at your new school." Then she succumbed to weeping and collapsed into Dad's arms while he shushed her and tried to offer comfort.

Doris's breakdown prevented Chief Perry from asking me any of the questions he had been saving. The disappointment was clear on his face, and he took a deep breath and blew out a sigh as Dad left to deliver Doris home.

Or maybe to an insane asylum.

They refused to release me into Dad's custody, said I had to stay at least until the county prosecutor returned from a fishing trip the following day. The idea of a seventeen-year-old murderer was too foreign in Ashland for anyone to know the rules, but they were pretty sure they didn't want to turn me loose onto the streets of Ashland to maim anyone else.

Chief Perry gestured for me to stand up as he held the door to the conference room open and waited for me to walk out of the room. "I'm going to put you in a holding cell," he said. "I'll have someone bring you some supper."

"I'm not hungry," I said woodenly. The stress was making my stomach ache, and my throat burned from the bile that kept creeping up my esophagus.

The holding cell was only about ten feet square, with a single cot bolted to the wall, a thin mattress rolled and stowed at the end. I paced and sat, paced and sat. I spent ten minutes trying to coax a pee into the stainless steel toilet with no seat, even though I had to pee so badly I couldn't focus on anything else.

Everything had been taken from my pockets, and there

was no clock within view of my cell. For a long time I was afraid to shut my eyes because when I did, all I saw was Grant's twisted, broken body at the bottom of the grease pit. Finally I was so exhausted that I had to lie down, though I kept my eyes open until sleep overtook me like a wave.

23

"Luke," someone whispered, and for a second I thought I was imagining it. I was still lying on my back on the thin mattress in my jail cell, one arm draped across my eyes. Normally I would sleep on my side, but the metal cot was only comfortable if I stayed flat on my back. My throat burned with acid reflux, but I had refused all food and drink other than water since being taken into custody.

"Luke." Definitely not a part of my dream. A girl's voice whispering my name.

I sat up and twisted toward the sound of the voice in one motion. The feeling of having no privacy, of being on display for the world to see me in my cage, was almost unbearable.

My first reaction to seeing Delilah was relief. It was good to see a friendly face, even if she had never really been all that friendly toward me. It didn't occur to me to wonder how she had managed to get into the prisoner area. She was as sneaky as she was clever.

"Does your dad know you're here?" I asked as I craned my head to peer through the bars, afraid Chief Perry would come storming at us any second and bludgeon me to death.

"Of course not," she said with a roll of her eyes.

"How did you know I was here?" I asked.

"Dad's radio at home. I heard everything from the paramedics and the dispatcher."

"Do you know if Grant's okay?" I asked, relieved to finally be able to ask the question.

She bit her lip and turned her head to one side, looking at the hall door instead of at me. "He was alive when he got to the hospital," she said finally. "That's all I know."

"They think I threw him. Pushed him," I said. "I didn't do anything. He fell. Just . . . tripped and fell. I thought he was dead." This all tumbled out in a rush as I felt comfortable speaking for the first time since the accident, as if I was finally in the presence of an ally.

"I'll talk to my dad," she said. "I'll tell him it had to have been an accident. There's no way you would kill someone, no way you would have hurt Grant on purpose. I mean, I know you . . . sort of." As she said this last part her expression changed and she paused for a moment, as if to consider how well she actually knew me. "Anyway, there's no way you could kill someone."

"Do me a favor and don't say a word to your dad about me," I said quickly. "He already hates me because he thinks

I'm trying to get into your pants. If you take up my side, he'll do whatever he can to make sure my ass goes to jail for a long time."

"Are you?" she asked.

"Am I what?"

"Trying to get into my pants?" Her eyes were wide with the question as she waited for my response.

"No," I said. "I have no interest in getting into your pants. Can we not talk about anything to do with you and me right now? Please. Grant Parker is seriously fucked up. And everybody thinks I'm the one who fucked him up."

"So, what did happen, then?" she asked. "Did you hit him with something?"

"I didn't hit him at all," I said too loudly, and lowered my voice as I leaned in closer to the bars, still with an uneasy eye on the hallway. "He came after me. I moved out of the way and he slipped and fell. That's it. There was no fight."

"Did you tell my dad that?"

"Look, you should go before anyone finds out you're here. Don't say anything to your dad. Please don't make it any worse than it already is."

"I told you not to mess with Grant Parker," she said, taking the last word for herself and not giving me time to argue that I hadn't messed with anyone. Everyone else kept messing with me.

Before I could say any of that to her, she left as quietly as she had come, and I was back to my pacing and worrying.

About thirty minutes after Delilah left, Chief Perry came back to see me in my cell, this time with Roger in tow. I stood quickly at the sight of Roger, and my hands moved nervously from my back pockets to my thighs as I tried to find a natural way to rest my arms.

"Hey, kid," Roger said in his gruff way as Chief Perry started to unlock the door to my cell.

"Hey, Roger. What are you doing here?" I asked, my eyes darting nervously between him and Chief Perry.

"Turns out that Mr. McElroy has a closed-circuit television system in his shop," Chief Perry said, though his words didn't mean anything to me in my current state.

"Used to have a guy working for me who would steal parts, sell them out the back door, and pocket the money," Roger said. "Got the cameras installed then but never had much use for them since." He shrugged and tilted his head, one eyebrow lifted. "Until now."

"You mean . . . ," I started, not daring to hope.

"The whole thing was caught on tape," Chief Perry said, by his tone conveying clear disappointment that I would not be going to the state penitentiary for life.

My heart had started to hammer crazily, and my breath was coming in short pants. "So you saw? You saw that I didn't do anything to hurt Grant. He came after me. He fell. Just like I told you." I waited expectantly, wanting to hear Chief Perry say that he had been wrong.

"Your story checks out," Chief Perry drawled. "But this isn't the end of it. Not by a long shot. I'm going to be watching you, boy. I get even a whiff of trouble from you and I'll be on you like stink on manure. You hear me?"

"Am I free to go?" I asked, hating him so much at that moment I wanted to scream.

"I called your dad," Chief Perry said. "He's taking care of your mom. Doesn't want to leave her. Your dad said I could release you to Mr. McElroy's custody. He's going to take you home."

"Stepmom," I said through clenched teeth. "She's my stepmom. Not my mom."

"Come on, kid," Roger said as he put a rough hand on my shoulder and gave me a tug toward the exit.

When we emerged from the police station Roger directed me to his truck, an old Ford F-250 with the garage name and number stenciled on the side paneling.

"Can you just drive me back to DC?" I asked as we both slid into the cab.

Roger chuckled at that, a bark muffled by his bush of beard. " 'Fraid not," he said.

"My life is over," I said with a moan as I leaned forward and ground my forehead into my palms.

"Yep," Roger said with a nod. His eyes never left the windshield, but I detected a note of sympathy in his voice. "Just be glad the Parkers aren't Baptists," he continued. "It would be worse if they belonged to your daddy's church."

"I have to leave the country," I said. "It's my only real option."

"Leland Parker is not the type of man to forgive and forget," Roger said in agreement. "You lie low until the police have a chance to explain what happened, show him the tape."

"Oh, I'll lie low," I said as I rested my head against the cool glass of the window. "I'm never coming out of my room again."

24

The next day the local paper broke the news of the whole debacle under the splashy headline LIFE HANGS IN THE BAL-ANCE FOR LOCAL HIGH SCHOOL HERO. The article included a laundry list of Grant's awards and accomplishments as well as the win-loss record of the Wakefield Wildcats for the current and two most recent past seasons. Leland Parker made a statement to the press that he and his wife were "overcome with grief," and were "concerned about public safety" with the influx of people moving to Ashland from the big city.

As a minor, I was not mentioned in the article by name, my identity cleverly disguised as the "son of a local promi-nent pastor, and a recent transplant from a large city, now attending Wakefield High School." I scanned the article quickly, looking for an update on Grant's condition. That he had survived the night, I took as a good sign. At least a hopeful sign.

I made the executive decision to stay home from school that day. Dad either didn't notice or agreed with my decision, though even if he had tried to force me to go, there was no way I would have shown my face at Wakefield. Dad was still overcome by the situation and was in full damage-control mode. Neighbors called and dropped in throughout the day in a show of expressing concern, but really they were just digging for gruesome details to share at the hair salon or the bank.

Even Penny's mother, though she was a lifelong Presbyterian, showed up with a green-bean casserole. Doris navigated the social awkwardness of the casserole offering with stoic and cold civility. I wasn't sure what help Mrs. Olson thought food would be. And green-bean casserole turned out to be a disgusting mixture of green beans and cream-of-mushroom soup. Worse even than the ambrosia salad that southerners ate by inexplicable choice.

Dad called Mom to try to explain to her what had happened. I stood in the kitchen doorway watching Dad's end of the conversation. He fumbled for a while, and I could hear Mom's voice, high-pitched and asking rapid-fire questions peppered, I was sure, with gratuitous swearing.

Dad finally gave up and handed the phone to me.

"Luke, what the hell?" Mom said as her opener.

"It wasn't my fault," I said.

"Are you okay?"

"I'm . . . fine. Sort of."

"Were you hurt?" she asked, and at the same time I

swore I heard a cork popping out of a bottle of wine on her end.

"No. Not at all. Things are just . . . awkward right now."

"I'm supposed to be catching a flight to L.A. in exactly"—a pause while she checked the time—"forty minutes. But I can cancel my trip if I have to. I can be there tonight. Or maybe tomorrow. How far is DC from Tennessee?"

"Really fucking far, Mom." I glanced up at Dad, who stiffened at my use of a curse word. And not just any curse word. The king of all curse words. But he said nothing.

"Yeah. Okay. I can be there by tomorrow."

"No," I said quickly. "Don't come. Just go on your trip."

"Luke, seriously, what is happening there?"

I sighed wearily. I thought about telling Mom all about Grant and how everything had unfolded, but the idea just made me really tired. I had already spent too much time talking about it.

"It's nothing I can't handle. Okay? Go on your trip. I'll talk to you in a couple of days."

I managed to get her off the phone with only a few promises to call with an update the next day.

Reporters from local papers were relentless as they called the landline seeking a quote from Dad or me. By midafternoon Dad turned the landline off and stopped answering the door.

Doris went to bed with a wet rag on her forehead, overwhelmed by the strain of being polite to nosy busybodies all day. Dad went to the hospital to check on Grant's family.

The house was now as much a prison to me as the police station had been. I couldn't leave the house, expected any minute for a crowd with torches and pitchforks to materialize in the front yard. Maybe they would burn a cross on the lawn or throw a rock through the bay window. I was never going to be able to leave the house again.

25

The news Dad brought home was grim. Grant Parker was in a coma and was suffering a swollen spinal cord and a severe concussion. A full recovery was not expected, but possible.

A prayer vigil was scheduled for that night. People had been leaving flowers and mementos outside the hospital and on the Wakefield home goalpost all day, a tribute to their fallen knight. At dark they would light candles and sing hymns outside Grant's hospital window to invite the healing grace of the Lord.

The Lord was obviously someone who cared more about Grant Parker than he did about me. Which made him something less of a god in my eyes. If this was how God conducted himself, he was no better than Principal Sherman.

Dad and I argued about whether I should attend the prayer vigil or not. I said no way. No way in hell. Dad argued that if I didn't go it would look as if I didn't care about Grant or his family, didn't care about whether Grant recovered from his injuries. But I held my ground and refused to even consider the idea of attending the vigil. I knew I would be publicly crucified if I showed my face so soon after the accident.

Dad never raised his voice because it wasn't in his nature, and he finally gave up. He did coax Doris out of bed with a rousing sermon about the community responsibilities of a preacher's wife, and she mustered the etiquette to select a conservative gray dress and flat black shoes.

I sat home that night and watched news coverage of the gathering, recognizing my classmates and teachers among the crowd. There were no pitchforks or torches present, which I took as a good sign. The cameras kept cutting back to Dad and Doris, and, inevitably, Dad was asked for comment.

"It was a terrible accident," Dad said earnestly. "My family and I are in pieces about it."

"An accident?" the reporter asked skeptically with an exaggerated lift of her eyebrows. "We were under the impression that this was a case of self-defense."

"No, no," Dad answered quickly as I squirmed urgently in my seat. "It's all a misunderstanding. It was just an accident."

"You mean, Grant Parker was accidentally almost killed during an altercation with your son?" the reporter pressed.

"Jesus wept!" I yelped at the television, sitting up so quickly my drink sloshed onto my pants, but I barely took any notice of it.

"No, I . . .", Dad started to yammer, when the camera

cut away suddenly to capture an image of the entire cheer-leading squad, crying and holding each other in a distract-ingly sexy group hug.

The reporter promised further updates on Grant's con-dition and the "alleged assault" before returning to one of the nineteen or so *CSI* spin-offs already in progress. At the mention of murder and forensic evidence, I quickly shut off the television and sat staring at the fireplace, contemplat-ing the least painful method for suicide.

With my tail between my legs, I retreated to my bedroom and lay on the bed in the dark. As testament to just how miserable I was, I didn't even think about looking at my phone or jacking off before sleep.

I was in a world of suck.

Though I didn't remember even feeling tired, I woke sud-denly to a scratching noise outside my window. Azalea branches tapped insistently against the siding as Delilah fought her way through the shrubs.

"What are you doing here?" I asked as I opened the win-dow sash.

"Let me in," she said simply.

I popped out the screen with the side of my fist and held out an arm to her as she struggled to get her leg up to the windowsill.

"Why are you here?" I asked again. "Don't you think I'm in enough trouble already?"

"I brought you a shit-ton of crystal meth," she said. "Fig-ured you'd want to off yourself."

"You have no idea," I said. I collapsed back onto my bed with a weary sigh. "Is that why you came? To help me kill myself?"

"No," she said, her voice softening with something that sounded almost like compassion. "I figured you would need a friend."

The night in the meadow when she told me about her brother was the only other time I had ever heard genuine emotion in her voice. It surprised me to hear it there now.

"I don't have any friends," I said bitterly. "I hate this fucking place."

Even though Delilah said plenty of crazy shit, like all girls, she was one of the few who knew how to be quiet too. On the nights when she had sat in the driveway watching me work on the Camaro, we often sat in silence. And neither of us ever asked what the other was thinking. I hated it when girls did that, since most of the time I was either thinking about sex or whether I had a skid mark in my underwear left over from a really potent fart.

Delilah came to sit on the edge of my bed and kicked off her shoes. She fought with my arm until I realized what she wanted and put it out so she could nestle under my armpit. We lay there with her head on my shoulder, her hand on the side of my chest, her hair tickling my chin. I had to admit that the warmth of her body comforted me and I felt less alone than I had in weeks.

"Did you go to the prayer vigil?" I asked.

"Yeah," she murmured into my armpit.

"I can't ever leave the house again," I said. "What if he dies?"

"Then it won't be your fault," Delilah said, her voice sleepy. "There's a big world outside of Ashland. You can get out, one way or another. Like Jeremy. He just came back sooner than he expected."

At the mention of her brother I felt a pang of sympathy and stroked her hair a few times.

"It will be okay," she said, and now I was slipping toward sleep.

When I woke in the morning, Delilah was gone. Her side of the bed was cold, and I ran my hand along the bedspread to find some evidence she had really been there the night before. The whole thing had felt like a dream. And maybe it was. I couldn't tell what was real anymore.

26

By Wednesday night I had started to succumb to the anxiety of cabin fever. I hadn't showered or changed my clothes, had barely left my room since Roger brought me home from the police station on Monday night. I wondered if Delilah would come to see me again after Dad and Doris went to bed. I was surprised to find myself hoping that she would.

Though I had not discussed it with Dad, I had skipped school again Wednesday. In fact, I had no intention of ever going back. There had been another vigil held to pray for Grant's recovery that afternoon during school. I would never have survived it.

I waited, hoping Delilah would come to bring me news of the world beyond my window.

Close to midnight I heard the familiar scratching of the azaleas against my window and rolled out of bed to open the sash. I was dressed in sweatpants and no shirt, my eyes clotted with sleep, though I felt as if I had only dozed for a minute.

When I opened the window I got the shock of my life. More shocking even than Grant's swan dive into the grease pit. Penny Olson stood below my window, her eyes bright even in the dim glow from the streetlight.

"What are you doing here?" I asked, realizing as I did that this was a recurring question I had about the two girls in my life.

"Let me in," Penny said softly.

She moved toward the front door without waiting for an answer from me. Delilah was a girl who climbed through windows. Penny walked through doorways.

I crept quietly out to the foyer to let her in, every pop of the hardwood floors sounding as loud as gunshot in the quiet house.

Penny followed me to my bedroom and didn't speak until I shut the door behind us and pressed in the button lock on the doorknob.

"I'm so sorry this has happened," Penny said as she threw herself into my arms. "I've been so upset, knowing what you did to Grant . . . and all because of me."

"Wait. . . . no . . . what?"

"It's okay," she said as she took a small step back and picked up my hand to hold it against her chest. Even though I was pretty sure Penny had on a bra that maximized the appearance and feel of her breasts, it didn't really matter. They looked amazing and felt even better against my hand. "I know you were just doing what you had to do. To protect yourself. To protect what we have."

"Uh . . ." Anything Penny and I had together was news to me. We hadn't even spoken since the night Chief Perry all but accused me of sexual assault.

"I don't think any less of you as a person," she continued without a pause for me to reply. "In fact, I think more of you. Grant was a bully. He needed someone to put him in his place." Her expression turned sharp as she said this, her nails digging into my arm.

"He's not dead," I said.

"What do you mean?" she asked.

"You said Grant *was* a bully. Past tense. He's not dead."

"Oh," she said with a flutter of her hand. "I just meant that Grant always got away with bullying whoever he wanted. Including me. He won't be doing that anymore." She cocked her head as her eyes searched my face in a practiced way. "Because of you."

"Look, Penny," I said as I held her by the arms just above her elbows. "About what happened . . . it's not what you think."

"Shh," she said, and put a finger to my lips to silence me. "I know. You were just defending yourself. It wasn't intentional. You don't have to tell me what I already know. Grant came looking for the fight. He just didn't count on someone getting the better of him."

"Is that what you think?" I asked. "Is that what everyone thinks?"

She shrugged one shoulder, and as she did, managed to sidle in closer to me. "Pretty much."

I took a moment to think. Maybe Penny's interpretation of what happened wasn't so terrible after all. Maybe I had been looking at the whole thing wrong.

"But everyone was at the prayer vigil. People were really upset. If they think I'm the one who's responsible for Grant's condition, everyone is going to hate me." I wasn't really saying any of this for Penny's benefit. I was just voicing the thoughts I had struggled with for the past two days. Grant was Ashland's answer to Superman. Which made me a villain. Not just a villain, but a supervillain.

"I mean, Grant was popular, but only because he was rich and good-looking and a great football player. . . ." Penny trailed off while I waited for her to finish cataloging all of Grant's assets. "We didn't have a choice but to like him," she said, giving me a pointed look, wanting me to understand her side of things. I just gave her a noncommittal nod as I waited for her to continue. "But Grant was also a bully. He was used to getting his way." She paused. "But not anymore. You proved that to me. To everyone. You showed everyone that Grant can't treat people any way he wants to and get away with it. You're, like, a hero."

Maybe just a slight overstatement.

But, no—Penny was right. I had to stop casting myself as the bad guy. I was the underdog. Not a loser but an unlikely hero. I was David to Grant's Goliath.

The truth? The truth didn't matter. It was what everyone believed that mattered. Truth had nothing to do with faith.

The whole school—hell, the entire town—knew Grant was an entitled prick. If people wanted to believe I was a hero, or at the very least not a complete coward, then that was fine with me.

"Do you like me, Luke?" Penny asked, interrupting my

thoughts with her sudden change in trajectory. She sounded hopeful.

"Of course I like you," I said with some surprise. After all, Penny was beautiful. She was nice to me. She treated me like I was smart and strong. She treated me like I was somebody.

Not like Delilah, who would, more often than not, point out my faults, and never let me forget them. Penny knew how to talk to a guy. To make him feel like he was the man.

Maybe that was part of Grant's secret—how he was able to keep everyone convinced that despite being an asshole and not a nice person, they somehow had to like him, had to treat him like he was something special. He expected to be treated like a god . . . and so he was.

And now, here Penny was, telling me I was her champion, practically asking me to kiss her. Standing so close to me, in fact, I was surprised she couldn't feel exactly how much I liked her. "I'm just . . . not sure what's going to happen now that everyone thinks I'm an attempted murderer," I said. "Maybe nobody really liked Grant, were just afraid of him. But I did just single-handedly take out the captain of the football team and the student council president."

Okay, now who's overstating things?

Penny ran her delicate hand up my arm, up under the sleeve, and squeezed my triceps. I suppressed a shudder as my stomach went cold, and I felt my dick pressing against my sweats with interest. The top of her head came to just below my chin, and I had to admit, I liked the fact that she was so much smaller than I was. It made me feel strong and powerful, like I could kill a wolf with my bare hands to protect her while she cowered behind me.

Though I was not a virgin, the one time I'd had sex the whole thing was over so quickly I'm not even really sure what happened. Since then I had been afraid to attempt it again, afraid to let go and lose myself completely with another human being present to bear witness.

Penny was clearly experienced. I knew she had been sleeping with Grant. She had told me that much.

So, there we were, in my room, Dad and Doris asleep upstairs on the other side of the house, and Penny looking up at me with those big green eyes, her head tipped back and her full, luscious lips parted slightly.

"Tomorrow we can worry about it," she said. "Let's just forget about it tonight."

27

The better part of valor prevents me from telling you everything that Penny and I did with and to each other in my bedroom that night while Dad and Doris slept. But the next morning I felt like a new man, humming to myself as I stood under the shower.

Truth be told, I was still terrified of the prospect of facing anyone at school or on the street, still a prisoner in Dad's house, but there were people who believed I was innocent or, as in Penny's case, even noble. I felt a momentary twinge of guilt that I had not disclosed the full truth to Penny. I should have interrupted her, made her sit down and listen to the full story.

Somehow, the right moment just never presented itself. There was no graceful way to launch into the story, and with the way she thought of me now, I couldn't risk disappointing her. Penny could love a bully like Grant. She could even love a murderer-in-self-defense. But she could never love a coward.

I had fooled around with her under false pretenses. I *was* a coward, not the murderer-in-self-defense she wanted me to be. It would be impossible to tell the truth now without making myself the bad guy.

And, as much as I wanted to, I couldn't bring myself to regret any of it. Having sex with Penny was the best thing that had ever happened to me.

With my new status as suspected attempted murderer I became completely isolated, alone in a way I had never felt before. Not just lonely, but without any allies. Despite what Delilah or Penny or anybody thought, no one understood the humiliation and loneliness I had felt those first two months in Ashland.

That first Friday after the accident, the football game was canceled as a show of deference to Grant's grieving family. The whole community was in mourning, maybe as much for the impact Grant's absence would have on the football program as anything else.

Dad was feeling the strain of our sudden celebrity. Attendance numbers rivaled those of a Christmas or Easter service at his church that Sunday. I was forced to attend and hated every minute of being on display in a front pew. I felt the gaze from hundreds of eyes boring into the back of my neck and hid in the bathroom for most of the coffee hour after the service.

Neighbors and busybodies from his church were relentless in their badgering phone calls and drop-by visits. The veil of concern was smothering. Doris stayed in bed to avoid everyone, and I only left my room when absolutely necessary for survival, so Dad faced them all on his own.

A reporter from the local paper had stopped by soon after the accident, wanting a statement from me about Grant and his condition. I stood with the door to my bedroom cracked to overhear as Dad tried to get rid of the reporter politely. Then I watched from my window as the guy stood in the driveway and took a few pictures of the house. The pictures showed up in the Sunday paper attached to an in-depth article about Grant. The story was still first-page news since nothing else had happened in Ashland and national news didn't seem to generate much interest in Ashland's isolated community. The article mentioned the Wildcats 4–0 season record and speculated about the upcoming homecoming game against the Benton Bulldogs, rivals from the neighboring county.

Grant smiled out at me from the sidebar of the article. Though grainy and dark, Grant's senior portrait was still clear enough to show off his charismatic smile and perfectly coiffed hair, his chiseled jaw perched on his fist in a casual way. The picture had been taken only a week before the accident, when Grant was still on top of the world—his future rosy and his place at the top of the pyramid still intact.

The latest article wasn't very long. There wasn't much to say about Grant's condition. He was still in a coma, still in stable condition, but there was no mention of his long-term prognosis, whether he would be in a wheelchair or would be a quadriplegic. There was no speculation about whether he would be confined to bed for the rest of his life, or to one of those electric wheelchairs that had to be controlled by a joystick. A shudder passed through me as I pictured Grant, years from now, sitting at the diner in his wheelchair alongside the other regulars talking about old football glories over a cup of coffee and a piece of pie.

The diner really does have good pie.

As much as I wanted to leave the house, escape Dad and Doris, I was afraid to face the judgment of the towns-people. Though I no longer worried about pitchforks and burning crosses, I couldn't bring myself to walk into an en-vironment where people would stare at me and talk about me behind their hands.

When I thought about it, I couldn't imagine life beyond my four bedroom walls now. Couldn't imagine a return to school or my job. Now I was like one of those kids who had to be raised in a sterile bubble. Maybe a tutor would come to the house and I would live out my days with no contact from the outside world.

Other than Chief Perry, Roger, and Delilah, no one else seemed to know or accept the turn of events that had led to Grant being comatose. Had I told Penny the truth, told her the real story, she might have spread the rumor through town about what had really happened.

The only people who knew the truth were not the ones who would gossip about it at church or the diner. I thought about reaching out to the media, had thought about calling the reporter who had come looking for a quote from me for his article. The article did mention me. Again, not by name, but there was a picture of the house. In black and white, the image of Dad's house looked almost sinister, the azaleas crouched along the foundation as if concealing some ugly truth. It reminded me of the photos you see of a serial killer's house after the FBI has removed all of the body parts from under the porch.

Part of me wanted to tell my side of the story, but there was something nagging there. I couldn't bring myself to admit my cowardice—to speak openly about Grant's mistreatment of me and the humiliation I had suffered at his hands.

The more I thought about the whole situation, the angrier I got. Grant was a fool. He had started the whole thing—set me up to be covered in cowshit, circulated the story about it to humiliate me at school, driven Penny away by treating her like crap, and taken every opportunity to make me look like a fool in the eyes of everyone. He led us to the showdown at Roger's garage, and then had thrown himself into the grease pit without any assistance from me. And now I was branded a troublemaker and an attempted murderer, while he rested comfortably on life support in the hospital, the whole town weeping crocodile tears for him.

I held on to that sense of indignation. As long as I was angry with Grant, there wasn't room to feel anything else. The anger banished embarrassment for myself and pity for him and gave me strength.

Ultimately it was the anger that fueled me when it came time to face the people at school again. Monday morning

Dad forced my return to school by threatening to call the sheriff's office to have me escorted if I wouldn't go willingly.

I summoned the anger and indignation, used it as an internal pilot light, and decided I would return to Wakefield High School not as an attempted murderer, the way I had felt since the night of Grant's accident, but as a victim of circumstance. I would return as David who had slain the giant. The way Penny saw me.

If anybody thought I was really guilty of something, well . . .

. . . *fuck them.*

The Camaro was road-ready now, and I drove it to school for the first time that Monday. As I passed Main Street, the road that would lead out of town, I hesitated at the stop sign. I could turn right, follow Main Street out of town toward the ribbon of highway that would deliver me to a hundred cities where I could be a nobody, instead of the boy who tried to kill Grant Parker.

It didn't take long for me to calculate how far the ten dollars in my pocket would get me. With the gas mileage of the Camaro I might make it as far as the next town. But I would still be in Tennessee. Still in hell.

My attitude of confidence and disinterest in the opinions of others slowly waned on the ride to school. As I pulled into the student parking lot, my heart began to thunder in my chest. By the time I cut the ignition, my hands were shaking and I had trouble catching my breath.

"Shit. Shit. Shit," I said in a hoarse whisper as I put my

forehead against the steering wheel and squeezed my eyes shut.

My body betrayed me again and I was motivated out of the car by the sudden and desperate need to go to the bathroom. The stress of the whole situation had been making my stomach ache, and everything I ate had the same effect—powerful cramping and the need to shit almost immediately after every meal.

So there I was, walking toward school, backpack over one shoulder, earbuds set at top volume, and asshole clamped tight for fear of crapping my pants—an act that would have been one hundred times more mortifying than killing one of my classmates.

As I approached the main entrance, the needle scratched across the record and everything . . . everything . . . stopped. People stood in awe as they watched my approach in slack-jawed silence.

Welcome to hell.

28

If you've ever had the sense that someone is watching you, imagine that feeling multiplied by one million. Actually, imagine that feeling amplified to the millionth power, and you will get a sense of what I felt like that morning, my first day back at school after the maiming of Grant Parker.

On my way to homeroom I walked with my head down, eyes on the floor. I hesitated at the doorway to homeroom, took a deep breath, then dove in headfirst.

All conversation halted when I walked in, and the squeak of my shoes against the linoleum tile echoed like a siren through the room. Even Ms. Bartlett was still, her eyes tracking me as I passed through the room.

I took my seat in the third row, and every head in the room swiveled at the same time to turn and stare at me. It was impossible to keep my gaze focused on something neutral, like the top of my desk, with everyone watching me.

The final bell rang, and the loudspeaker in the room crackled as the office began morning announcements. I imagined the morning announcements would include a moment of silence or a prayer for Grant Parker, but there was no mention of Wakefield's fallen knight.

When the bell rang, dismissing us to first period, the spell was broken. The volume in the hallway was back to normal as people chatted at their lockers and hurried to class. And as when I had returned after my first altercation with Grant, people treated me like I was one of their own. Hell, people were downright friendly—said hello to me in the hallways, even greeting me by name.

At the very least I had expected anger and alienation from Grant's friends. But no one came after me, no one said anything rude or mean, and . . . no one really seemed to miss Grant Parker.

I passed Skip or Chet in the hallway, and he even gave me a friendly, "What's up, brah?" with a nod and a crack of his gum.

There was still a mountain of flowers and mementos piled around the home goalpost from the prayer vigil and memorial assembly at school. In a way, it was like Grant Parker was dead.

But he wasn't.

Grant had been like a god to the students at Wakefield. But not the sympathetic, compassionate God of the New Testament. He had been like the Old Testament God—a God of power and intimidation. He ignored the needs of the students at Wakefield while demanding their worship and sacrifice.

I expected to get called into Principal Sherman's office that morning, for him to give me some warning about not assaulting or murdering any of my other classmates. But the summons never came.

I did see Principal Sherman once between morning classes, as I passed through the lobby. But instead of a warning look or a frown, he merely turned his head, pretending as if he didn't see me, and busied himself with straightening a banner suspended from a hook on the brick wall.

At lunch I went quickly to the table I had shared with Don, Aaron, and Josh since the first day of school. The three of them were already there, Aaron and Don leaning toward each other over the tabletop in such earnest conversation that I knew they were talking about me.

Don and Aaron both sat back when they noticed my approach, their guilty expressions letting me know they really had been talking about me. At first they appeared scared, all three with eyes wide, as I took my place among them. I started to unpack my lunch without even saying hello, but after a minute they were all staring at me so intently I couldn't keep my cool.

"Stop staring at me," I hissed as I cut my eyes to the tables around us to gauge if we were being watched.

"Holy. Shit." A nervous smile played at the corners of Don's mouth as he said this.

"No shit," Aaron said in agreement.

I ignored them. "Where the fuck have you been?" I asked Josh, noting this was his first return to our lunch table since Grant had started harassing me.

Josh still didn't speak, but he seemed more relaxed in his seat, his torso no longer hunched forward to protect his soft underbelly.

"It's safe now," Don said, "with Grant gone."

"Thanks to you," Aaron added, and Don and Josh both nodded eagerly in agreement.

"*Not* thanks to me," I said. "Grant came after me. . . ."

"I know," Don said. "And you stood up to him. We never have to worry about Grant Parker again."

"He's not dead," I shot back defensively.

"He's in a coma," Don said.

"Probably paralyzed for life," Aaron added.

"Shut your mouth," I said with too much force. Aaron winced, his body retreating from mine instinctively, and it startled me. He really was scared. Was convinced I had faced Grant one-on-one and bested him.

I let my anger cool before speaking again. "All I'm saying is, he's not dead. He could still come out of the coma. Be okay."

Don and Aaron exchanged a look full of meaning, and they quietly chewed their food while they considered my reaction.

"If"—Don caught my look and quickly edited himself—"*when* Grant comes out of his coma, I don't think he'll be bothering you anymore."

Because he'll be a vegetable.

I was learning to hate the voice inside of me. It was always there, providing editorials that stole my calm.

"Look," Don said, "everyone knows it was self-defense. Grant was a bully. He came after you at Roger's garage. It's not like anyone thinks you're a murderer or something."

"Right," I said. "Because Grant *isn't* dead. It was just a stupid accident."

"Of course," Don said, his tone placating, soothing.

"I don't want to talk about it."

I was so intent on my conversation with them that I didn't notice as Penny approached our table.

"Luke," she said, her tone questioning as she looked at Don, Aaron, and Josh, then back to me with bewilderment. "What are you doing?"

My body reacted to Penny's proximity with alarm bells in my stomach and groin. I was instantly transported back to last Wednesday night in my bedroom.

"I'm . . . eating," I said, my voice rising with a question.

She laughed, almost nervously, and looked quickly over both shoulders, as if to make sure no one was within earshot.

"Here?" she asked, her tone questioning but at the same time clearly disapproving.

"Hello, Penny," Don said, obvious pride in his voice as he greeted her boldly.

"Oh . . . uh, hi . . . Don." The veneer of politeness was there, but she seemed unsure how to react to one of the lowly LARPers addressing her directly.

"Did you want to sit?" Don asked as he grabbed his lunch and slid down eighteen inches to make room for her on the end of the bench.

Penny looked stricken and her eyes turned to me, pleading. Then she composed herself and straightened her shoulders, her delicate collarbones shifting under her shirt-front. "I was just coming to get Luke." She said this with a meaningful widening of her eyes and a small jerk of her head, summoning me toward her. "Aren't you going to sit with me, Luke?" she asked.

"I . . . yes. Sure," I said as I rose partway from my seat, watching her face for approval.

I untangled myself from the bench and awkwardly gathered my sandwich and bag of chips.

Her face smoothed with relief, and she turned her body away from the table as I took up my place by her side. "See you guys later," Penny said cheerily.

As we walked away from the table, I realized where we were headed, straight for the table next to the window, the table usually reserved for Grant and his disciples.

29

I was welcomed like a long-lost brother at the table where Grant once held court. There was only a moment of uncomfortable quiet as everyone adjusted to the new social order. Grant was gone—at least temporarily—and they seemed to want me to take his place among them. These people were all Grant's friends, had known him since birth. These were the same people who had laughed at my expense during the cow-tipping incident. They were my sworn enemies, my tormentors.

They reminded me of a pride of lions. The king of the pride loses his seat of honor when a younger lion beats him in combat, and the old lion is killed or slinks away to lick his wounds in solitude. The pride then naturally coalesces around their new leader as he takes the alpha female as his mate.

As much as I wanted to be angry or dislike them for their former treatment of me, they quickly drew me in with their small talk. When someone dropped an inside joke, one of them would offer me an aside, lean in to quickly explain the foundation of the joke so I could be in on it. They were bright and witty and fun with their banter. And all of them were impossibly good-looking.

The girls all had names like Blanche or Josephine or Annette, old-fashioned names that had once belonged to their great-grandmothers, and they nibbled carefully portioned meals with restricted calories. Skip and Chet were there, though I was still unsure which was Skip and which Chet. I tried to focus, pay attention to the conversation to determine which was which when the others addressed them, but the conversation was so fluid and their reactions to the mention of their names so ambiguous that I never did manage to place a face with a name.

They laughed about the cow-tipping incident as if I had been in on the joke from the beginning. I was chided playfully for being a city boy, but now it came across as a compliment rather than a curse.

Tony was there, and I had spent the most time worrying about him, what he would do or say in defense of his best friend upon my return to school. But he only gave me a silent nod of greeting as I took my place at the table beside Penny. He returned to his lunch without comment.

"Delaine's parents are out of town this weekend," one of the girls, whose entire lunch consisted only of raw carrots and a Vitamin Water, said to me. "She's going to have a big party. Are you going to come?"

"Uh . . . maybe," I said. I had been told nothing of the party before that minute but played it off as if it had already been an option I was considering.

"You should totally come," she said with an unbelievable amount of enthusiasm.

"Of course he's coming," Penny interjected as she put a hand on my elbow. "I already told Delaine you would," Penny said to me. "I promised her I would bring you."

"O-okay," I said. I had no idea who Delaine was.

"I'm going to get a Diet Coke," Penny said as she started to rise.

"I'll get it," I offered quickly. I wanted to show Penny that I was a gentleman, and she seemed pleased by it.

"Thanks," she said with a smile and exchanged a look of *I told you so* with one of her friends.

Penny dropped a kiss on my cheek as I rose from the table to get us both sodas. It was when I was leaving the line after paying for the drinks that everything came crashing back to earth with a thud. I was hurrying to return to Penny's side when I ran smack into Delilah, literally ran into her, and fumbled the cans of soda while reaching out to steady her with my other hand.

"Sorry," she said breathily. "I wasn't looking where I was going." Her eyes widened when she realized it was me she had collided with, and her cheeks flamed red. "Hi," she said quietly, as if worried that her dad would overhear our conversation even here.

I was struck dumb, had not seen her or spoken to her since the night after I almost killed Grant Parker. Time slowed, then stopped altogether, the din of the lunchroom around us fading into the distance. Delilah was wearing her rocker-chick boots with the tall heel, so we were eye-to-eye, her dark hair casting a blue shine under the fluorescent lights of the cafeteria. Her eyes stood out today against the yellow of her shirt—a T-shirt with an image from the cover of a Nancy Drew book. She wore it under a brown Mr. Rogers–style sweater that she may have purchased at a Goodwill or possibly rescued from the trash.

"I . . . How are you?" she asked as if she genuinely wanted to know.

"I'm okay," I said, wondering as I did what kind of facial expression was appropriate. It didn't seem appropriate to smile. Her brow wrinkled in confusion as she watched my face shift through half a dozen emotions. I wasn't sure how I was supposed to be feeling. Societal standards probably dictated that I feel remorseful about Grant's condition, sympathetic toward his family, maybe embarrassed about being the center of attention.

In all honesty, I felt great. I had gotten to sleep with the hottest chick I had ever seen in person. People were being nice to me. Grant Parker, my nemesis, was in a coma.

Grant Parker is in a coma, and all is right with the world.

"My dad has strictly forbidden me from even talking to you," Delilah said with an apologetic smile. "He's been watching me like a hawk, so I've had to lie low. But I can sneak out tonight, maybe."

"Uh . . ." I was searching my brain for a response when Penny stepped up and slid an arm around my waist.

"Luke, I was waiting for you," Penny said with some reproach, her lower lip pooching out into a delicious pout.

"Sorry," I said, "I just ran into Delilah."

Delilah's eyes widened with surprise as she looked at Penny and then cocked her head at me with a questioning gaze.

"Hello, Delilah," Penny said as she rested her head against my arm and rubbed her hand suggestively along my flank at the top of my waistband. I was instantly turned on and wished Penny and I were alone somewhere instead of in the crowded lunchroom.

"Are you serious?" Delilah asked me, ignoring Penny's pleasantries.

I waited, hoping the question was rhetorical. There was nothing I could say that wouldn't make Delilah mad. I had fantasized about Penny since the first time I saw her. Delilah was a familiar, comforting presence, but she didn't set my heart racing or make my mouth go dry when I saw her.

"You are fucking serious, aren't you?" Delilah pressed.

Side by side, Penny and Delilah were a study in opposites. Penny was petite and delicate, her hair styled and makeup carefully applied, her eyebrows waxed into an artful arch. Delilah was tall, almost my equal in height. In her high boots her gaze was level with mine. I shied away from her gaze, unwilling to face the judgment with a clear conscience.

Finally I said, "It's a long story," somewhat lamely. That was the best I could come up with. If Penny hadn't been standing there listening to every word, I might have made up some bullshit about how Grant was gone and it was my fault, sort of, and so I had an obligation to look after Penny and comfort her as best I could.

The reality, which I freely admitted to myself and which, by the look on her face was clear to Delilah, was that I was completely infatuated with Penny and would do anything to keep her.

"Save it," Delilah said, her words icy and short. "I'm sure I've heard better."

She stalked away with a toss of her hair, her boot heels grinding into the linoleum with each step.

"God, she is so weird," Penny said with a sigh. "I mean, it was sad about Jeremy and all. Everybody loved Jeremy. But she's been like a crazy person since he died. I guess the stories about her family are true."

Penny's comments caught me by surprise. Even if a person had thoughts like that, the rules of decency dictated that they shouldn't be spoken aloud. It was a joke, of course. The kind of thing that people say without thinking about how it made them sound. I didn't correct Penny or call her out for saying something so mean about Delilah, and it made me feel a little ashamed.

After all, Delilah was my friend.

Sort of.

30

I was one of the last people to emerge from school that afternoon, dawdling at my locker and making an unnecessary pit stop. The stress and anxiety from seeing my classmates for the first time since Grant's accident had left a residual exhaustion. I wanted sleep and solitude to recover.

The buses were gone when I walked out into the afternoon sun, but there were clumps of people standing around talking in the student parking lot. Most of them, no doubt, discussing my now almost mythical idiot-hero status.

Penny had told me to show up at Parr's Drive-In, where everyone would be hanging out after school. I had been noncommittal, but she kept telling me I had to show, that everyone would want me there. I was mystified by this. After all, I had just single-handedly killed their football program and ousted their student council president. I wasn't sure what responsibilities were held by a student council president, but I figured everyone would feel some loss about it.

Tony Hurst was leaning against the passenger door of his red American-made truck. My knees buckled at the sight of him, and I knew my distress was in full display on my face.

His truck was parked only two spaces away from the Camaro. There was no way to get to my car without engaging him in conversation. It wouldn't be socially acceptable to ignore him.

"Hey, Tony," I said. I was going for casual and confident, but my voice betrayed me and came out as a garbled squeak.

He gave me his characteristic nod in greeting but didn't bother with any pleasantries.

"I wouldn't have figured you for a tough guy," Tony said as he stowed a wad of chewing tobacco between his lip and gum. His manner of speech was a lazy drawl, as if the words were made of taffy.

"I'm not," I said. "I never said I was tough."

"Yeah?" Tony asked. "I wonder what Grant would say about that. If he could talk, that is." He added this last comment as a barb, and whether he was trying to be funny or start a fight, I wasn't sure.

"Grant was the one who liked to start fights," I said hotly, forgetting, as I did, to refer to Grant in the present tense—still very much alive.

"Yeah, Grant liked to start fights," Tony said with a nod of agreement, ". . . and he liked for me to finish them."

My scrotum shriveled at the implied threat, but Tony

didn't move toward me. Just kept his lazy stance against the truck and spat a stream of tobacco juice with the grace of long practice.

"I don't have a beef with you, Tony," I said.

"True enough," he said, squinting off into the middle distance. "Your beef was with Grant. And Grant's not here."

I wasn't sure how to interpret this little speech, but it seemed friendly enough. "No, he's not. And I'm sorry about that," I said.

Really? Are you really sorry about that?

"But it wasn't my fault," I continued.

"Sure, I can see that," Tony said. "Grant was asking for it. He just didn't count on you being a ruthless son of a bitch."

"No, that's not—" I reflexively started to deny any responsibility for Grant's condition, but Tony cut me off.

"Stepping in to make time with his girl? That's more ruthless than throwing a guy into a grease pit. Ruthless as shit."

"It's not exactly—"

"I suppose it could have been worse," Tony said, ignoring my protest. "I'm not faulting you for it," he continued without any other objections from me. "Grant came after you. All you did was defend yourself."

I didn't correct him, let the lie hang there between us. As long as Grant hung in limbo between life and death and was not there to testify to the truth, I was a different person in the eyes of everyone. And, if I was being completely honest, I liked that people believed that I had faced the giant and I had won.

If you've ever lived through a tragedy, you know that the

first road toward crazy is imagining all the ways that things could have happened differently. Had I left with Roger and Tiny that night instead of staying behind to clean and close the shop myself, Grant's accident never would have happened. I could have left with Roger and Tiny that evening. I could have run as soon as Grant came into the garage. I could have tried to fight back.

And what would the end result have been?

Grant would have come after me another time when I was alone. Grant, with his superior athleticism, would have caught me as I tried to run. It would have been me who had plummeted into the grease pit and ended up in a coma or a wheelchair.

Or a coma and then a wheelchair.

I took my reaction to the thought of Grant returning to school as a paraplegic—a sudden physical sensation in my stomach of guilt and empathy—as a good sign. I could still feel pity for Grant, had not completely dehumanized him. More than anything, I wanted to believe I was a good person.

I had never been one to believe in fate or a higher power, but now I questioned the probability of coincidences. Maybe Grant had been destined to end up at the bottom of that grease pit. Maybe our fates had been tied together since birth and nothing could have changed the inevitable.

This desire of bowing to a higher power, to believe that it was God's will, was almost intoxicating. I wanted to let go of personal responsibility. Up until and including Grant's accident, outside forces had imposed themselves on me. I had not been in control.

But now control had been handed back to me. I had the power to tell everyone, with Roger and Chief Perry and God as my witnesses, that I had not been at fault.

It was still my choice.

And yet I didn't take the opportunity to tell everyone the truth. I allowed everyone to go on thinking that Grant's accident was proof of my superior strength or intelligence, my bravery. Hindsight is twenty-twenty, but on that day, my first day back at school after the accident, I wasn't able to see even a minute ahead. I had no idea how my actions and choices would affect the course of my life. It was so brief, that moment of control, when I could still choose the path of the innocent victim.

And I let it slip away.

31

When I got to the garage that afternoon, Roger and Tiny greeted me as they usually did, and I was grateful for that. It was a relief to be in their company because I didn't have to pretend. They knew the whole story about my run-ins with Grant and knew the truth about what had happened after they left the night of Grant's accident. Roger was almost gentle in the way he spoke, his expression holding the appearance of guilt whenever he looked at me.

It hadn't occurred to me to think about the fact that it was in Roger's grease pit where the accident took place. It seemed to weigh on him, and I wondered if he thought about it every time he had to descend into the pit to work on a car.

"How was it?" Roger asked. "Your first day back at school."

"It was . . . weird," I said. "I thought everyone would be angry, but everyone was nice to me."

Roger's eyebrows shot up with a question, but he said nothing.

"They invited me to come to Parr's Drive-In after work, to hang out."

"Are you going to go?" Roger asked with as much interest as he usually reserved for episodes of *Law & Order*.

"I don't know," I said with a shrug. "It feels wrong somehow."

The way it felt wrong to sleep with Grant's girlfriend?

The question startled me. I *had* slept with Penny, under false pretenses and while Grant languished in his coma. But it hadn't felt wrong at the time. In fact, it couldn't have felt more right.

"What I want to know is," Roger said as he worked a socket wrench, "who are they going to play as starting quarterback now."

"That's it?" I asked. "That's what you're worried about? Football?"

"Hey, a four-zero record for the season is nothing to sneeze at. We could have gone all the way this year. I'm talking state championships."

"So is that it, then?" I asked with some disgust, happy to be in a position to question someone else's moral compass instead of studying my own. "If it wasn't football season, no one would even notice Grant was gone?"

"Oh, they'll notice, sure enough." Roger stood and took a step back from the car, idly wiping his socket wrench with his rag. After so many weeks hanging around the garage, I didn't think about Roger's meticulous nature when it came to his tools anymore. It was the one thing he valued.

He didn't pay attention to his personal appearance, his clothes, or his hair, and he kept his office a mess. I had never seen the inside of his house, but with his lifelong bachelor status, I imagined it was littered with empty beer cans, the trash bin a leaning tower of pizza boxes and frozen-dinner trays.

"They'll notice that they don't have to live in fear anymore. It's no secret Grant was a bully. His daddy has always been a mean little son of a bitch," Roger said thoughtfully. "Like I said, he's a few years younger than me, so he didn't give me any trouble in school, but he was the star quarterback in his day. The Parkers have always had money and influence. They like being the big fish in a small pond. The Parkers got rich during the Civil War. They've run this town ever since."

"Got rich during the Civil War?" I asked. "How? I thought the South lost."

"The Parkers had a foundry. Made shovels. They got rich off of death."

My expression must have conveyed my confusion, because Roger shook his head and rolled his eyes at my idiocy. "They needed shovels to bury the war dead," he said with some impatience. "There was a big market for shovels during the Civil War."

"Oh," I said, rearing my head back with sudden understanding.

As Roger and I stood talking, a car pulled up in front of one of the open bay doors. We both turned to see who the visitor was, and my heart leapt into my throat as I recognized Leland Parker's Cadillac.

Speak of the devil, and he shall appear.

"Get on in the office," Roger said. "Stay out of sight."

I quickly complied, grateful to Roger that he would face my demons for me.

I kept the door to the office cracked, straining for the most minute sound over my breath, which was loud in my ears.

"Roger," Leland Parker said as he hiked his pants up from the back in an unconscious motion. For anyone else it would have been humbling, but Leland Parker did it with such unselfconsciousness that it was barely noticeable.

"Leland," Roger said, his tone guarded.

"I'm not going to beat around the bush," Leland Parker said. "I just came from a meeting with Jim Perry."

"Is that right?" Roger asked, his rag continuing to work its way around the socket wrench, even though it no longer needed his attention.

"He said he isn't charging that boy with any kind of crime. He showed me your video." The way Leland said it, it was like Roger had doctored the video, rather than it being a portrayal of the events as they had really happened.

"Is that right?" Roger asked, playing the dumb yokel.

"It showed my boy . . ." Leland's voice became choked with emotion, but he cleared his throat and continued. "It showed when my boy went into where you change the oil." Leland said this with a nod toward the gaping maw of the grease pit.

"Yeah," Roger said, with an almost apologetic glance over his shoulder at the offending hole in his shop floor.

"That video is what got that city boy off. Vindicated him," Leland said with disgust.

"It is what it is," Roger said with a shrug. "The video only showed what happened."

"What are you saying?" Leland asked.

"I'm not saying anything," Roger said. "Just stating a fact."

"Well, what *I'm* saying," Leland Parker said with impatience, "is that boy is a menace. I don't care what Jim says," he said. He was the first person I had heard use Chief Perry's given name. Everyone else called him Chief Perry. "That boy is a troublemaker."

"He's never made any trouble for me," said Roger coolly, and I was grateful for his loyalty.

"He still working for you?" Leland Parker asked.

"He is."

"Well, I'll tell you, you should fire that boy. Don't reward him by giving him a paying job. Not after what he did to my boy."

"The kid didn't do anything to your boy, Leland. If you saw the video, then you know that."

"Are you defying me?" Mr. Parker asked, and his voice had gone cold.

"Last time I checked," Roger said with a nod of his head, "I only had to answer to God and the US government."

"Well, just so you know," Leland Parker said, "I'll be taking my business elsewhere. I won't be bringing any cars to get worked on here as long as that boy is employed by you. And I'll be asking all of my friends to do the same."

"You do whatever you feel you need to do, Leland," Roger said, and he almost sounded sorry for him.

Leland Parker's jaw bunched as he ground his teeth with restrained fury. He left without another word, spinning on the worn heel of his cowboy boot.

Once he had gone I emerged from the office, but Roger didn't look at me or say anything about his exchange with Mr. Parker.

"Is that going to hurt your business?" I asked, still marveling that Roger had come to my defense in the way he had. "If you lose Leland Parker as a customer?"

Roger dismissed my question with a wave as he went to the cooler and dug out a can of beer. "Leland Parker is a bully. Grant came by it naturally. Learned from his daddy."

"Will he kill your business? Do you want me to stop coming around?" I asked.

Maybe you should push Leland Parker into the grease pit. That would solve your problem.

"Don't worry about it," Roger said. "He'll go to that swindler pothead one time and then come crawling back. He loves that Cadillac more than you love that Camaro."

"I just don't want you to have problems because of me," I said. "But I appreciate that you stuck up for me."

"Just keep your head down and your nose out of trouble," Roger said. "This too shall pass. If you keep to yourself, this will blow over soon enough. Grant will recover, and everything will go back to normal."

Roger was trying to make me feel better, but I realized that Grant coming out of his coma was the last thing that I wanted. Not that I wanted him to die—I tested that idea, rolled it around in my head for a minute, and decided that, no, I really didn't want Grant to die—maybe if he could just stay in a comatose state, then make a full recovery sometime after graduation. I would walk across the stage to collect my diploma, and exit straight out of town.

32

I was the last to arrive at Parr's. The seniors who drove their own cars to school showed up at Parr's most afternoons after practice. They would take up all of the parking spaces along the sides of the building, and people would mill around or sit on the hoods and tailgates of the trucks and cars. A few came who did not have their own transportation, but it was a disgrace not to arrive in a vehicle. Only the socially desperate, who clung to the edges of the popular circle, came on foot. Some of them were lowerclassmen who played on the football team. Just about any girl, even a freshman girl, could get a ride from someone.

When I pulled the Camaro into the lot, I had the top down, and I found one vacant spot waiting for me next to Tony's truck. I was listening to The Smiths and left the ignition on to keep the music going after I got out and walked over to greet Penny and her friends.

Penny squealed when she saw me and put an arm around my waist. Tony and Skip and Chet were standing around the tailgate of Tony's truck, so I went to say hello to them.

"What is that music?" Tony asked by way of greeting.

If the local radio stations were any indication, everyone in Ashland listened to either country, pop-country, or Christian rock. I had tried, in vain, to find a local music station that played anything worth listening to. There were one or two stations from the nearby Atlanta metro area that played the latest hip-hop and pop, but it was all the crap Top 40 stuff I hated. Sometimes I found myself getting sucked into the local Christian talk-radio shows.

"Good Christ," Tony said as he cocked his head to listen to the song pumping from the Camaro's speakers. "What's he saying?"

"Uh, 'heaven knows I'm miserable now,'" I said helpfully. "It's the title of the song." My favorite Smiths song, in fact. I had listened to it on repeat since I had moved to Ashland. Morrissey was the only one who seemed to get where I was in life.

Tony's expression was mystified, but he didn't pursue the subject. He seemed uncertain about me, as if I were speaking a foreign language. I felt the same way when Tony, Skip, and Chet started talking about the upcoming hunting season and their excitement about going for large racks of antlers on their own.

In a place like Ashland, families found it perfectly reasonable to place rifles and shotguns in the hands of boys long before they needed a regular shave. I had never held a gun or even seen a real one in person, and the idea of shooting a deer was both disgusting and terrifying.

As long as we avoided the topics of music, guns, or football, I could get along with Grant's former friends. That pretty much left beer or girls to talk about. But there is always plenty to say on the subject of beer and girls.

And in truth, even though my conversation with Tony and the guys was limited, I had even less to say to Penny and her friends. They discussed reality television shows I didn't watch and celebrities I had never heard of. There just wasn't much to do in Ashland. Since it turned out that cow tipping wasn't even a real thing, that mostly left getting drunk in the middle of a field or at a house party. No wonder the LARPers worked so hard to create an alternate reality.

Tony and the others were now discussing hunting lures like toe musk and hot-doe urine.

"What the hell is hot-doe urine?" I asked.

Tony's expression was bemused as he said, "Just what it sounds like. Urine from a doe that's in heat."

"How do they get it?" I asked. "The urine, I mean."

"You probably don't want to know, city boy," Tony said.

He was right. I didn't really want to imagine the process by which hot-doe urine could be acquired.

"What do the hunters do with it?" I asked. "Wear it?"

"Only if they want to get raped by a buck," Tony said, and Skip and Chet laughed in appreciation of this joke.

Clearly I was out of my depth when discussing any of the male preoccupations in Ashland: I knew nothing about hunting or football. So I left Tony and the others and went inside Parr's to get a soda and some French fries. As I was waiting for my order, Annette, one of Penny's friends, approached me.

"Hi, Luke," she said with a smile.

"Hey."

"So, who's your date for the homecoming dance?" she asked.

"Uh . . . I don't have one," I said. "I hadn't really thought about going, actually."

Her eyes widened with disbelief, but then she giggled. "Oh, I see. You're joking. Everybody goes to homecoming. Even most of the parents, which is kind of lame."

"Yeah. Lame," I agreed.

"If you don't already have a date for homecoming, you'd better get on it," she continued, though I was unsure where this conversation was going. "Some people go just with a group of friends but not anybody who's anybody."

"Uh. N-no. I don't have a . . . date," I said, the statement coming out almost like a question.

"Well," she said, flashing me a winning smile, "you should ask someone."

"Uh . . ."

"You know, I don't have a date yet either," she offered helpfully.

"Oh," I said, really losing at this whole conversation thing now.

"Annette!" Penny's voice behind me was shrill, and I jerked with a start. I hadn't sensed her walking up behind us. "What's going on?" Penny asked. "What are you two talking about?"

"Nothing," Annette said at the same moment I said, "Homecoming."

"Oh?" Penny asked with a pointed look at Annette. "What about it?"

"Uh . . ." I was back to not knowing what to say. Fortunately, Penny had enough to say for both of us.

"We really need to start making plans, Luke." Penny directed her comments to me, but they were said for Annette's benefit. "Everyone is already making dinner reservations for that night, and you're going to have to wear a nice suit. Some people wear tuxedos, but I think it's much more stylish to wear a suit instead of a rented tux. Don't you think?"

Honestly, I had never considered the topic either way, but Penny obviously had strong opinions, and I wondered if I was going to be left to manage the whole situation myself. My job didn't actually pay money, so I was going to have to go to Dad if I needed money for clothes and dinner. Crap. The whole situation seemed overwhelming, and I didn't really want to think about it—the fact that Penny expected me to take her to the dance.

Maybe if she had strong opinions about the situation, I could let her manage the whole thing. But I had a terrible suspicion that I was going to be expected to figure out a lot of this on my own.

33

I was leaving fourth period one morning that week and heading to Penny's locker to meet her for lunch when I was stopped by a kid in glasses who barely reached my shoulder in height. He wore a button-down shirt and khaki pants, looking oddly out of sync with the other students in his business-casual attire.

He pushed his glasses up his nose with a knuckle and didn't beat around the bush. "I'm David Greene," he said. "I'm the student council vice president. Well," he said, quickly correcting himself, "I guess technically now I'm the student council *president*. It's my job to assume the role if the president resigns or is . . . unable to perform his duties."

"I'm aware of how the system works," I said, though David seemed oblivious to my sarcasm.

"I have the necessary experience to fill the role," he continued. "In a situation like this, normally the treasurer would step up to fill the role of vice president, but what with homecoming just around the corner, the treasurer has a lot of responsibilities."

"Okay," I said, unsure why he was telling me any of this.

Maybe he mistakenly thinks I give a shit.

"The reason I'm telling you this," he said, as if he could read my thoughts, "is that if the treasurer maintains her current position, we'll be without a vice president. I was thinking that your input might be valuable on the student council. You're an outsider," he said with an apologetic shrug, "so to speak, so you would have a fresh perspective. I can appoint you as the temporary vice president. That is, assuming, of course, that Grant recovers and returns to his duties."

"You want me to serve on the student council?" I asked, skeptically.

"Sure," David said. "I was thinking you could take over Grant's role overseeing the preparations for the homecoming dance. There's a committee. You wouldn't have to do all of the work yourself. In fact, Penny has been really helpful with organizing everything. She was the one who suggested you might be a good fit for working with the homecoming committee."

"Uh . . . okay," I said, not really sure this was a job I wanted to take, but not knowing how to say no. I was already busy procrastinating about getting a suit and making dinner reservations, hoping that if I put it off long enough Penny would take the reins and manage the details.

"Great," he said, and pulled his phone from his pocket. "I'll put your number in my phone and text you details about meetings and stuff later."

As I walked to Penny's locker I thought about this new development. I was still mystified by how easily Grant had been cast aside, forgotten by his classmates now that there wasn't a daily physical reminder of him.

After school and practice that day everyone was headed to the lake to party on the secluded beach that was accessible only by foot. Chief Perry and his deputies were unlikely to navigate the rocky terrain, if they even knew kids went there to party.

I had time to kill while everyone was at practice and after-school activities, so I drove around in the Camaro for a while, enjoying the freedom of being out on my own. I cruised slowly down Main Street, appreciating, for once, the brightly painted shops and the leafy boughs of the old-growth trees that lined the street. The leaves had changed color, and the bright splashes of orange and red and yellow were really pretty impressive. I felt a pang of homesickness for DC. I knew Rock Creek Park, where I would sometimes ride my bike on weekends, would be a lush valley of autumn colors at this time.

I was homesick for more than just my hometown. I missed the anonymity of a city, a place where I could blend in and no one would know my name.

As I drove past the diner on Main Street, I saw Delilah strolling along, the hood on her sweatshirt covering her black hair. I looked back over my shoulder as I passed her, almost driving the Camaro into an elderly couple as they stepped off the curb at the intersection.

I slammed on the brakes, and the Camaro rocked on its suspension as the man looked up at me with a concerned frown. At the sight of me he lifted a hand in greeting but bent his head to murmur something in his wife's ear. She looked at me now, too, and from the look in their eyes I knew they recognized me, the boy who had almost killed Grant Parker.

Ignoring them, I looked back again in time to see Delilah ducking into the small, family-owned grocery store. There was no large chain grocery store in Ashland, just the small independent grocery that offered a bewildering selection of basic necessities—everything from milk to mousetraps to peanut butter—to tide people over between monthly trips to the Walmart Supercenter one town over.

I backed the Camaro into a space and walked casually down the street, stopping to look into the window of the grocery, as if I were just idly window shopping on a fall afternoon. I didn't see Delilah through the window, so I let myself into the store. A young woman, maybe barely out of high school and the only employee in sight, sat behind the register reading.

She looked up and smiled a greeting at me but went back to her book as I ducked into an aisle of the floor-to-ceiling shelves. The lower shelves held items of regular demand, like cat food and hot dog buns. The upper shelves housed a motley collection of seasonal supplies, like fishing nets and lawn chairs.

Delilah was contemplating the condiment section when I found her at the back of the store. She didn't see me right away, so I had a minute to study her without her knowing I was.

Or maybe not.

"Are you lost?" she asked without looking away from the shelf in front of her.

"Maybe," I said.

"Don't you have an awesome party to go to? Down at the lake?"

"Later. After practice. How did you know about that?" I asked.

"Tony invited me," she said.

"He did?"

"Yes."

"Why?" I asked with genuine curiosity.

"Why shouldn't someone invite me somewhere?" she asked, suddenly angry. "What's wrong with me that someone shouldn't invite me somewhere?"

"That isn't what I meant," I said. The conversation was quickly degenerating, so I hurried to mend things between us. "I just . . . I didn't think you liked him. As a person, I mean."

She shrugged. "Tony isn't so bad . . . when Grant isn't around."

A grim silence descended, as it always did when someone mentioned Grant's efficacious absence in my presence.

I was dimly aware of the girl at the register chatting with someone who had just come in off the street. I was so focused on my exchange with Delilah, wondering what she thought of me—if she bothered to think about me at all—that I wasn't thinking about anything else.

Delilah's eyes widened suddenly with surprise, and I turned hesitantly to track her gaze over my shoulder. I'm not sure what I was expecting to see, but certainly not what—or rather who—had managed to render Delilah speechless.

Leland Parker stood behind me, his expression a confusion of anger and something that resembled fear.

"You," Leland Parker said. "You have some nerve showing your face around town, boy, after what you've done." He hiked up his pants from the back, the same gesture I had seen him perform the day he came by Roger's garage to tell Roger to fire me. I recognized it as a nervous habit now, and it humanized him in a way that made me self-conscious for both of us.

My mouth went dry, and I gulped involuntarily as my heart started to beat crazily. A blush crept up my cheeks and I was rendered speechless.

"It's a free country," Delilah said, matter-of-factly.

Now it was Leland Parker who turned red, but from restrained anger instead of the terror I felt.

"Your father and I," Leland Parker said, ignoring me now and facing off with Delilah, "seem to be the only two people who realize that this boy is nothing but a . . . a . . . sociopath."

"Luke never did anything but defend himself against Grant," Delilah said, her voice and eyes both lowering with involuntary apology.

"That," Leland Parker said, stabbing a finger in my direction, "is for a jury to decide."

I could almost feel Delilah physically restraining herself from rolling her eyes as Leland Parker said this.

"Don't think that just because your daddy is the police chief you can speak to me any way you please," Leland Parker started in. "I know that brother of yours was nothing but trouble. . . ."

"Hey," I said, reacting without thought to his mention of Jeremy, whose memory, while not mine, was still a raw wound from the night Delilah had invited me to his posthumous birthday party. "Hey," I said again. "Don't."

Leland Parker and Delilah both looked at me with some surprise and, really, I was as shocked as anyone that I had reacted the way I did.

"It's . . . uh . . . this had nothing to do with Delilah," I said, not wanting to backpedal, but unsure where to go from here. "She's not part of this."

"Your daddy is an outsider in this town," Leland Parker said, turning his ire on me, which, while not comfortable, at least redirected the threat from Delilah to me. "You aren't one of us."

Thank God.

"I don't want to be one of you," I said hotly. "Your son was . . . I mean, is . . . he *is* a bully. I don't want to be one of you."

The pause that followed felt like an eternity but was probably only a few heartbeats. Delilah and I both held our breath as we watched him, like waiting for a kettle to blow steam. "Get out of here," Leland Parker said shortly.

Now, anger was the only emotion he was able to express, but I saw the tightness of grief in the way his jaw was set.

Without even exchanging a look, Delilah and I took the invitation to exit the encounter. Delilah dismissed the errand that had brought her to the grocery store, and I followed on her heels to the door.

We escaped the close quarters of the grocery store and arrived on the street into fresh air, which suddenly represented freedom. I turned to her, wanting to share in the emotion of what we had just endured, maybe with the exchange of a sympathetic smile or an eye roll. But when I looked at Delilah I was struck by her expression, usually so passive, impossible to read. But the lines of worry and sorrow were etched so clearly, and I felt only impotent, knowing any words I could offer had no power to fix anything.

"I'm sorry," I said. "That was wrong of him to say anything about your brother."

She didn't answer, just dug her fists into the pockets of her hoodie, and ignored me.

"I'm sorry," I said again, though now I was apologizing for a lot more than what Leland Parker had said. "Can I give you a ride home?"

"No," she said, refusing to give me her eyes.

"C'mon," I said, nudging her elbow in the direction of the Camaro.

"No," she said, this time with more force. "I don't want anything from you."

With that, she turned on her heel and headed for the direction of our neighborhood. I thought about calling after her. I thought about what I could say to make things right between us. I thought about so many things that I couldn't think of a single thing to say before she made it two blocks, then turned down a side street and disappeared from my view.

34

The football game that Friday night was a somber event. Dad had not been invited to deliver the opening prayer this time, though the home fans were overwhelmingly of the Baptist persuasion. This was probably done as a show of respect for the feelings of Grant's family, who attended the game despite Grant's absence.

I didn't want to attend the game, but Penny and Tony had pressed me, making me promise to go. We would all go out to party after the game. A great time, they promised.

Sitting in the bleachers, the field was the only safe place to train my eyes. I sat in the front row so I couldn't see the way people in the crowd studied me, or look at Grant's mother, who kept a handkerchief pressed to her mouth as if to hold in her grief.

The Methodist preacher who led the opening prayer

mentioned Grant and asked everyone to observe a moment of silence, but it felt more like a show than it did genuine regret about his absence. The home side seemed to be more upset about the implications for the team's season record than it did about grief over Grant's accident.

The flowers and mementos had been removed from the home goalpost, but Grant was there with us in spirit. His absence was a looming presence for me.

Delilah was doing a really good job of ignoring my existence. I saw her at the game when I was waiting to buy snacks from the Booster Club booth during halftime, but even with steely glances in her direction I could not get her to acknowledge me in any way. It was as if she could render me invisible. Like it was her superpower. I wasn't sure what I would say to her even if I could get her attention, but I didn't think about it too much. I was quickly caught up in the excitement everyone had for homecoming plans.

No one talked much about the game itself other than to lament the fact that the team would be in sore shape without its captain. The role of captain had fallen to Tony, who played a receiving position. With his reserved, quiet nature, he was better suited as a second-in-command. But with his commanding officer dead, or in a coma at least, Tony had stepped into the role with stoic dread.

I was just at the game to kill time before the after-party, unsure where to put myself so that I was inconspicuous. It was almost impossible not to draw attention, since everyone was still talking about Grant and his accident. People maintained a veneer of politeness by not staring at me constantly, but I could sense them nod their heads in my direction, whispering to the person they were with. "There he is. That's the boy who tried to kill Grant Parker." I could almost hear them saying it, until the din of the crowd just became a repeat of their murmured convictions and sentencings of my character.

It was an isolating feeling. I hadn't spoken to Don or Aaron since I started hanging out with Penny and her crowd, and I didn't feel comfortable seeking out the dork squad to sit with. Besides, Penny would kill me if Don and Aaron got the idea they could go to the party with us after the game.

Though I could maintain a stoic public face, the anxiety was with me all of the time now. As the new kid I had felt as if I was constantly under scrutiny, everyone watching and judging every move I made. Now I was the new kid who had tried to kill the Wakefield football program with a single stroke, and it was distinctly . . . uncomfortable. I wanted to grab the mic from the sound booth and relate my story from the beginning—tell everyone about Grant's mistreatment of me and that, while I wasn't a coward, I certainly wasn't the kind of person who would intentionally attempt murder. There was just no entry point for a conversation like that.

I thought about gaining access to the video of my alleged assault on Grant and posting it on social media so people could see the truth. The one thing holding me back was the truth. The truth was . . . I was a coward. Not just a coward, but a victim. It wasn't who I wanted to be, even if that's who I really was.

After the game there was no time to worry about Grant or about my place in the cosmos. After the players and cheerleaders changed in the locker room we caravanned to the after-party. Penny rode shotgun with me with two of her friends in the backseat. I kept looking at Penny and the two cute girls in the backseat of the Camaro, thinking to myself, how did this happen? How did I end up this lucky? From dork squad to righteous dude. How the fuck did this happen?

Delaine's house was remote from the center of town—the perfect location for a high school party. A distant glimmering porch light was the only evidence of a neighbor. There was no one to be offended by the noise and call the sheriff to shut down the festivities.

The yard backed into the slope of a hill, but the side yard was littered with the typical detritus of country living—trampoline, aboveground pool, industrial-grade satellite dish.

I wandered the yard with Penny, who kept by my side the whole time. With her on my arm I felt stable among so many strangers. The people at this party did not interact at school with Don and his friends, were barely aware of their existence.

The only reason I was somebody was because I was the boy who had almost killed Grant Parker. Everyone else at the party had attended the same school since kindergarten. I was the "x" in the equation.

And before I knew it, I was high. An amazing body buzz that made me feel as if I might be able to take flight. Coupled with the four beers I had before hitting a joint, I was pretty far gone into the wilds of my own uninhibited self.

When I left Penny's side to go in search of another beer, I found Tony, along with Skip and Chet, in earnest consultation standing over the galvanized metal tub full of icy water.

"What's up?" I asked, breaking the conversation.

"We're out of beer," said Skip or Chet.

"Sucks," I said, realizing as I did that it really was a huge letdown. I had been wanting that fifth beer.

"Grant used to always get his older brother to buy for us, but since Grant's . . . not here . . ." The look he gave me was almost apologetic. "We just were trying to figure out where we can get some."

"I know where we can get some beer," I said.

"Yeah?" Tony asked. "Where?"

I spoke without thought. And now everyone was looking to me to solve our dry-party dilemma. The idea had risen in my mind fully formed. It was the kind of impulse that would be immediately quashed by a rational brain, but because of the beer, my instincts weren't bound by logic.

"The LARPers," I said, alcohol loosening my tongue. "At their fort. They always have tons of beer."

"What the hell is a LARPer?" Tony asked.

"I . . . I can't really explain," I said. "You kind of have to see it for yourself."

When we parked on the dead-end street, I had been unsure if I could find the LARPer fort without Don to guide me, but the path became familiar once I entered the woods.

"Ho-oly shee-it," were the first words out of Tony's mouth when we made it to the clearing and he saw the LARPer fort for the first time. As advertised, the Land of Misfit Toys was in full swing. Swords and magic-infused Ping-Pong balls and even (*good Lord*) a costumed dragon were on full display. From the outside, where we stood hidden by the tree line, it was like watching a movie or a play. It gave me a small rush to be standing there watching them, the LARPers, who were blissfully unaware of our presence. Hogwarts was in session and all of the freaks were there.

"Yeah," I said in emphatic agreement. I imagined Tony was as surprised as I was the first time I saw the LARPers in their natural environment.

"What are they doing?" he asked.

Excellent question. Who the fuck knows?

"Live-action role-playing," I said simply.

"Like they play dress-up?"

"Something like that."

"Are they queers?" Tony asked, for the first time sounding concerned, maybe afraid.

I thought about making a rude comeback, calling Tony out for being a homophobe. His "queer" comments made me uncomfortable, like being confronted with overt racism. Yet I held my judgment to myself and just said, "No more than Skip or Chet."

Tony laughed in appreciation at my joke. Skip and Chet didn't catch the irony and took this, like everything anyone said, at face value.

Don wore only a subdued cloak, like a Hobbit or a Jedi, and he approached me as I broke the circle of trees ahead of Tony and Skip and Chet.

"Hey, Luke," Don said, "I didn't think we'd see you." As he said this last part Tony and the others stepped into view and Don's eyes widened. "Hey . . . guys," Don said while looking a question at me. He didn't seem upset. Just bewildered. He didn't even have sense enough to look embarrassed about being caught in his masquerade. "Uh, welcome . . . I guess."

"What the hell is going on here?" Tony asked, the "queer" moniker implied in his tone.

"Not much. Just hangin' out," Don said.

"Yeah? You guys got any beer?" Tony asked.

"Sure. Come on over," Don said, as if he were offering someone a drink in his own living room.

The four of us followed him into the glow from the bonfire. The LARPers had all stopped to stare at us, as if we were the ones in freakish costumes. No one spoke or hailed us in greeting, just watched us walk across the clearing to where the coolers and tubs held chilled beer.

"We've got a few different kinds," Don said as he waved a hand over the collection of coolers in offering. "You want a Bud or a Schlitz or—"

"We'll just take all of it," said Skip or Chet, and Skip or Chet snickered at that.

Don was still recovering from his shock over seeing Grant Parker's outlaw gang at the fort. Now he was completely confused. It hadn't dawned on him yet that we were not there to take bets on the sword battles. But he was about to find out the ugly truth.

"I don't know what . . ." Don looked a question at me again, and I just gave him a soothing smile.

"Maybe not all of it," I said. "We'll leave you a six-pack or something."

I was trying to do this nicely, but the words came out sounding condescending and oily.

I had set in motion the wave that was about to take over. I knew, of course, that it was wrong. In order, the Bible places "Thou shalt not steal" lower on the totem pole than "Thou shalt not kill." But it's still a numbered offense—one of only ten.

This wasn't really stealing, I told myself. Don and his buddies would enjoy their swordplay and witchcraft with or without booze. Our party needed it. And I had a promise to fulfill to everyone there.

Skip and Chet quickly lost interest in our conversation and drifted over to the knights' arena. One of them shoved a boy who was so slight in stature he probably weighed less than his chain mail. The shove was playful, but with their superior strength and size, the boy was sent toppling and gave up his sword. Both Skip and Chet took up swords and started to drunkenly swing at each other and the other combatants, giggling as they did so.

They swung the swords wildly, not attempting to use proper broadsword fighting form the way Don and his friends did. There were a few startled cries as Skip and Chet whacked someone with the flat of a sword or swung the fake-though-still-able-to-cause-serious-harm weapon in a wild arc near people's heads.

"How much have you got?" Tony asked Don. "It's going to be a bitch and a half to carry it all back to the cars."

"You came to take our beer?" Don asked, the idea finally clear to him.

"Well, not exactly," I started diplomatically, but Tony cut me off.

"Yeah. You got a problem with that?" he asked with the confidence of someone who knows no one is going to give him a problem.

"I don't. . . ." Don stopped as he considered the question. There were only four of us. If the knights of the Round Table decided to fight us, they had superiority in numbers and in weaponry. But none of them were prepared to stand up and fight for themselves.

"If you want," Tony said, his tone a quiet threat, "we can go back to the party. Round up everyone and just bring them back here. We can drink the beer here." His smile was both fluid and sly. "Of course, then you guys would have to leave."

Don was staring at me. Hard. And I let my gaze wander so I didn't have to answer the question in his eyes.

"No," Don said, a little loudly. He cleared his throat and said it again. "No."

"No, what?" Tony asked.

"No, you're not taking our beer. It's ours. We stole it fair and square. Get your own beer."

"You see what happens," Tony said, directing his comment toward me. "You upset the natural order of things. Don here thinks it's his turn to put me in a coma."

Hoo boy. You see what you started?

"Just let us take the beer, Don," I said. "It's no big deal. We'll make it up to you."

"Forget it," Don said to me. Then to Tony: "I'm sick of the way you treat us."

Don took a breath, as if he was going to continue his speech, but before he could get another word out Tony quickly reached out and grabbed Don by the collar of his shirt and gave him a shake. "That's a mighty bold statement," Tony said as Don's eyes bulged from surprise and sudden lack of oxygen. "You want to take it back."

The squeak that emitted from Don's throat was impossible to decipher. Maybe a yes, maybe a no. Tony shoved him away, and Don took two stumbling steps but kept his feet.

The clearing had grown quiet as Skip and Chet and the LARPers all stopped to see what Tony was going to do next. I silently begged Don to back down and just let us take the beer and go. Time stood still as Don rubbed at his throat, his head down as he caught his breath.

I hoped this was the end of it, that Don would step aside and give in to us, and just when I thought things were going the way I hoped, Don surprised everyone, maybe even himself, by lashing out and swinging a punch at Tony's jaw. He was shorter than Tony so his fist had to fly up at an awkward angle, and there wasn't a lot of power behind it. It was probably the first time in his life he had swung a fist at another person in anger.

Though Don's fist did connect with Tony's chin, the punch was so weak that the gesture was more pathetic than threatening. Tony put a hand on Don's head and held him just beyond arm's length as Don cried out and swung his arms wildly, his fingertips barely grazing Tony's chest and sides.

Tony laughed and Skip and Chet joined in. I just watched in amazement as Don quickly wore himself out, wasting all of his energy on screaming and throwing wild punches. Tony kept his hand on Don's head and circled each time Don tried to step out of his hold, laughing the whole time.

None of the LARPers came to Don's aid, just watched him in fascination. I thought about saying something, telling Tony to stop.

But I didn't.

Though it seemed like Don's humiliation lasted an impossibly long time, he was soon too tired to keep lifting his arms and staggered back away from Tony's mocking control.

"You're a little shit," Tony said, and I thought the moment had passed, that now we could just take the beer and walk away. But Tony wasn't done yet. Almost without any effort at all, he pulled his arm back and swung at Don's cheek. Tony's fist connected with a disquieting splat, and Don went down like a pile of bricks. One second Don was standing there catching his breath, the next he was lying flat on his back.

"Anybody else?" Tony asked as he turned to survey the LARPers.

No one ran to Don's side, no one spoke up to answer Tony.

"That's what I thought," Tony said.

Skip and Chet took their swords and swung at the fire, knocking burning logs throughout the clearing, and embers flew up in sprays, drifting up to reach their place among the stars. In a confusion of shouts and yelps the LARPers scattered to avoid the burning projectiles bouncing around the clearing. It was a melee of fire and terror as the three attackers pulled apart the planks of wood that made up the sheltered part of the fort. The LARPers scattered into the woods, leaving their fallen knight behind on the field of battle. Don was lying still, though whether he was really unconscious or just playing possum I wasn't sure.

Skip and Chet and Tony laughed as they tore apart the fort and threw the lumber into the remains of the fire. Then we were loading all of the beer into the big cooler, the last permanent fixture of the fort, and we started back through the woods.

Skip and Chet each took up a handle of the cooler, their shoulders straining under the weight. But they didn't seem to mind the burden as they laughed their way back to the car. The cooler went into the back of Tony's truck, and Skip or Chet rode shotgun with me in the Camaro while the other climbed into Tony's truck cab.

"You believe that kid who was talking shit to Tony?" Skip or Chet asked me as he pulled the car door shut. "What was that little shit thinking?"

He was thinking someone actually stood up to Grant Parker. And won.

35

The next morning I woke with the feeling that something had crawled into my mouth and died. The sound of my hair rubbing against the pillow was enough to make my head pound with a terrible pain. I wanted ibuprofen and bacon and orange juice, but I couldn't bring myself to get out of bed. God, I was so hungover.

I didn't even really remember much of what had happened the previous night. Unfortunately, what I did remember was that I had led Tony and Skip and Chet to the LARPer fort, had stolen the LARPers' beer, and watched passively as the fort had been destroyed and Don was knocked on his ass.

I rolled onto my side, feeling like I might puke. I felt around under the covers looking for my phone and finally found it in the back pocket of my jeans, which were in a wad on the floor next to the bed.

Since I had used all of my energy to find my phone, I lay recovering for a minute while I tried to decide what to do. I wanted to call Don to apologize for what had happened. I never meant for anyone to get hurt, for the LARPer fort to get destroyed.

I unlocked my phone, deciding I would just send Don a text, but as soon as I saw the notifications on my phone I forgot all about Don.

There were seventeen texts waiting for me to read. Three were from Penny and the rest were from numbers that weren't programmed into my phone. People were asking me where I was and what I was doing, or making comments about what a crazy, fun night we had at Delaine's party. All of them wanted me to call or text so we could hang out.

I had two dozen friend requests on Facebook and dozens of new followers on Instagram. I pulled up my Instagram account and scrolled through selfies with people I barely recognized from Delaine's party. I had a big, goofy grin on my face in all of the photos, my eyelids at half-mast, clearly wasted. There was even a picture of me standing in just my underwear beside Delaine's aboveground pool.

Bits and snatches of the night before returned as I studied the pictures. I remembered being in the backseat of the Camaro with Penny, but my mind couldn't hold on to any concrete sequence of events.

Penny's texts had escalated from asking me where I was, to reminding me that I had made a promise to show up for a homecoming planning meeting and was now reneging on that promise. I made it to the homecoming meeting at

12:30, thirty minutes late, my head still pounding, wishing I could go back to bed for a few more hours.

The homecoming dance was being held in the Benevolent and Protective Order of Elks Lodge, a massive wooden structure built into the hillside above the lake. It was a popular site for weddings, the only place near town that could hold several hundred people at one time.

I wasn't sure what the Benevolent and Protective Order of Elks was, but I assumed the Elks were, in fact, humans. I wondered idly if LARPers grew up to become Elks.

As it turned out, other than wearing funny hats, the Elks were pretty normal guys, even though they went by titles like "Grand Exalted Knight." Maybe they really were just LARPers all grown up.

The gazes of the men who had once been Grand Exalted Knight followed me from their portraits as I wandered until I found Penny in a large meeting room with a group of about twenty people. There were pizza boxes and two-liter bottles of soda on one table, and everyone sat in a circle of metal folding chairs, Penny standing in the middle of the circle with a clipboard in her hand. Clearly I had missed lunch, and they had moved on to the official meeting.

"Luke," Penny said, her smile forced, though still seemingly genuine. "Finally."

"Sorry," I said as everyone shifted their seats to make room in the circle for me. The groan of metal folding chairs against the floor and the shuffling of papers that accompanied my awkward interruption seemed to last an eternity, but Penny waited patiently until everyone was re-settled before starting again.

"So," she said breathily, with dramatic effect, "we're seriously behind schedule at this point, what with . . . everything that's been going on. We need to finalize the theme and decide on a band or a deejay right away."

"I still think my cousin, Ron, would be great as a dee-jay," Annette said with a look of appeal around our circle.

"Annette," Penny said, her voice strained with impatience before anyone could respond, "your cousin does weddings and his playlists are seriously lame. We're not going to dance to a bunch of eighties music at homecoming. I want the whole event to be cutting edge, not catering to the geri-atrics."

"I'm just making the suggestion," Annette said acidly. "I'm part of this committee."

"And we already discussed the idea and decided Ron wasn't the right person to play at our event," Penny said, maintaining the veneer of passive-aggressive politeness that made talking to anyone in Ashland complicated. I realized that the reason why I had gravitated toward Roger, of all people, more than anyone, was that he told it like it was. Never said anything just to appease anyone's feelings.

"So, what's our theme, then?" Annette asked, clearly bristling at Penny's dismissal of her cousin.

"I don't know," Penny said. "Does anyone have any bet-ter ideas than the list of failures we came up with the last time we met?"

No one spoke. Everyone studied their laps or the walls around us, their foreheads wrinkled in feigned or real con-centration.

"Luke," Penny said, startling me. "You're new to the

committee. Do you have any ideas for a good theme for the homecoming dance?"

I wasn't prepared for her to suck me into the debate, and in my hungover state I had been more focused on the pizza boxes and sodas than I was on what anyone was saying.

"Uh . . ." This was a bad start. People were looking to me to say something clever and creative, and I didn't have any idea what they wanted in a theme for a dance.

Nor do I really give a shit. I should have taken four of those ibuprofens.

I cleared my throat, stalling for time. "What if we went . . . old school," I said, feeling the idea was completely lame as I said it. "I mean, old school like Biggie Smalls and N.W.A. and Tupac—that kind of thing. . . ." My voice trailed off uncertainly as everyone's brows wrinkled. People waited for someone to have the courage to shoot down my idea. After all, no one wanted to end up in a coma like Grant, or with their fort burned down like Don and the LARPers.

"I like it," Penny said, so suddenly that a few people jumped with a start, including me. "I mean, maybe not the idea of old school in the hip-hop sense." She said this with an apologetic tilt of her head in my direction. "But what if we made the theme old school like in the sense of the history of the school. 'Old school' is our theme," Penny said, annunciating "old school" by making quotation marks in the air with her fingers, "and we feature music and clothing styles from the past of Wakefield High School. Like styles that were in when our parents and grandparents went to school."

"I like it," someone said, and there were a few murmured agreements.

"Great idea, Luke," Penny said with a broad smile just for me.

It hadn't been my idea, really, but Penny made it seem like it was, and that felt pretty good. After that I sat back to nurse my hangover while trying to look interested in the brainstorming session that followed.

36

On Monday I saw Don in the hallway sporting a scab on his split cheek, his left eye puffy and swollen. He looked right through me as he passed me in the hallway, as if I were vapor. I thought about stopping him to ask if he was okay or to say that I hadn't intended for things to go down the way they had, but anything I tried to think to say felt inadequate and stupid.

At lunch I sat with Tony and Penny and the others, like I always did now, but I kept looking at the table where Don and Aaron and Josh sat.

I was at my locker at the end of the school day when I sensed someone behind me. I turned to find Delilah staring coldly at me, her eyes narrowed.

"Hello, Delilah," I said.

"Don't you 'Hello, Delilah,' me," she said, her tone threatening. "I know what you did on Friday," she said. "You and Tony and Skip and Chet."

"I didn't do anything," I said. "I was there, but I didn't do anything."

"Spare me, okay? They wouldn't have even known about the fort if you didn't tell them."

"We just wanted some of their beer. It was no big deal."

"No big deal? Tony gave Don a black eye and Skip and Chet tore apart the fort. They could have started a major forest fire."

I rolled my eyes at this. "I seriously doubt a forest fire was ever a real risk. Hey," I said as it occurred to me that Delilah could help me out, "can you tell me which one is which?" I asked. "I can't figure out which one is Chet and which one is Skip."

"What?" she asked, her brow wrinkling in confusion.

"I mean I can't tell Chet and Skip apart. It would be weird to ask now. If I asked now they would know I haven't known their names from the beginning."

"You can't be serious," she said.

"I tried to figure it out by asking them their real names, you know. But one of them is named Edward and the other is named Walton, and I couldn't figure how they would get Skip or Chet out of either of those names, so . . ." I trailed off into a shrug to illustrate my bewilderment.

"I mean," Delilah said, her voice rising, "I can't believe you are asking me which of your henchmen is Skip or Chet after what you did on Friday night."

"It really wasn't a big deal," I said. "Don got some crazy idea in his head to stand up to Tony. What an idiot, right?"

She planted one hand firmly on her hip, and her eyes narrowed even more. It was hard to believe that she could still see me through the slits of her eyelids. Like a newborn kitten. But a seriously pissed-off newborn kitten.

"You destroyed the fort, stole their beer."

"There were, like, a dozen of them there," I said impatiently. "And they had swords. I can't help it if they let Tony and those guys take their beer. If they wanted it so badly they should have stood up for themselves."

"Like the way you stood up to Grant?" she asked coolly.

"This was different."

"How is it different?" she shot back quickly.

"It just is," I said lamely. I knew she was right, but that fact just made me angry. I didn't like her calling me out.

"They've been terrorized by Grant and his friends their whole lives," Delilah continued. "You think they were going to stand up for themselves? You think they want to spend their lives looking over their shoulders? Waiting to see which one of them ends up trapped in a gym locker for the night?"

"Nobody knows for sure that Grant was the one who did that to Josh," I said, coming quickly to Grant's defense.

"Uch." She threw up one hand in disgust, the other still on her hip. "You're an asshole. You can't stand the thought of your precious Penny not thinking you're the bomb diggity. And now the fort is ruined. That fort has always been a sacred space. The one place people could go to avoid Grant Parker and his posse. And now you're one of them. You're a traitor to your own kind."

"I'm not a fucking LARPer," I said, too forcefully. "And

anyway, we were desperate. Our party ran out of beer. What were we supposed to do?"

"Try not being an asshole, for starters."

Who does she think she is?

"Are we done here?" I asked coldly.

She was making me mad—didn't have any right to accuse me of anything. Even if it was something of which I was actually guilty.

"Oh, yeah," she said, matching me for cold. Arctic, in fact. "We're totally done."

"Good," I said, because I had no better comeback.

"Prick," she said to my back as I walked away.

I let her have the last word and banged my way out of the exit.

37

"You've got to be kidding me," I said.

"I wouldn't joke about something like this," David Greene said earnestly. "We have an independent committee that counts the ballots. This was all confidential before now, but you won hands down."

"Homecoming king?" I asked, my voice rising to a squeak.

"Yes. So we'll need to talk about the events for homecoming night. The presentation of the homecoming court . . ."

"That's impossible," I said. "I can't be homecoming king."

But David misunderstood my objection and said, "The votes don't lie."

"No, I mean I *can't* be homecoming king. I can't do it. I can't get up in front of everyone. If Grant were"—*conscious and able to eat solid food*—"here . . . he's the one who should be homecoming king. I can't do it."

"I don't understand what the problem is," David said.

"My problem—" I said forcefully, then stopped. What was my problem exactly?

If they make you homecoming king, it will look like you pushed Grant Parker into a grease pit, stole his girlfriend, stole his friends, and then stole his crown.

That was exactly what it was going to look like.

It's kind of what actually happened.

"No," I said with such sudden force that it startled David. "Absolutely not. You'll just have to give it to the person with the second most votes."

"You want to turn down being homecoming king?" David asked, now looking at me as if I had completely lost it.

"That's it. That's exactly what I want to do. You'll just have to give it to someone else."

"But tha-that's never happened before," he said.

"That you know of."

He shrugged, unconvinced. "Look, just take a day or two to think about it. Penny is going to be homecoming queen, and it would be great to have you two up there together. Everyone thinks of you as a couple now."

"Wait a minute," I said, a thought suddenly occurring to me. "If I was voted homecoming king"—I paused as it took my brain a minute to catch up—"then that means I won before I almost killed Grant . . . I mean before Grant had his accident . . . I mean . . ."

"Yeah," David said. "That's right. You were voted homecoming king before Grant . . . had his accident."

"But that doesn't make any sense," I said, not really talking to David at this point, but thinking aloud.

David was talking again, but I wasn't listening. My mind had started to trip down the rabbit hole.

If I was voted homecoming king before Grant's accident, that would mean . . .

That I was popular enough to win homecoming king before I ever tried to kill Grant Parker.

Or at least, before people *believed* I had tried to kill Grant Parker.

Semantics. As long as people believe you tried to kill Grant Parker, then that's what happened.

Just because I was voted homecoming king didn't prove anyone actually *liked* me. It just proved that my classmates wanted someone other than Grant Parker to be king.

Nobody really liked Grant.

Right. And now I was going to be homecoming king—the ultimate measure of worth in the high school ecosystem.

"So," David said, eyeing me now like I might be a bit unstable, "we'll discuss the ceremony at the next planning meeting. You'll be there, right?"

"What? Uh, yeah—yeah. I'll be there," I said.

David's expression conveyed mystified concern as he walked away, but I had retreated back into my own thoughts.

38

"Do you hear that?" Penny asked as she pulled her lips away from mine with the smack of a wet suction cup separating from a pane of glass.

"Hear what?" I sat up and swung my head to look out the side and rear windows of the car. We were parked down by the lake just off the gravel road that serviced the private boat slips, where I always expected to be assaulted by either a serial killer or Chief Perry. "Hear what?" I asked.

"The song," Penny said as she pulled herself out of my embrace to reach over and turn up the volume of the radio. Taylor Swift? Had to be. Taylor Swift had a unique variation of suck. And this was the more countrified version of one of Taylor Swift's songs. So, uniquely suckier.

"What about it?" I asked. I sighed out a breath of relief

that I was not about to withstand more abuse from Chief Perry.

"Our song?" She said it like a question, her voice rising expectantly. "Have you already forgotten?"

"I'm sorry. I . . ." I was unsure what to say, since she wasn't making any sense, so I just leaned in to kiss her again on the jaw. But this time she pulled away completely, at arm's length to search my face for understanding.

"The first time we made out," she said with a little huff. "We made out to this song."

"Oh," I said, since there didn't seem to be much else to say about it. Had I not been in the middle of making out with a girl there was no way (*No. Way.*) a Taylor Swift song would have stayed on in my car. I would have changed the station immediately. And now this was our song?

"Why do I feel suddenly as if all you care about is us having sex?" Penny asked, her voice rising to a whine that set my teeth on edge. My boner was disappearing more rapidly than it did when I thought about my mom. "You don't even know our song. I shouldn't have to *tell you* something like that, Luke. You should just *know.*"

"I'm sorry," I said again. "Penny, if I'm holding you, it's not as if I would notice anything else going on around me."

Wow. Good one.

While I thought this was an almost genius bit of improvisation, it was exactly the wrong thing to say.

"So, what does that mean?" she snapped, now pulling away from me altogether. "You're only interested in sleeping with me? You don't care about anything else we share?"

Okay, now that was a loaded question, since Penny and

I never actually shared anything besides bodily fluids. When we weren't engaged in making out we were usually doing something that didn't involve a whole lot of conversation. Bowling, a movie, going to the drive-in or a party—we weren't philosophizing or talking about our futures.

"What do you want me to say?" I asked, starting to lose my temper.

"Nothing. Just take me home." She retreated into her corner and crossed her arms over her chest, all but telling me not to even try to touch her.

Not that it mattered. I was angry now too. Just about every girl in school, other than Delilah, that is, would gladly take Penny's shotgun seat in the Camaro. I didn't have to waste my time listening to her whine and complain about me forgetting "our song."

I turned on the Camaro's engine and revved it once before I spun out of our parking space, gravel spitting up from the back tires as a balm to my anger. We rode in silence as I rolled through stop signs, gunning the engine for jackrabbit starts after each.

As we approached her street I lost the silent game, unwilling to let her go without some closure to our anger.

"Seriously, Penny. I have no idea what you're so mad about. I told you how I felt. I wouldn't have noticed some random song on the radio the first time I got to hold you."

I cut a glance at her face to gauge how my words were affecting her. She was looking out the window, refusing my gaze. She stayed silent for another minute before speaking again. When she finally did speak her emotions had cooled, but there was a hollowness to her voice that told me she was holding a grudge.

Her anger clouded the interior of the Camaro until she broke the silence by saying, "You could at least act like you care about homecoming. Act like it's important to you."

"What are you talking about?" I asked. "What does homecoming have to do with anything?"

Her shoulder twitched in a shrug of annoyance. "I'm just saying you haven't really been interested when I talk about it. You were practically falling asleep during our committee meeting the other day."

"I was hungover," I said, wondering how I had gotten sucked into this line of conversation. "I never said I didn't care about homecoming."

"You didn't have to. It's obvious."

"So what do you want me to say?" I asked, my voice rising with frustration.

"I want you to say you're sorry for being an insensitive asshole," she said. "What's gotten into you? You used to be such a gentleman."

You used to put out without making a federal case out of it.

"I'm still a gentleman. I pick you up for school five days a week, don't I?" I realized I was raising my voice and reached out to turn the radio down, as if I had only been speaking loudly to be heard over the soundtrack.

"Well," she huffed as the Camaro slid to a stop at the curb in front of her house, "if it's such an *inconvenience* for you, then don't bother picking me up on Monday!" Her anger returned, white hot in the confined space, and she spun toward me in her seat as she reached for the door handle.

"Fine," I said to her retreating back as she slammed the door of the Camaro and hurried up the front walk. "And by the way," I shouted after her, "I hate Taylor Swift!"

39

Now that I had the demands of homecoming and preparations and a social schedule, I spent very little time at the garage. It was unclear whether I still owed Roger anything for the Camaro. He hadn't kept any records of the hours I worked or, for that matter, ever told me what he credited for each hour I spent enduring *Law & Order* episodes or picking up empty beer cans.

The Camaro ran like a dream now, and when I pulled into the parking space in front of one of the open bay doors, Roger came out to listen to the engine for a minute before I shut it off.

"Sounds like the day they rolled her off the assembly line," he said with an approving nod. "Too bad you don't know now to work on current models."

"I'm sure I could figure it out," I said. "How hard could it be?"

His eyebrows shot up in surprise at my comment, but he didn't remark on it. "You actually showing your face to do some work today?" he asked instead.

"Work like what?" I asked. "Pick up beer cans?"

"The office is a mess. Tiny spilled a whole coffee on the desk calendar, and I can't make out any of the writing with it all in pencil."

"Everything on the calendar is on the computer, too," I said. "Just look on there."

"Yeah, well, the computer doesn't work."

"Let me look at it," I said as I followed him inside. "Did you turn it off and turn it back on again?"

"Why would I do that?" Roger asked. "It doesn't work."

I suppressed a sigh as I followed him through the open bays to the office. The only evidence of Tiny was the clang of tools and the drone of one of the dozen local country-music radio stations. I still hadn't developed an appreciation for the pop-country sound many of my classmates listened to, but I tolerated it at parties without much choice.

It took me about two seconds to diagnose the problem with the computer. The password lock screen was engaged. As soon as I put in the username (Roger) and the password (password) the computer hummed to life, louder than many of the engines under Roger's care in the shop.

"How did you do that?" Roger asked, sincere in his amazement.

"I put in the username and password," I said with some impatience. "Jesus, Roger."

"Well, I'll be," Roger said. "So it wasn't broken?"

I sighed and rolled my eyes, then got to work straightening and cleaning the office. I copied the schedule in black

Sharpie marker onto the desk calendar so it was legible through Tiny's coffee stains.

I was in a hurry, wanted to get in and out of there as quickly as possible. Penny was waiting for me, along with some other people, at Parr's Drive-In. Penny and I had made up after our fight via a complicated series of dissertation-length texts from her, with mostly single-word responses from me. I acknowledged that I had been insensitive, even though I still didn't understand how my behavior had been so. I agreed to her request that I try harder to be an attentive boyfriend, though I wasn't sure what exactly that should entail. After all, I spent almost every free moment I had in her company. I saw her between classes and after school and on weekends just to hang out.

"You should be all set for a while," I said to Roger as I passed through the garage bay on my way to the Camaro. The grease pit was covered by a car, Tiny just a tinkering sound from below. I studiously avoided looking at the grease pit as I passed, though I felt it lurking there, morbidly beckoning.

"You heard any news about Grant Parker's condition?" Roger asked me. Just a casual question, but I could sense he wasn't asking simply for information.

Most of the time I didn't have to think about Grant. His name rarely came up anymore, and even the local paper could only report on his unchanged condition of stable and in a coma for so long before people lost interest.

"Nothing new," I said. "My dad goes to check in on the family every couple of days."

"The homecoming game ought to be interesting," Roger said, and I sensed he was still leading, trying to draw some reaction out of me.

"Yeah," I said, eager to change the subject. "Well, I've got to go. I'm meeting some people at the drive-in."

"You're not sticking around?" Roger asked with some surprise.

I shook my head. "No, I just came by to check on things. You don't really need me here. There's nothing much for me to do."

"I see," Roger said.

"I set up the calendar again so you don't have to get on the computer. If someone calls, just write it in. You don't really need me," I said again to make it true.

"Alright then," Roger said, and he almost sounded hurt. Almost as if he wanted me there to watch *Law & Order* and drink beer. "Does that mean we won't be seeing you for work this week?"

"Well," I said, letting regret seep into my voice, "I've just got a lot going on. I'm on the student council now, and there's homecoming, and I pick Penny up most days after cheerleading practice."

"I see," he said. "That Penny Olson. She was Grant's girl, wasn't she?"

"They dated," I said noncommittally.

"Did you at least wait for the body to get cold?" he asked, and his question startled me.

"Grant treated her like crap," I said, hating how defensive I sounded. "They were fighting all the time before he . . . before his accident anyway."

"Uh-huh," Roger said. "Well, I guess as long as you've justified it to yourself, you don't need to worry."

"What's that supposed to mean?" I snapped back.

"Easy, tiger," Roger said. "I'm on your side, remember?"

But I wasn't so sure anymore what my side was. To Chief Perry and Principal Sherman, I was a delinquent; to the LARPers, a bully; to Delilah, I was an asshole; to Penny, I was an insensitive jerk of a boyfriend; and to everyone else, I was some kind of false idol, liked and accepted only because people thought I was something I wasn't.

And now, I was no longer sure what was real and what was make-believe.

40

Homecoming evening I picked up Penny at five o'clock. It felt odd to be wearing a tuxedo in the late afternoon sunlight. To calm my anxiety over the evening events, I had drunk two beers before leaving the house, then vigorously chewed gum on the drive to Penny's to mask the smell.

Though they had not graduated from Wakefield, as most of the parents in Ashland had, Dad and Doris were attending the homecoming dance. It was Dad's obligation to the community to ensure that the event did not degrade into some den of Satan.

Penny's mother greeted me at the door dressed in a long evening gown, the color and shimmer of the fabric garish in the fading afternoon light. I kept my distance in case the smell of beer lingered on my breath.

"Well," she breathed as she opened the door and pressed

a hand to her impressive bosom, "don't you look handsome, Luke."

"Thank you, Mrs. Olson," I said, knowing that I should find something complimentary to say to her, too. Grant would have had the charm to carry off this moment, but I was still lacking compared to almost any boy raised in the south. "You look . . . nice," I finally said, since she was clearly waiting for her return compliment.

"Well, I didn't keep the dress I wore to homecoming, but I did wear this to the prom too many years ago for me to want to tell you," she said as she lifted her skirt and gave it a small shake. "Penny looks really lovely. She's a vision."

"I'll bet," I said as I stepped inside.

And when Penny appeared on the stairs, she really did look beautiful. Her hair was swept back from her face and fell in buttery curls down her back, her arms and shoulders bare.

"Hi, Luke," Penny said, her smile radiant.

Penny's dad sat at the dining room table reading the paper while her mother fussed over us, making us stand by the fireplace for a dozen or more pictures. There were photos of me pinning Penny's corsage to her dress, pictures of us both standing with our hands at our sides, with my arm around her waist, and with us both facing the same direction with my hands on Penny's shoulders. Mrs. Olson would show us the photos after every few she took, and I hoped I was the only one who noticed how fake and forced my smile was. By the end of the ordeal a film of sweat covered my forehead and my hands felt clammy.

Penny's parents took us out to dinner at the Italian

restaurant on Main Street. Penny and I rode in the Camaro, following her dad's Buick at a safe distance. At dinner I tried to make polite conversation but spent most of the meal staring enviously at the carafe of wine the Olsons shared with their veal piccata and salad. When Mr. Olson put down cash for the bill, I was the first one out of my seat.

By the time we reached the Elks Lodge I was ready to experience a full-blown anxiety attack. We were among the first to arrive, since Penny was running the homecoming committee.

Miss Mitze and Miss Tucker were working the main entrance as greeters, both in evening gowns yellowed with age and wearing heavy white corsages on their wrists. Reflected light on her glasses obscured Miss Tucker's expression, but Miss Mitze was watching me with the spark of anticipated drama. "Hello, Luke," Miss Mitze said eagerly.

He's the boy who almost killed Grant Parker. What will he do next?

"Hello, Miss Mitze, Miss Tucker. How are you?" I said with nods to both of them.

"It's such a lovely night for the dance," Miss Mitze gushed. "Isn't it lovely, Tucker? Tucker and I were just saying how lovely it is."

"It is nice," I said.

"And we're really enjoying the theme for this year's dance," Miss Mitze said, her eyes wide with genuine delight. "Old school. People have started to arrive and have been coming in the gowns they wore for their own past homecoming dances or proms. Such a delightful idea."

"Of course," Miss Tucker continued, an extension of her sister's commentary, "not everyone can fit into the dress or suit they wore to their own homecoming, even with the aid of a good tailor." She said this with a pointed look in the direction of a woman who was handing off her coat to the attendant in the coatroom and who wore a sheath dress that was obviously designed for a figure slimmer than hers.

"Just between you, us, and the lamppost," Miss Mitze said in what was supposed to be a whisper but was still audible from twenty paces, "that's Mrs. Brenner of Brenner's Bakery. I think he feeds her extra éclairs because he likes roomy women. And that seems perfectly natural, of course. If anyone, a baker would be the kind to appreciate a woman with a fuller figure."

"I suppose he would have to," agreed Miss Tucker. "Perhaps it's an acquired taste."

I immediately cut off the conversation with a few pleasantries before Miss Mitze or Miss Tucker could make any additional commentary about bakers and their fetishes.

The activity hall at the Elks Lodge had been transformed by the homecoming committee into a bewildering accumulation of balloons and streamers and tinsel. The walls were lined with blown-up images from homecoming dances of Ashland's past.

Within thirty minutes the party was in full swing, a crush of people arriving at the same time. Penny was flitting around the room, overseeing the refilling of the punch bowl or greeting people.

The homecoming committee had managed to find a band out of Chattanooga that would play cover songs from the seventies and eighties, not all of them country hits, thank God. I had a terrible feeling I was going to be expected to dance, and I had no idea how to even begin dancing to a country song. I would have preferred a wallflower position, but people kept singling me out for conversation.

A lot of country songs seemed to have choreographed line-dancing steps that everyone knew but me. I took frequent trips to the bathroom to avoid the embarrassment of dancing, but in actual fact I was making trips to my car to shotgun one of the beers in my trunk. The drunker I got, the better I felt. Or maybe the drunker I got, the less I felt. Feeling less was feeling better, as far as I was concerned.

As I walked back into the building on my last trip to the car, the faux-lantern lights along the walkway to the entrance burned trails of light as I passed them, letting me know that maybe I was too drunk. I took a few deep breaths before opening the door to the side entrance and tried to slow the beating of my heart. "Almost over, almost over," I muttered to myself. "You can do it."

I have my doubts.

41

This was what I had been dreading the most. The presentation of the homecoming court. Now I was drunk, and nervous to the point that my hands trembled and my pulse boomed in my ears.

The last thing I wanted to do was climb onto the stage and be put in the spotlight. I had spent the past month with a glaring spotlight following me everywhere. My accidental-hero status had left me exhausted and suffering all the symptoms of overstress. My acne had started to return along my jawline, and I had not slept through the night in weeks.

As acting student council president, David Green took the stage to welcome everyone and thank the homecoming committee, the faculty, the school administration, the local businesses that had contributed to the event, and God.

God was almost mentioned as an afterthought, and I hoped that wouldn't piss him off.

After what seemed like an eternity, David finally got down to the business of announcing the members of the homecoming court, beginning with the royal representative from each underclass. There were squeals of delight and applause from the crowd as each member of the royal court was announced.

Penny was announced as queen, and she did a great job of feigning absolute surprise and amazement. She pressed one delicate hand to her chest, her eyes and mouth wide with delight as she climbed the short staircase to the stage.

Penny's acceptance speech included a lot of "oh, my God"s and "thank you guys so much," and there were even real tears at the corners of her eyes as David placed the tiara on her hair.

And then, the moment we'd all been waiting for . . . my turn.

This is going to suck.

"Your new homecoming king!" David was shouting into the mic over the murmurs of the crowd. "Luke Grayson!" He flung out an arm in my direction, and the spotlight shifted to track my ascent to the stage.

As I climbed the stairs, David gave me an encouraging nod and I tried to force a smile onto my face. He was holding the cheap plastic crown in both hands as if it were made of actual gold. I was going to look ridiculous wearing it. Somebody else, Grant Parker, maybe, could wear the plastic crown and not look or feel foolish, but there was no way I could carry it off.

I looked out into the crowd, remembering that I should give them a wave and a smile the way I had seen Grant do at the opening pep rally, but when I looked out at the sea of faces, Delilah's grim expression was the only thing I saw, so I quickly trained my eyes back on David. The walk across the stage seemed to take an eternity, and then, when I reached the podium, things got super awkward.

As David turned to greet me, I started to dip my head to accept the crown. He had placed the tiara on Penny's head, so I just assumed he would do the same to me. But that wasn't his intent, so at the same time I was lowering my head to be crowned, he held it up for me to take it from his hand. He ended up whacking me in the nose with the plastic band, and a murmur of giggles swelled from the crowd.

Our second attempt was worse as David realized his mistake and tried to put the crown on my head, just as I realized my mistake and went to reach for it. The result was that I had to hold my hand up near my forehead to snatch the crown from his grasp. The applause had long since diminished and I coronated myself in front of a silent room.

Then there was a standoff between David and me as he was clearly waiting for something, but I had no idea what he wanted me to do.

After a silence that was broken by only a few coughs and one or two uncomfortable snickers from the audience, David leaned in to murmur to me, "Don't you want to say something?"

"Like what?" I whispered.

"Whatever you want. You're the king."

"I don't want to say anything," I said, like a ventriloquist, barely moving my lips.

David turned back to the mic and said—an unnecessary repeat of his previous announcement—"So, this year's homecoming king, ladies and gentleman, Luke Grayson." He took a step back from the podium and started to clap, and soon everyone, with palpable relief that the uncomfortable moment had passed, joined in to clap politely.

David had left the podium for me to take his place, but I just stood there with a wooden grin plastered on my face.

The room became a kaleidoscope of light and sound as my gaze traveled quickly around the room. I didn't want to see any recognizable faces in the crowd. Didn't want to see Delilah's silent judgment or Don's sense of betrayal or Principal Sherman's look of disapproval.

For a fleeting moment, I thought I caught a glimpse of Grant's face in the audience. One second, I was looking at his face. The next, I saw only a gap in the crowd between two girls in dueling pink and sea-foam satin. Between the girls, I could just make out the retreating sandy brown head of hair atop a pair of broad athletic shoulders as Grant turned his back on the room and was leaving.

Holy shit.

It was Grant.

He was here.

By some miracle, or epic cosmic tragedy, Grant Parker . . . was alive.

And maybe more importantly . . . he's here.

I dropped the mic, and David fumbled to catch it before it hit the floor with a bang. The speakers coughed with the sound of his hands and sleeves scraping across the mesh of the microphone, and a few people covered their ears against the offending sound. But I didn't care and hopped off the front of the stage to follow Grant's retreating figure. I crossed the open dance floor just as Grant pushed through the fire doors into the entrance hall. He turned his head to one side as he exited the room, and I could make out his features clearly now, in profile, as the brighter light from the lobby cast him in silhouette.

People watched me in silence as I roughly pushed my way through the throng. I threw myself against the heavy fire door that had just shut behind Grant, and then stumbled into the vacant entrance hall.

Mrs. Schnabel had replaced Mitze and Tucker at the greeting table and sat in the metal folding chair with her hands folded primly in her lap. She was eighty-five and sometimes thought that Eisenhower was still president. The fluorescent lights cast half-moons on the lenses of her thick glasses as she watched me twirl first one way, then the other, looking for Grant.

"Did you see . . . ?" I started to ask her if she had seen Grant Parker pass through the lobby. But the question suddenly seemed so absurd that I bit off the rest of the sentence. "Did you just see someone pass through here?" I asked, trying to mask the hysteria in my voice.

She looked around the room, her head bobbing like a bird of prey, then turned back to me and just shrugged. I could hear through the door the muffled sound of David talking into the microphone, and then there was subdued applause from the crowd.

I wasn't sure what was happening, but the one thing I did know, there was no way I could go back inside to the dance. Wakefield High School was going to have to make do without a king.

The alcohol had entered my bloodstream completely now and was putting me over the edge. I was having trouble walking straight. I lurched toward the exit doors, hit the crash bar with my hip, and fled into the night.

I didn't think I could drive in my condition. Or maybe I could, but shouldn't.

The cold night air lifted the sweat from my face and made me shiver as I dug in my pocket for my keys.

I looked forward to the relief I would feel once I was within the safety of the Camaro, the only place in the world I ever felt any solace now. I promised myself that once I was in the car, the stereo on, I would allow myself to forget everyone in the Elks Lodge. They would melt away like sand under my feet at the beach.

When I saw the Camaro waiting, she wasn't alone. I stopped in my tracks. If I hadn't been so drunk, my heart might have reacted more, might have started to pound in my chest from fear. But the alcohol formed a hazy buffer, coated my brain so that it slid from one thought to the next without focus.

Waiting for me, leaning against the side of the Camaro with no regard for the original cherry finish I had buffed lovingly with Turtle Wax, was Grant Parker.

42

"It *was* you," I said. "I saw you. Inside. What are you doing here?" I asked, possibly the least coherent or useful of all possible questions. I staggered a little to one side, off balance from both the alcohol and the unexpected sight of Grant.

"You didn't think it would be this hard, did you?" Grant said as he studied the nails on his right hand.

"How . . . ? What . . . ? I don't . . ." There were so many questions it was impossible to form just the right one with mere words.

Grant watched passively as I stabilized myself and regained control of my feet. Beads of sweat popped, fully formed, from every pore on my body, but I was shaking with cold and fright. One corner of his mouth was lifted in a bemused smirk as I labored to find composure.

"You thought it would be easy. Because you thought you were smart and I was dumb," Grant said. "Isn't that right?"

"I-I . . . I don't know what you mean," I said. And really I didn't. I was still so overcome trying to process the presence of Grant, my mind couldn't process much else. "You're okay," I said. "I mean, you look okay. Did you just get out of the hospital?"

Grant's gaze shifted away from my face, and I waited for his answer with nervous anticipation.

"Are you disappointed?" Grant asked. "Would you prefer that I was dead or a vegetable or something?"

"Of course not!"

Even if I had never really done anything to hurt him, if Grant had died I would still be a murderer in the eyes of most people. Only a few people knew the real truth, and their protests would not be enough to quell the tide of public opinion. Besides, I wasn't even sure people like Delilah and Roger would stand up as my allies at this point.

There was still the video that proved my innocence, but if everyone saw the video, then the real truth was almost as harmful as the myth. It was my cowardice that had almost killed Grant Parker.

"Are you . . . ?" I asked. "Are you okay?"

He considered the question for another few seconds as I held my breath.

"What I am," he said, "is necessary. You see it now. They've done the same thing to you that they did to me."

"Did what?" I asked.

"They put you on a pedestal. They made you homecoming king," he said, this with a meaningful glance at the plastic crown still perched on my hair. "It doesn't really suit you, you know?"

"Of course I know. I didn't ask for any of this. All this . . . this . . . bullshit," I said, holding my hand out in an expansive gesture to indicate the Elks Lodge. I took the crown from my head and threw it to the ground. It didn't shatter, just hit the gravel and bounced harmlessly away. "I don't even know how I got here."

"The same thing happened to Jesus," Grant said, ignoring my outburst. "They elevated him to a position that made him feared and hated by the people who didn't follow him. And they crucified him for it."

"Are you comparing yourself to Jesus Christ?" I asked. "Because I'm pretty sure Jesus didn't play high school football or date a cheerleader."

Grant shook his head, as if my ignorance disappointed him. "Am I comparing myself to the son of God? No. I'm just using him as an example. Any person with power is victim to the same thing. Like you. Once I was gone they needed someone to take my place. They elevated you to the status of a superstar, and what did you do with that power?"

"I . . . there . . . I don't have any power," I said, feeling as if I was talking in circles. "There is no power. All I did was step out of the way to avoid getting my ass kicked."

Grant ignored my protest and held up one hand to tick off his points on his fingers. "You took the prettiest girl in school as your girlfriend, even though you don't really like her. . . ."

"She listens to Taylor Swift," I said, my voice rising in protest.

"You bullied the people who showed you friendship when you were new in town." Another accusing finger tick.

"I didn't touch any of them. It was Tony and Skip and Chet who did that."

Grant ignored me and kept on rattling down his list.

"You threw away Delilah's friendship."

"She always makes fun of my shirts," I said. My protests were becoming weaker and my head was starting to ache. I didn't want to talk about any of this. Grant had to know my actions had hardly been dictated by choice. They were dictated by a lack of choice.

"That's what you did once you were handed the power. And now they'll destroy you for it. The same way you destroyed me."

"I didn't do anything!" I shouted, my voice now a high whine. "I never asked for any of this. I wanted to fade into the background, do my time in this hellhole, and then leave for college. And now—what college is going to accept me once they do a Google search on my name? I'll tell you what college—none. I never asked for any of this."

"Really?" he asked, one eyebrow arched skeptically. "You wanted to hang out with Don and his buddies? Acting out the latest episode of *Game of Thrones* or whatever the hell it is they do? No. You wanted to be popular, you wanted the prettiest girl in school. You wanted all of it."

"I don't want it," I said, my voice shaky now. "Everyone thinks I'm an attempted murderer. That's your fault." I pointed an accusing finger at him as I said this last part.

I felt bile rising in my throat and I tried to fight it. The alcohol was a poison now, no longer my friend that would protect me from feeling or thinking shitty thoughts about my situation. It was eating away at my insides, fighting to get out.

"You believe what you want," Grant said indifferently. "Believe what you want about me. About yourself. What truth do you want people to know?"

"I want . . . I want . . . I want to throw up," I said miserably. Then I bent over, and that's what I did.

It was mostly liquid. There wasn't room in my head to think about much besides the burning in my throat, the pain in my stomach, as I bent double and puked onto the gravel. The vomit splashed on my pants and shoes, but I was too sick to care.

I spat a few times, trying to remove the offending taste from my mouth, a violent reminder of the thirty dollars Mr. Olson spent on the steak and fries for dinner. When I finally felt well enough to stand again, Grant was gone, almost as if he had never been. I looked this way and that, trying to find him. I hadn't heard a car engine, so I assumed he must have gone back into the Elks Lodge. Maybe he had stepped in to assume the throne as homecoming king. The heir apparent wasn't qualified to hold the title.

Comforted by the idea that with Grant's return everyone would be too busy to care what had happened to me, their fallen leader, I got into the Camaro and started the engine. The smell of vomit lingered on my shoes and my breath, and I wished for a bottle of water.

I decided there was no way I could safely operate a vehicle, and perhaps for the first time since this entire ordeal had started, I made a sound decision and got out of the

Camaro. The car was still running, and I thought about getting back in to shut off the ignition. But I was beyond caring at that point and just slammed the car door. The effort of shutting the car door upset my balance again, and I stumbled against the car next to mine, banging my shoulder painfully.

I took a minute to gather myself, then started the long walk home.

43

My hand was slimy against my face. I didn't want to wake up, but now that I had moved, the cold wetness of drool on my hand and pillow forced me to take action.

I rolled onto my back, my eyes squeezed shut against the pain in my head, as the night's events slowly came back to me in bits and pieces. It played out like a movie reel in my head, with essential scenes cut out. I scrounged in the back of my brain as I tried to think of what I had said when I was onstage, tried to think if there was any way to salvage my reputation. I could say that I had become ill suddenly. True enough. My mouth still held a dim memory of the vomit I had spewed in the parking lot. I scraped my tongue against my front teeth, trying to remove and swallow what was left of the taste.

Then I remembered Grant, who had appeared out of

nowhere—like a ghost—and disappeared the same way. If I had seen him in the Elks Lodge, why didn't anyone else notice him? The return of Grant Parker would have been a major event, and everyone would have recognized him immediately. Why hadn't anyone else noticed?

Had I imagined him?

But he had spoken to me. At my car. I even remembered most of the conversation.

Mostly.

If Grant Parker had really been at homecoming, someone had to have seen him. I couldn't be the only one.

And if I *was* the only one who saw him, that could mean one of two things. Either I was crazy . . .

Totally believable.

. . . or Grant Parker had been a ghost.

And if Grant Parker was a ghost, that meant he was . . .

Go on, you can think it. Definitely dead.

I was already dressed and standing in the driveway when I remembered that I had left the Camaro idling in the parking lot of the Elks Lodge the previous night. Yet somehow it had found its way home, the driver door unlocked, the key in the ignition. It occurred to me to wonder who had delivered the Camaro, but I was too desperate to resolve the issue of Grant and his ghost status to give it much thought.

I reached the hospital in record time, skidding the Camaro into a space reserved for doctors. In the stillness of the parking lot there was sudden quiet when I cut the ignition. The inner voice, my constant companion over the past few weeks, was quiet. My breathing was loud in the privacy of the Camaro.

The lobby of the hospital was virtually empty. There was just one old guy, hands clasped behind his back as he surveyed the window display of the gift shop, and a lone woman in pastel hospital scrubs who sat behind the reception desk. Neither of them gave me more than passing notice.

I poked my head around corners in the lobby, as if looking for a bathroom or a person who might be waiting there, but the receptionist took no notice of me. When she turned her back to place a file in a cabinet behind her, I headed for the double doors marked with a sign advertising the cafeteria and the main hospital.

I wandered the labyrinth of hallways, unsure where I was going. With each step my feet almost reached the ever-shifting puddles of light cast by fluorescent bulbs on the buffed linoleum floor. The ache behind my eyes started up again from the fluorescent glare, but I couldn't tear my eyes away from the floor. I followed the glowing mirages, my step falling short each time I tried to land my foot in one of the puddles of light. It put me in a trance as I thought about what I was hoping to find.

With sanity restored, at least for the moment, I decided what had brought me here. I needed to know if Grant was alive or dead. If I had been visited by the real Grant Parker, then that would mean shit was about to get real. If I had been visited by a ghost, then that meant Grant Parker was dead . . . and shit was about to get real. If the vision had been just that, only a vision, then that would mean I really was crazy . . . and shit was about to get unreal.

But a crazy person can't know he is crazy. Right?

No answer from the voice, still eerily silent.

Crazy or sane, I followed the same quandary in circles, like a dog chasing its tail. If Grant was dead, I didn't know who or what I would become in the eyes of everyone. If he lived . . . well, the same question applied.

I couldn't remember now why it had seemed so necessary for everyone to think that I had bested Grant in an act of self-defense, rather than just telling everyone the truth. What had been so critical to me that I would lie by omission? Had it been just to gain the acceptance of people like Tony and Penny and Skip and Chet? I didn't even know who was Skip and who was Chet. So why did I care so much what they thought of me?

The only real friends I had in Ashland were Roger and Don and, possibly, Delilah. They all hated me now. Hated me because of the lie. Not because of the truth.

I entered a waiting area on the second floor and knew immediately I was in the right place. A tattered banner wishing Grant a speedy recovery hung by duct tape from the drop-ceiling tile. The banner had been neglected since the first days after Grant's accident, when everyone still gave a crap about his fate.

There was no one at the nurse's station and there was only one path to follow. Double wooden doors led from the waiting area, small panes of glass in each door revealing the deserted corridor beyond. I pushed through the double doors and walked the length of the hallway, glancing into each room as I passed. Most of the rooms were empty. Only a few housed patients, all of them watching television, the noise from each room mixing in a swirl of directionless echoes in the hallway.

After I had exhausted my search without finding Grant, I stood in the middle of the hallway contemplating my game plan. Maybe Grant had been moved to an intensive care unit or I hadn't recognize him. Or maybe he really was dead and his room was now vacant.

The thought of Grant being actually dead brought on a violent physical reaction. Beads of sweat formed on my brow, and the puddles of light on the linoleum started to waver in a rhythmic way. It was as if I were dosing on some horrible drug, desperately wishing I was sober when there were still hours left on my trip.

A panic attack was rising when a nurse arrived, seemingly out of nowhere. Her soft-soled shoes had masked her approach, and I yelped in fright at her question of "Can I help you?"

Her eyes were wide with shock at my reaction, and I struggled to regain my composure.

"Grant Parker," were the only words I could muster.

"What about him?" she asked.

"Where is he?" I asked. "Is he . . . did he . . . ?" I couldn't bring myself to say the words.

Say it, you fucking pussy.

"Is he dead?" I asked.

"Not unless he died on the way home," she said and stifled a small laugh. "Sorry. That was terrible. Hospital humor." Her smile was quick and apologetic.

Her joke reminded me of Delilah. Of course, Delilah would have delivered it deadpan. No laugh. But it was the kind of thing she would have said.

"You mean he . . ."

"Was discharged," she said. "Early this morning."

"Nobody told me," I said as the meaning of her words began to ping through my brain. It was a stupid, nonsensical thing to say. It's not as if I were a blood relation to Grant, but this woman had no way of knowing who I was.

"He woke from his coma a few days ago. The doctors thought he would recover more quickly at home. His parents didn't want anyone to know that he woke up from the coma. Didn't want to get the local media excited again."

She said "local media" as if Grant were an L.A. Laker or a Kardashian.

"So . . . he's . . . does that mean he's okay? He's not paralyzed?"

She hesitated, which at first I interpreted as acknowledgment that Grant was indeed a cripple. "Look, unless you're part of Grant's immediate family, I can't really discuss it with you. I shouldn't even be telling you that he was discharged. Patient confidentiality."

"Sure," I said. "Of course."

She read the disappointment on my face and her expression softened. "Is he a friend of yours?"

Sure, we just haven't been hanging out much since I tried to kill him and stole his girlfriend and his best friend.

"Not exactly," I said.

"Wait a minute," she said, her eyes narrowing with sudden

recognition. "Aren't you that boy who moved here from the big city? The one who tried to kill Grant Parker?"

"It's the other way around," I said with a sigh. "He tried to kill me. And I think he succeeded," I added, knowing that now I sounded as crazy as I felt.

44

I left the hospital in a daze. The Camaro was waiting patiently in its parking space, sitting at an awkward angle, one of the front tires all the way up on the wheel stop. I had been too out of it to even notice the horrible parking job when I arrived at the hospital. But now, alone in the quiet parking lot, I felt the Camaro's judgment. It had been witness to all of my actions over the past month, watched me lie every time I didn't correct someone for assuming I had defended myself against Grant. Had watched me embrace Penny and take advantage of her belief in that lie. The car had seen Skip and Chet load the back of Tony's truck with beer stolen from Don and his friends. It had taken me on an almost nightly detour to cruise by Delilah's house on my way home.

As I sat behind the steering wheel I realized I didn't know where to go. My first thought, a crazy one, was to go to Grant's house and try to talk to him, to continue the conversation we started in the parking lot of the Elks Lodge.

Instead of taking me to Grant's house, the Camaro took me to Delilah's. I cut the engine at the curb and sat watching her house for evidence of life. Chief Perry's patrol car was in the driveway. I thought about going to the front door and facing Chief Perry directly, asking him to let me see Delilah.

It occurred to me that Delilah might not even be home. I decided to text her even though every text I had sent her since the raid on the LARPer fort had gone unanswered.

I sent her a simple message, just asking where she was, then sat impotent and unsure while I waited for a response.

No answer.

I checked to make sure that my message showed up as delivered. Of course, if she had blocked me, I wouldn't know it.

So I sat. And waited. And checked my phone obsessively to make sure notifications were turned on and that it wasn't silenced.

Nothing.

I got out of the car and walked up the sidewalk, trying to catch a glimpse of the interior through the front bay window. No sign of Chief Perry. No sign of Delilah. No movement in the house. Nothing.

I paced the length of the sidewalk in front of Delilah's house a few times, my eyes fixed on the windows, hoping for some sign of where they were within the house or which window opened onto Delilah's bedroom.

"What are you doing?"

The voice came out of nowhere, and I yelped in fright as I jerked reflexively and almost stumbled over a clump of ornamental grass.

"Jesus," I said as I panted and put my hand to my heart. Delilah was standing in the middle of the sidewalk. She glanced toward the house as I tried to collect myself.

"If my dad sees you out here he is going to shoot you," she said matter-of-factly.

"I know," I said.

"I might shoot you myself."

"I wouldn't really mind at this point," I said.

She ignored my comment, even though I really was feeling closer to suicide than I had since the day after Grant's accident. "So, what are you doing here?" she asked.

"I don't know," I said.

"That was some stunt you pulled last night," she said, and the corners of her mouth twitched with a suppressed smile.

"I'm glad I was able to amuse you with the travesty of my existence," I said, the sudden reminder of last night's humiliation hitting my gut like a physical blow.

"Poor David tried to salvage the situation, but it was no use. Everyone spent the rest of the night talking about how crazy you are, wondering what stunt you'll come up with next."

"This isn't a joke, you know," I said. "This is my actual life."

She was quiet, considering that, and I thought I saw the glimmer of sympathy again behind her eyes.

"I came here because I needed to talk to someone," I said finally.

"So go talk to your precious Penny," Delilah said.

"She's not my precious anything," I said. I wasn't angry. Just weary. And Delilah seemed to hear it in my voice.

"What's wrong with you?" she asked, and I thought I detected concern. Or maybe I just wanted to believe she was concerned, that she cared about what happened to me.

"I think I'm crazy," I blurted suddenly.

"Crazy people don't know they're crazy," she said, dismissing my confession. "That's what makes them crazy."

"Maybe," I said. "But last night I talked to Grant Parker's ghost."

"He's not dead. At least," she said with some hesitation, "not that we've heard. Someone has to be dead to be a ghost."

"He's not dead," I said. "That's what makes me crazy."

"You're talking in circles."

"I know," I said with a nod. "I went to the hospital after I talked to Grant's ghost. . . ."

Her eyes widened when I said this, and she seemed to be thinking that maybe I was right, maybe I really was crazy. I hurried to explain myself before she started hollering for her dad to come out and shoot me like a rabid dog.

"Grant isn't dead," I said. "They sent him home from the hospital. He's out of his coma and they sent him home."

"And so . . . what? Why are you here?"

"I'm not sure," I said. "I just needed to talk to someone. And I guess I . . ."

She lifted one eyebrow and cocked her head toward me as she waited.

"I guess I kind of missed hanging out with you."

"You should have thought of that before you started dating Penny, hanging around those toolbags."

"I thought you used to go out with Tony," I shot back defensively. That little factoid had been nagging away at the back of my brain since Don told me.

"Used to," she said, stress on "used." "I was a kid, for Christ's sake. I know better now. Unlike some people."

"I'm not dating Tony," I said, my joke falling flat.

"You might as well be." We fell into a stalemate of silence, both of us thoughtful. Delilah was the first to break the silence. "So?" she said. "What are you going to do now?"

"I don't know," I said as I tucked my hands into the back pockets of my jeans and shook my head. "Run away from home, I guess. Leave town."

"That's what Jeremy did," Delilah said. "You see how far that got him."

"I'm not going to join the army."

"You could," she said, and after a pause, "*or* you could go to school on Monday and tell everybody the truth."

"What is the truth?" I asked. "That I'm a coward?"

She shrugged. "I guess you have to decide that for yourself."

"Don't give me your passive-aggressive bullshit," I said hotly. "I know exactly what you think of me."

"You really don't," Delilah said.

"Look, I don't know what to do. I just wanted to . . . to see you. To talk to someone who knew the truth about me and—maybe liked me anyway."

"Which truth are we talking about?" she asked.

"All of it."

She considered that for a few seconds, and the air shifted between us as she seemed to relent a little bit.

"So what are you going to do?" she pressed.

"I'm going to leave. I'm going back to DC. I can't stay here. Not with everything that's happened. And then there's that whole possibility that I'm completely crazy. . . ." I trailed off and gazed into the middle distance while I let a plan form and solidify in my head.

That's what I would do. I would leave Ashland and go back to DC. I would make an Irish exit and just go without telling anyone. By the time I got back, Mom would have to take me in. She wouldn't have a choice. And it's not as if Dad wanted me here anyway. All I did was create problems for him and his life.

"Yeah?" Delilah asked. "You're just going to leave? Just like that?"

"Just like that."

"And so—what? You just came to say good-bye?"

"Maybe," I said.

"And your dad and Doris are just going to let you ride off into the sunset?" she asked skeptically.

"Well . . . no," I conceded hesitantly. "I'll have to wait and sneak out tonight so I can take my stuff."

"Yeah," she nodded in agreement, "you wouldn't want to leave without that Beastie Boys shirt."

I cut her a warning look, but she ignored it.

"You know," she said, approaching her next attack in a roundabout way. "Maybe what's making you crazy is how hard you have to work at being something you're not. The stress is what's making you crazy. You could come back to school on Monday and just . . . start over."

"Start over? You were at homecoming, right? You saw me ditch like a psycho in the middle of my acceptance speech?"

"Yeah," she said, cracking a smile for the first time. "You should have seen the looks on everyone's faces after you left."

"I don't want to know," I groaned.

"You know what you need to do?" she asked, mercifully letting the subject of homecoming drop.

"No," I answered honestly. "Are you going to tell me?"

"Yes. What you need to do is face Grant Parker. Go and talk to him. Make it right with him. If you do that, or at least try, you might just salvage what little sanity you have left."

"That's a terrible idea," I said.

"And running isn't?" she asked. "Running is a terrible plan. If you run now, you'll be running for the rest of your life."

And, you know, it was a pretty grand statement, coming from the mouth of a seventeen-year-old girl. But for once, with Delilah talking, the voice in my head was silent. As if maybe, the voice agreed with Delilah.

45

I rubbed my hands along the tops of my thighs as if to warm them as I contemplated the Parker house. It was a blight on the landscape of golden rolling hills, with porticoes and columns and useless wooden decorative railings along the roofline, brick pillars flanking the front drive. I remembered what Roger had told me, that the Parkers had gotten rich over a century ago, capitalizing on death to make their fortune. The thought of all those shovels from the Parker factory turning fresh graves gave me a sick feeling, conjured an image in my head of hundreds or thousands of graves being dug along a battlefield. The dead tumbled into piles, while the factory churned out shovels faster and faster to keep up with death's demands. It gave me such a sick feeling that if Delilah hadn't been in the car with me, I would have turned tail and run.

But Delilah *was* there, sitting silently in the passenger seat as we both contemplated the imposing Parker mansion. Wealth and power oozed from the brick mortar.

"You think if I pull up the drive someone will come out with a gun?" I asked.

"Definitely," she said, no hint of irony evident in her tone. "Do you have the balls to find out?"

"Leave my balls out of this. They're totally innocent."

The withering glance she gave me was fleeting, and her expression turned to one of sympathy. "Do it," was all she said.

No one emerged from the house with a gun as we crunched up the gravel drive. Delilah's hands were buried deep in the pocket of her sweatshirt, mine in the front pockets of my jeans, and we both trudged slowly yet determinedly forward. At least, Delilah seemed determined.

I hesitated at the porch steps, but Delilah tugged at my sleeve impatiently and then put both hands in the middle of my back to push me toward the front door. She pulled at the bell chain, then stood, hands clasped behind her back, as she waited for a response.

A uniformed maid answered the door, which I had not anticipated. I thought I would have to face one of the Parker clan immediately and would, promptly, pee myself.

The maid looked at us questioningly, though with a pleasant smile, and Delilah asked if Grant was home. The woman hesitated, clearly made uncomfortable by our request. I pictured Grant in a first-floor bedroom, propped up in a home hospital bed, various machines beeping and blinking insistently around him.

"Grant isn't taking any visitors," the maid said with a glance over her shoulder.

"It would only be for a minute," Delilah said.

"I'm very sorry," the maid said, and she did sound sorry, but she had moved her body into a defensive position in the open doorway, as if Delilah and I might suddenly try to force an entry. "I have very strict orders."

I had only seen Leland Parker a few times, but I could easily imagine he ran his house the way Kim Jong Un ran North Korea.

"Okay," Delilah said pleasantly, her voice sweet in a way I had never heard before. "Thanks anyway."

Seemingly relieved, the maid shut the door gently, and Delilah turned as if to walk back to the Camaro. I was almost to the porch steps when I realized Delilah was not following me. Turning back, I saw her with her ear pressed to the front door.

"What are you doing?" I asked in a whisper.

She held up one finger, telling me to wait, then waved me back to the door.

"Come on," she mouthed silently.

"Come on where?" I hissed.

"Inside," she said with impatience.

"I'm not breaking into his house," I said, my voice rising with worry.

"The door isn't locked," she whispered. "It's not actually breaking in. We're just going to *walk* in."

"And do what?" I asked. "Are you crazy?"

"Not as crazy as you," she said. Then she ignored me as she gently pushed down the door lever. The noise from the door handle was barely audible, but to my ears it sounded as loud as a passing freight train.

"No," I whispered. "Delilah. Delilah!"

But she was still ignoring me as she pushed the door open six inches and stuck her head inside. I held my breath, expecting to be startled by a cry of anger or alarm. But no one objected as she put one foot through the doorway and slid into the foyer.

I thought about just turning on my heel and walking away. If Delilah wanted to get herself arrested by her own father, that was her problem. Just the thought of running into Leland Parker as an uninvited guest in his own home made me think about peeing myself again.

I wanted to grab Delilah by the arm and drag her to the Camaro, but it was too late. She had already disappeared into the house, and I either had to leave or follow. "What the fuck am I doing?" I moaned, then slipped through the gap of the open doorway. On the other side I found myself in a cavernous foyer, with a wide staircase and an unreasonable number of paintings featuring horses. I had not noticed any horses on the grounds of the Parker mansion, but if the decor was any indication, they seemed to really like them.

My hands were sweating and my heart beat loudly in my ears as I followed Delilah's confident stride past the docile gazes of the horses and up the grand staircase. On the walls of the stairway were family portraits and photos documenting every milestone of Grant's childhood. Grant as a baby, with dimpled cheeks and wearing a onesie covered in ducks; Grant as a towheaded child in blue seersucker; Grant on one knee, squinting against the sun for his Pee Wee football portrait.

Delilah seemed to know exactly where she was going, and I remembered Don saying that Delilah had once been part of the popular crowd. This probably wasn't her first visit to Grant's house. If we got caught, it would definitely be her last. But we hadn't heard any evidence of another human since entering. Our feet made only whispers on the plush carpeting of the stairs and upstairs hallway.

When Delilah stopped it was so sudden that I ran into the back of her, and she dug her elbow into my gut as she fought to keep her balance. She frowned at me, then pressed her ear to a closed door. I waited impatiently as she listened. She put a finger to her lips to warn me to be silent, and I narrowed my eyes at her, annoyed that she would treat me as if I were stupid enough to start making a ruckus. Again it was Delilah who took the courageous first step, opening the door to stick her head in, then giving me the all clear as she quietly entered the room.

The first sight of Grant startled me, not because he looked so different. He didn't. But he was changed somehow. He no longer looked like the person I remembered. For one thing he seemed smaller, and I realized I had built him up to be a colossus in my mind. He wasn't much over six feet and didn't have unnatural muscle bulk. He was just an average-size guy.

After over a month in the hospital he had grown thinner, and he was pale. I suppose this had a lot to do with the fact that he hadn't been eating solid food for a while. I cringed inwardly at that thought. He didn't look anything like he had when I spoke to him on homecoming night. . . .

. . . Which, I had to remind myself, had not really been him. On homecoming night he had been a hallucination. The figure who sat before me now was a weakened, stripped-down version of the Grant who had stood before me in the Elks Lodge parking lot.

Delilah and I stood side by side, she with her arms clasped behind her back, me with my hands hanging awkwardly at my sides. We stood gazing over Grant's sleeping form.

Grant lay on his back in a queen-size bed, a flat-screen television hanging on the wall across from him. A remote control and magazines and a PlayStation controller lay scattered on the duvet. There was a hospital-style table pushed to one side, but within easy reach to swing into place so he could take his meals in bed.

He looked so . . . innocent. Childlike. He wasn't the menacing figure who had haunted me for the months since I had moved to Ashland.

I was relieved that he was asleep. I didn't know if I had the strength to face him yet, to have a conversation with him. What would I say? That I was sorry? I wasn't sorry. I hadn't done anything to him.

I took a deep breath and a moment to think. Had I been wrong to think Grant was an ogre? Had I just overreacted to an innocent prank? After all, it was the kind of prank I might have played on some unsuspecting freshman at my old school.

But Grant was a monster. He had mistreated the LARP-ers and been a jerk to Penny and . . .

Was that Grant? Or was that you?

The question startled me, and I turned suddenly to Delilah, as if she were privy to my internal dialogue. Her eyes widened as she mouthed the word "*What?*"

I was rattled by the question, but I tried to shake it off. It wasn't my imagination—how ostracized I had felt when I first came to Ashland. It wasn't my imagination—the humiliation I felt when Grant pranked me in front of all his friends. But since I had seen Grant's apparition in the Elks Lodge parking lot, I had started to doubt everything I thought I knew.

And now, faced with Grant in this new light, I couldn't decide if he really was an ogre or if the ogre was me.

"Let's wake him up," Delilah whispered, but I shook my head no.

"Why not?" she pressed. "We came all this way."

"Let him sleep," I said, and for once Delilah didn't argue.

With one final look at Grant, I opened the bedroom door and we made our way back down the stairs and to the front porch without encountering anyone.

"You didn't even say anything," Delilah said as we descended the porch steps.

"He seemed so weak. I didn't want to wake him," I said. "It felt . . . wrong."

She was quiet for the rest of the walk to the Camaro, and

even as I held her door for her and she climbed into the car, she only thanked me quietly.

I didn't start the Camaro right away, just sat in the driver's seat with the keys in my lap. When I finally did start the car it broke the silence between us.

"What are you thinking?" she asked, usually the most annoying question a girl could ask, but in this instance, it was the only question that made sense.

"I was thinking . . . that I don't really remember. I can't remember what's real and what I imagined."

"There's a video of it," Delilah said matter-of-factly. "You didn't do anything other than get out of the way." I wondered if Delilah had actually seen the video. I didn't think Chief Perry would have let her see it, but knowing Delilah, she would have figured out some way on her own.

"That isn't what I mean. I mean I can't really remember how things played out between Grant and me. Between Penny and me," I added with an apologetic glance in her direction, but she seemed unmoved. "And maybe I didn't push Grant into that grease pit, but I wasn't sad about him ending up there. And I sure let everyone believe I *did* push him."

"Is that what you told everyone?" Delilah asked. "You told them you pushed him?"

"I didn't tell anybody anything," I answered truthfully. "People just kind of believed what they wanted to believe."

She considered that for a minute, then said, "Well, I guess that's where we are, then. People will just believe what they're going to believe."

46

Facing Grant Parker had been awkward and horrible, but I had never felt any real guilt about what had happened to him. Even if he wasn't the monster I had imagined, Grant had made my first weeks in Ashland hell. Maybe he didn't deserve to be put into a life-threatening coma, but that point was definitely debatable.

The real guilt I harbored was not about what had happened to Grant Parker. My feelings of uncertainty and dread were much more centered on facing people like Don and Roger. They had shown me friendship, of a sort, though in Roger's case it wasn't immediately obvious that he even liked me.

After we left Grant's house I dropped Delilah at home. Or, more accurately, I dropped her off four doors down from her house, a careful eye out for Chief Perry's patrol car as we said our good-byes.

"So?" Delilah said. "What now?"

"I don't know. I don't know about anything anymore," I said, wanting to glean as much sympathy as I could. But Delilah was never one to offer much sympathy. Self-pity only garnered weakness, and she wouldn't give me any more than she gave herself. And since she had lost both a mother and a brother before she turned seventeen, self-pity could fill every crease of her life like sand if she let it.

"So you'll be at school on Monday?" she asked.

"Maybe," I said as I chewed nervously at the skin on the side of my thumb, a habit that had been with me since the night of Grant's accident.

"Well," she said, "I suppose if this might be the last time I ever see you, I'll say good-bye. Just in case."

I was idly wondering what a good-bye from Delilah would be. Maybe a fist bump, or a punch on the shoulder if she was feeling really affectionate. I was thinking I should get out of the car, open her door for her, and give her a hug. And maybe Grant Parker could have pulled that off, would have taken charge of the situation and not fumbled it the way I did.

I was still thinking about what to do when Delilah slid across the seat and leaned in to gather the collar of my jacket loosely in her fist and put her mouth over mine. This time I remembered to breathe through my nose.

She pulled away abruptly and managed the door by herself.

"Hey," I said, calling her back as she started to swing the heavy door closed behind her. "Delilah?"

"Yeah?" she said, sticking her head back into the car, one arm rested along the top of the door.

"Thanks," I said. It was sort of a lame thing to say, but I couldn't wrap my head around everything I wanted—needed—to say to her. Before that moment, I hadn't really appreciated her friendship. She had tripped Grant to distract him from ridiculing me, stuck up for me against Tony when he came to deliver Grant's threat, and had kept me company when I worked on the Camaro all those nights. She had even called me out when I was being an asshole, which was something only a real friend would do.

"You're welcome," she said simply, then shut the door between us and turned to walk away.

The Camaro found its way home to Roger's garage. It wasn't until I got there that I really knew that's where I was headed or what I would say when I saw him.

Roger didn't greet me right away when I walked into the garage, but his expression said plenty.

"Grant's out of the hospital," I said.

"I heard," Roger said with a nod.

"I went by his house."

Roger's eyebrows shot up questioningly at that bit of information. "I'm surprised Leland didn't shoot you on sight."

"He didn't see me."

"Ah."

"So," I said as I pulled the car keys out of my pocket and held them out to him, "I wanted to return the Camaro to you. I don't know that I ever really earned it with the time I worked."

Roger considered the keys in my hand but didn't reach

out to take them from me. "That's what you want? To give the car back?"

"I think so. Like I said, I don't think I really earned it. It's still your car. Besides," I said, casting a forlorn look toward the Camaro, "every time I look at it, it just reminds me of all the shitty things I've done over the past few weeks."

"Well, you could try not being an asshole," he offered helpfully. "If that doesn't work out, you can always go back to being one."

"I am kind of an asshole, aren't I?" I asked, glad to have it out in the open.

"I wouldn't say 'kind of,'" Roger said.

"Yeah," I sighed. "Thanks."

"I'm not telling you anything you don't already know. Maybe it's better for you to keep the Camaro. You need to keep her as a reminder." He paused after he said this, waiting for me to catch up, but before the moment got too deep, he added, "And, of course, the office is a mess again, and you'll be working to the end of the school year to earn back what those tires and parts cost me."

"Yeah?" I asked.

"I suppose. Plus, Tiny misses having you around."

"He does?" I asked with some surprise.

"Nah, I made that up," Roger said, his face creasing into a smile. "I'm not sure he even noticed you were gone."

47

Monday I rode my bike to school despite the cold and a slick frost covering everything. I would have felt too conspicuous pulling up in the Camaro. Though Grant was convalescing at home and would not return to school right away, everyone in town already knew he was out of his coma and had been discharged by his doctors. Everyone in town had a cousin or friend or other informant who worked at the hospital. I had not heard from Penny or Tony or any of my new besties since the disaster at the Elks Lodge, since I had destroyed the purity of the Ashland homecoming tradition and left Penny a dowager homecoming queen.

My plan . . . well, I didn't really have a plan. My plan was to show up at school Monday morning and try to pretend like nothing had happened. I was still the boy who had almost killed Grant Parker, but I wasn't sure what that meant anymore now that Grant seemed on his way to making a full recovery. I just had to make it through the next six months, try to keep my head down and stay out of trouble. So my situation hadn't really changed all that much from where I began.

Delilah was loitering outside the entrance when I arrived at school, and my heart swelled with gratitude at the sight of her. I knew she was waiting for me and I was thankful for an ally. She walked me to class, distracting me with conversation as the needle scratched off the record and everyone stopped to stare.

Homecoming night was just a dim, hazy memory for me because of the booze. I knew I had made a fool out of myself, but unfortunately (or maybe thankfully) I did not have full recall of the sequence of events.

Penny was waiting for me at my locker when Delilah and I approached, and for the first time Penny seemed shy and uncertain.

She greeted Delilah in a friendly way but then turned her attention to me and in a soft voice said, "Luke, can I talk to you for a minute? Alone?"

"I'll see you in class," Delilah said without hesitation and walked on.

"How are you?" Penny asked, eying me warily. After the way I had acted at homecoming she was probably wondering if I was a complete lunatic. I had spent most of the weekend wondering the same thing. The jury was still out.

"Okay, I guess," I said with a shrug.

"You really gave everyone a scare at the dance," she said with characteristic tact.

"I can imagine," I said with an understanding nod.

"Well, I'm glad you're okay." She paused for a minute as she thought about what to say next, but since I already knew where this conversation was going, I tried to make it easy for her. After all, Penny really had always been nice to me. From the beginning.

"Listen, Penny," I said, launching in before she could continue, "you're an awesome girl and I appreciate how nice you've been to me and all, but I think it's probably better if we just try to be friends. Maybe not see each other anymore in a . . . boyfriend/girlfriend kind of way."

Her relief was palpable as I said this, and she let her breath go in a gust. "Yeah, I . . . I was kind of thinking the same thing. Not that I don't think you're great and all."

"Sure, yeah," I said with a nod. "I know. I just don't think I'm good boyfriend material right now. For anyone. I've got a lot of stuff to sort out."

She smiled brightly now that the hard part was over and gave me a soft pat on my arm. "I totally get it," she said. "Friends?"

"Absolutely," I said, knowing as I did that Penny and I would probably never do more than just smile at each other in the hallway at school.

"Great," she said, her whole manner transformed now that she had been let off the hook and no longer had to live as the girlfriend of the guy who had almost killed Grant Parker and then, as an opus, ruined homecoming before being shipped off to an asylum. "I have to get to class but I'll . . . I'll see you around."

"Sure," I said, but she had already turned and melted into the crowd of students moving through the hallway.

In my classes that morning people did stare, as if waiting for me to do something crazy. I couldn't blame them. And really it was no worse than my first few days at Wakefield when people had looked at me like I was an alien in their midst.

Delilah was waiting for me again after fourth period and accompanied me to the cafeteria. "Did Sherman call you into his office today?" she asked.

"Not yet," I said with a shake of my head.

She blew out a sigh, fluffing her bangs in the process. "Well, I suppose there are some advantages to being an assumed attempted murderer."

"I think that might be the only one."

I thought that Delilah and I would take up an innocuous seat together in a corner of the lunchroom at a vacant table, but she strode confidently up to the designated dork-squad bench where Don, Aaron, and Josh sat.

Josh and Aaron gave me weak smiles in greeting. More like grimaces, really. But Don just glared at me. "Hello, Delilah," Don said, intentionally omitting me from his greeting while still giving me a steely-eyed glare.

"Hey, Don," I said, waiting for an invitation to sit down among them while Delilah made herself comfortable on the bench between Aaron and Josh.

"You're a total dick," Don said, one of the few genuine things anyone in Ashland had said to me since my arrival.

"I know."

"So, what now?" Don asked. "Grant's out of his coma and you're back where you started? Back with the dork squad? Isn't that what you call us?"

"What do you want me to say?" I asked.

"How about that you're sorry?" Don said. "Say you're sorry for being a dick and wrecking the fort and generally acting like a major douche bag since you almost killed Grant."

"I am sorry," I said. "I never wanted anything bad to happen. I don't know how things got so fucked up."

"You did it to yourself," Don said. "It's like in *Spider-Man*, when Peter Parker's uncle tells him that with great power comes great responsibility."

"I think Peter Parker's uncle stole that quote from the Bible," I said.

"It doesn't matter," Don snapped quickly. "I'm making a point. You were irresponsible with the power you got from putting Grant in a coma."

"I didn't intentionally put Grant into a coma," I said. "I didn't want any power. It just . . . happened."

"Do you think Peter Parker wanted to get bitten by a radioactive spider?" Don asked in almost a shout. "Of course not."

"Jesus Christ," I muttered and gave Delilah a pointed look, but she just averted her gaze and ignored me. "I said I was sorry. Okay? I am sorry. I don't want to hang out with Tony and Chet and Skip and those guys. As much as it pains me to admit it, I would much rather hang out at the fort drinking beer and watching sword fights."

"There is no fort," Don said. "Not anymore, thanks to you guys."

"Well, maybe I could come by when I'm not working and help you guys rebuild it."

Don thought about that for a minute as he built a cracker sandwich from his Lunchable. "Yeah, okay," he said grudgingly. "We'll be down there during the day on Saturday putting things back together."

"I'll be there," I said.

That afternoon Delilah and I walked home from school together. I held my bike by the handlebars and wheeled it beside me as we strolled along.

"Just think," Delilah said, "in ten years we'll look back on this whole thing and laugh. I'll say, remember that time you almost killed Grant Parker? And it won't seem so terrible. Besides, now that you ruined homecoming, nobody really cares about you anyway."

"Are you trying to make me feel better, or worse?" I asked. "Sometimes I can't tell."

"I'm your friend. I'm only supposed to tell you the truth."

"You are my friend," I said, feeling suddenly sentimental. "Maybe the only one I have."

"Maybe," she said as she took my hand and twined her fingers through mine. "Or maybe the only one who knows you're a crazy person but likes you anyway."